T0304570

CLASSIC CHRISTMAS
CRIME STORIES

More short stories available
from Macmillan Collector's Library

Classic Dog Stories
Classic Cat Stories
Irish Ghost Stories
Standing Her Ground
Classic Science Fiction Stories
Classic Locked Room Mysteries
Round About the Christmas Tree
Ghost Stories by Charles Dickens
Complete Ghost Stories by M. R. James
Best Short Stories by W. Somerset Maugham
Prelude & Other Stories by Katherine Mansfield
The Awakening & Other Stories by Kate Chopin
In the Ravine & Other Stories by Anton Chekhov
The Third Man & Other Stories by Graham Greene
The Happy Prince & Other Stories by Oscar Wilde
The Best of Sherlock Holmes by Arthur Conan Doyle
Tales of Mystery and Imagination by Edgar Allan Poe
A Glove Shop in Vienna & Other Stories
by Eva Ibbotson
Sleepily Ever After: Bedtime Stories for Grown Ups
Tales and Poems by Edgar Allan Poe
All the Mowgli Stories by Rudyard Kipling
Just So Stories by Rudyard Kipling
Dubliners by James Joyce

CLASSIC CHRISTMAS CRIME STORIES

Selection and introduction by
DAVID STUART DAVIES

MACMILLAN COLLECTOR'S LIBRARY

This collection first published 2023 by Macmillan Collector's Library
an imprint of Pan Macmillan
The Smithson, 6 Briset Street, London EC1M 5NR
EU representative: Macmillan Publishers Ireland Ltd,
1st Floor, The Liffey Trust Centre, 117–126 Sheriff Street Upper,
Dublin 1, D01 YC43
Associated companies throughout the world
www.panmacmillan.com

ISBN 978-1-5290-9756-6

Selection copyright © Macmillan Publishers International Limited 2023
Introduction copyright © David Stuart Davies 2023
'Happy Christmas' copyright © David Stuart Davies 2023

The permissions acknowledgements on p. 305 constitute an
extension of this copyright page.

3 5 7 9 8 6 4

A CIP catalogue record for this book is available from the British Library.

Casing design and endpaper pattern by Andrew Davidson
Typeset in Plantin by Jouve (UK), Milton Keynes
Printed and bound in China by Imago

Visit **www.panmacmillan.com** to read more
about all our books and to buy them.

Contents

Introduction vii

ARTHUR CONAN DOYLE 1
The Blue Carbuncle

ROBERT BARNARD 37
Boxing Unclever

MARJORIE BOWEN 55
Cambric Tea

NICHOLAS OLDE 89
The Invisible Weapon

MARGERY ALLINGHAM 103
Murder Under the Mistletoe

DAVID STUART DAVIES 123
Happy Christmas

PETER LOVESEY 127
The Case of the Dead Wait

ROBERT LOUIS STEVENSON 181
Markheim

H. R. F. KEATING 211
The Case of the Seven Santas

NGAIO MARSH 245

Death on the Air

EDGAR WALLACE 293

Stuffing

Permissions Acknowledgements 305

Introduction

DAVID STUART DAVIES

Murder and mistletoe. Felony and the festive season. These might seem odd bedfellows, but in fact very few mystery writers worth their salt have not, at some time in their career, penned a story in which a fiendish crime has taken place during this season of goodwill to all men. These authors can provide impish fun and entertainment by presenting the perpetration of a wicked act set during the twinkly cheeriness of the Christmas holiday. The winter months are dark and inhospitable, and it seems that there are those out there who're intent on taking advantage of this vulnerable time of year.

Of course, the crimes presented in this collection are wrapped up with a jolly ribbon and are purely for your vicarious enjoyment. Rather like a chocolate selection box found under the tree, these tales come in a variety of flavours: some are comic, some very dark, and there's the odd rather nutty one too.

We have assembled an exciting range of mystery scribes for your delight, including some famed word-smiths from the Crime Fiction Hall of Fame. Our festive adventures begin with a classic tale involving a classic detective – Sherlock Holmes – in 'The Adventure of the Blue Carbuncle' by Arthur Conan Doyle (1859–1930). It is, as one critic noted, 'a Christmas story without slush'. It does however have an intriguing puzzle, a sly sense of humour and a conclusion that is in tune with the season of forgiveness.

Other star names featured in these pages include Ngaio Marsh (1895–1982), a New Zealander whose work was always praised for giving the reader pure detective stories. In 'Death on the Air' she created a cunning little mystery featuring her regular police detective Roderick Alleyn. It's a wonderful period piece with butlers, house maids and a puzzling murder involving a radio – of the old-fashioned valve type, of course.

Another accomplished female writer from the Golden Age of crime fiction we've brought to our party is Margery Allingham (1904–1966), who had a long career of writing detective stories, but whose later work gathered a greater depth and sophistication in works such as *The Tiger in the Smoke*. That novel, as well as the story we give you, 'Murder Under the Mistletoe', features her idiosyncratic sleuth Albert Campion, who performs 'a little armchair miracle' by solving the case of a man murdered on Christmas Eve whose body is discovered partially hidden by 'a large bunch of mistletoe'.

Robert Louis Stevenson (1850–1894) makes a guest appearance with the story 'Markheim', probably the most unnerving entry in our selection with its air of frantic nightmare. Although not known as a crime writer, Stevenson was most adept at creating very dark scenarios – one need only think of *The Strange Case of Dr Jekyll and Mr Hyde*.

Edgar Wallace (1875–1932) was the most prolific of authors, turning out hundreds of stories and novels before his early death. It seems that stories sprang from his imagination in a torrent. During his comparatively short life he produced 173 books, seventeen plays and numerous short stories, including 'Stuffing', which concerns dishonour among thieves and the surprising role a turkey plays in the proceedings.

Marjorie Bowen (1885–1952) was an author who wrote in a range of genres, including historical fiction and horror. She was also an accomplished crime writer. In 'Cambric Tea' a young doctor is summoned to the bedside of a man who believes his wife is poisoning him by lacing his Cambric tea with arsenic, but, as with all excellent mystery stories, there is more to this situation than first appears.

Nicholas Olde was the pseudonym of Amian Lister Champneys (1879–1951) and is best remembered for his creation of a Holmes-like detective who appeared in *The Incredible Adventures of Rowland Hern*, a volume of short stories published in 1928, copies of which are now hard to find and exchange hands for hundreds of pounds. Hern also appears in 'The Invisible Weapon', where he is faced with an apparently impossible crime when the police officer informs him, 'There is only one man who could have done it – and he could not have done it.'

'Boxing Unclever' by Robert Barnard (1936–2013) is typical of the author's novels in that his mysteries reflect the style of the Golden Age of crime fiction. In this witty and amusing tale, he takes us into the world of theatrical feuds and revenge and provides a cheeky surprise ending.

Rosemary & Thyme was a popular British mystery-thriller television series which was screened from 2003 to 2007. It starred Felicity Kendal and Pam Ferris as Rosemary Boxer and Laura Thyme – two gardening detectives – in a sort of murder and mulch, corpses in the cabbage patch scenario.

In 2004, respected crime writer Peter Lovesey was asked to write a festive story featuring the green-fingered duo for the *Daily Mail* newspaper over Christmas. This is the first time the story 'The Case of the Dead Wait' has appeared in book form and it is a real treat, keeping readers guessing until the very last minute.

Introduction

H. R. F. Keating (1926–2011), a number of whose acclaimed mystery novels featured Inspector Ghote of the Bombay CID, provides an English rural mystery in 'The Case of the Seven Santas'. It has a faint Dickensian flavour and is both witty and quirky. The problem lies in deciding which of these Santas murdered old Mr Ebenezer, who was found up at the Manor 'with a neat little bullet hole in the middle of his forehead'.

I have also slipped a small story of my own into this collection with the ironic title 'Happy Christmas'. I hope that the twist in the tale will give readers a pleasing jolt.

So there you have it: a rich festive menu of murder, mayhem and mischief for your delectation. I will not delay you further from sampling these juicy crimes at Christmas. Enjoy.

CLASSIC CHRISTMAS
CRIME STORIES

The Blue Carbuncle

I had called upon my friend Sherlock Holmes upon the second morning after Christmas, with the intention of wishing him the compliments of the season. He was lounging upon the sofa in a purple dressing-gown, a pipe-rack within his reach upon the right, and a pile of crumpled morning papers, evidently newly studied, near at hand. Beside the couch was a wooden chair, and on the angle of the back hung a very seedy and disreputable hard-felt hat, much the worse for wear, and cracked in several places. A lens and a forceps lying upon the seat of the chair suggested that the hat had been suspended in this manner for the purpose of examination.

"You are engaged," said I; "perhaps I interrupt you."

"Not at all. I am glad to have a friend with whom I can discuss my results. The matter is a perfectly trivial one"—he jerked his thumb in the direction of the old hat—"but there are points in connection with it which are not entirely devoid of interest and even of instruction."

I seated myself in his armchair and warmed my hands before his crackling fire, for a sharp frost had set in, and the windows were thick with the ice crystals. "I suppose," I remarked, "that, homely as it looks, this thing has some deadly story linked on to it—that it is the clue which will guide you in the solution of some mystery and the punishment of some crime."

"No, no. No crime," said Sherlock Holmes, laughing. "Only one of those whimsical little incidents which will happen when you have four million human beings all jostling each other within the space of a few square miles. Amid the action and reaction of so dense a swarm of humanity, every possible combination of events may be expected to take place, and many a little problem will be presented which may be striking and bizarre without being criminal. We have already had experience of such."

"So much so," I remarked, "that of the last six cases which I have added to my notes, three have been entirely free of any legal crime."

"Precisely. You allude to my attempt to recover the Irene Adler papers, to the singular case of Miss Mary Sutherland, and to the adventure of the man with the twisted lip. Well, I have no doubt that this small matter will fall into the same innocent category. You know Peterson, the commissionaire?"

"Yes."

"It is to him that this trophy belongs."

"It is his hat."

"No, no, he found it. Its owner is unknown. I beg that you will look upon it not as a battered billycock but as an intellectual problem. And, first, as to how it came here. It arrived upon Christmas morning, in company with a good fat goose, which is, I have no doubt, roasting at this moment in front of Peterson's fire. The facts are these: about four o'clock on Christmas morning, Peterson, who, as you know, is a very honest fellow, was returning from some small jollification and was making his way homeward down Tottenham Court Road. In front of him he saw, in the gaslight, a tallish man, walking with a slight stagger, and carrying a white goose slung over his shoulder. As he reached the corner of Goodge Street, a row broke out between this stranger and a little knot of roughs. One of the latter knocked off the man's hat, on which he raised his stick to defend himself and, swinging it over his head, smashed the shop window behind him. Peterson had rushed forward to protect the stranger from his assailants; but the man, shocked at having broken the window, and seeing an official-looking person in uniform rushing towards him, dropped his goose, took to his heels, and vanished amid the labyrinth of small streets

3

which lie at the back of Tottenham Court Road. The roughs had also fled at the appearance of Peterson, so that he was left in possession of the field of battle, and also of the spoils of victory in the shape of this battered hat and a most unimpeachable Christmas goose."

"Which surely he restored to their owner?"

"My dear fellow, there lies the problem. It is true that 'For Mrs. Henry Baker' was printed upon a small card which was tied to the bird's left leg, and it is also true that the initials 'H. B.' are legible upon the lining of this hat, but as there are some thousands of Bakers, and some hundreds of Henry Bakers in this city of ours, it is not easy to restore lost property to any one of them."

"What, then, did Peterson do?"

"He brought round both hat and goose to me on Christmas morning, knowing that even the smallest problems are of interest to me. The goose we retained until this morning, when there were signs that, in spite of the slight frost, it would be well that it should be eaten without unnecessary delay. Its finder has carried it off, therefore, to fulfil the ultimate destiny of a goose, while I continue to retain the hat of the unknown gentleman who lost his Christmas dinner."

"Did he not advertise?"

"No."

"Then, what clue could you have as to his identity?"

"Only as much as we can deduce."

"From his hat?"

"Precisely."

"But you are joking. What can you gather from this old battered felt?"

"Here is my lens. You know my methods. What can you gather yourself as to the individuality of the man who has worn this article?"

I took the tattered object in my hands and turned it over rather ruefully. It was a very ordinary black hat of the usual round shape, hard and much the worse for wear. The lining had been of red silk, but was a good deal discoloured. There was no maker's name; but, as Holmes had remarked, the initials "H. B." were scrawled upon one side. It was pierced in the brim for a hat-securer, but the elastic was missing. For the rest, it was cracked, exceedingly dusty, and spotted in several places, although there seemed to have been some attempt to hide the discoloured patches by smearing them with ink.

"I can see nothing," said I, handing it back to my friend.

"On the contrary, Watson, you can see everything.

You fail, however, to reason from what you see. You are too timid in drawing your inferences."

"Then, pray tell me what it is that you can infer from this hat?"

He picked it up and gazed at it in the peculiar introspective fashion which was characteristic of him. "It is perhaps less suggestive than it might have been," he remarked, "and yet there are a few inferences which are very distinct, and a few others which represent at least a strong balance of probability. That the man was highly intellectual is of course obvious upon the face of it, and also that he was fairly well-to-do within the last three years, although he has now fallen upon evil days. He had foresight, but has less now than formerly, pointing to a moral retrogression, which, when taken with the decline of his fortunes, seems to indicate some evil influence, probably drink, at work upon him. This may account also for the obvious fact that his wife has ceased to love him."

"My dear Holmes!"

"He has, however, retained some degree of self-respect," he continued, disregarding my remonstrance. "He is a man who leads a sedentary life, goes out little, is out of training entirely, is middle-aged, has grizzled hair which he has had cut within the last few days, and which he anoints with lime-cream. These are the more patent facts which are to be deduced from his hat. Also, by the way, that it is extremely improbable that he has gas laid on in his house."

"You are certainly joking, Holmes."

"Not in the least. Is it possible that even now, when I give you these results, you are unable to see how they are attained?"

"I have no doubt that I am very stupid, but I must confess that I am unable to follow you. For example, how did you deduce that this man was intellectual?"

For answer Holmes clapped the hat upon his head. It came right over the forehead and settled upon the bridge of his nose. "It is a question of cubic capacity," said he; "a man with so large a brain must have something in it."

"The decline of his fortunes, then?"

"This hat is three years old. These flat brims curled at the edge came in then. It is a hat of the very best quality. Look at the band of ribbed silk and the excellent lining. If this man could afford to buy so expensive a hat three years ago, and has had no hat since, then he has assuredly gone down in the world."

"Well, that is clear enough, certainly. But how about the foresight and the moral retrogression?"

Sherlock Holmes laughed. "Here is the fore-sight," said he putting his finger upon the little disc and loop of the hat-securer. "They are never sold upon hats. If this man ordered one, it is a sign of a certain amount of foresight, since he went out of his way to take this precaution against the wind. But since we see that he has broken the elastic and has not troubled to replace it, it is obvious that he has less foresight now than formerly, which is a distinct proof of a weakening nature. On the other hand, he has endeavoured to conceal some of these stains upon the felt by daubing them with ink, which is a sign that he has not entirely lost his self-respect."

"Your reasoning is certainly plausible."

"The further points, that he is middle-aged, that his hair is grizzled, that it has been recently cut, and that he uses lime-cream, are all to be gathered from a close examination of the lower part of the lining. The lens discloses a large number of hair-ends, clean cut by the scissors of the barber. They all appear to be adhesive, and there is a distinct odour of lime-cream. This dust, you will observe, is not the gritty, grey dust of the street but the fluffy brown dust of the house, showing that it has been hung up indoors most of the time, while the marks of moisture upon the inside are proof positive that the wearer perspired very freely, and could therefore, hardly be in the best of training."

"But his wife—you said that she had ceased to love him."

"This hat has not been brushed for weeks. When I see you, my dear Watson, with a week's accumulation of dust upon your hat, and when your wife allows you to go out in such a state, I shall fear that you also have been unfortunate enough to lose your wife's affection."

"But he might be a bachelor."

"Nay, he was bringing home the goose as a peace-offering to his wife. Remember the card upon the bird's leg."

"You have an answer to everything. But how on earth do you deduce that the gas is not laid on in his house?"

"One tallow stain, or even two, might come by chance; but when I see no less than five, I think that there can be little doubt that the individual must be brought into frequent contact with burning tallow—walks upstairs at night probably with his hat in one hand and a guttering candle in the other. Anyhow, he never got tallow-stains from a gas-jet. Are you satisfied?"

"Well, it is very ingenious," said I, laughing; "but since, as you said just now, there has been no crime committed, and no harm done save the loss of a goose, all this seems to be rather a waste of energy."

Sherlock Holmes had opened his mouth to reply, when the door flew open, and Peterson, the commissionaire, rushed into the apartment with flushed cheeks and the face of a man who is dazed with astonishment.

"The goose, Mr. Holmes! The goose, sir!" he gasped.

"Eh? What of it, then? Has it returned to life and flapped off through the kitchen window?" Holmes twisted himself round upon the sofa to get a fairer view of the man's excited face.

"See here, sir! See what my wife found in its crop!" He held out his hand and displayed upon the centre of the palm a brilliantly scintillating blue stone, rather smaller than a bean in size, but of such purity and radiance that it twinkled like an electric point in the dark hollow of his hand.

Sherlock Holmes sat up with a whistle. "By Jove, Peterson!" said he, "this is treasure trove indeed. I suppose you know what you have got?"

"A diamond, sir? A precious stone. It cuts into glass as though it were putty."

"It's more than a precious stone. It is *the* precious stone."

"Not the Countess of Morcar's blue carbuncle!" I ejaculated.

"Precisely so. I ought to know its size and shape, seeing that I have read the advertisement about it in *The Times* every day lately. It is absolutely unique, and its value can only be conjectured, but the reward offered of £1000 is certainly not within a twentieth part of the market price."

"A thousand pounds! Great Lord of mercy!" The commissionaire plumped down into a chair and stared from one to the other of us.

"That is the reward, and I have reason to know that there are sentimental considerations in the background which would induce the Countess to part with half her fortune if she could but recover the gem."

"It was lost, if I remember aright, at the Hotel Cosmopolitan," I remarked.

"Precisely so, on December 22nd, just five days ago. John Horner, a plumber, was accused of having abstracted it from the lady's jewel-case. The evidence against him was so strong that the case has been referred to the Assizes. I have some account of the matter here, I believe." He rummaged amid his newspapers, glancing over the dates, until at last he smoothed one out, doubled it over, and read the following paragraph:

"Hotel Cosmopolitan Jewel Robbery. John Horner, 26, plumber, was brought up upon the charge of having upon the 22nd inst., abstracted from the jewel-case of the Countess of Morcar the valuable gem known as the blue carbuncle. James Ryder, upper-attendant at the hotel, gave his evidence to the effect that he had shown Horner up to the dressing-room of the Countess of Morcar upon the day of the robbery in order that he might solder the second bar of the grate, which was loose. He had remained with Horner some little time, but had finally been called away. On returning, he found that Horner had disappeared, that the bureau had been forced open, and that the small morocco casket in which, as it afterwards transpired, the Countess was accus-tomed to keep her jewel, was lying empty upon the dressing-table. Ryder instantly gave the alarm, and Horner was arrested the same evening; but the stone could not be found either upon his person or in his rooms. Catherine Cusack, maid to the Countess, deposed to having heard Ryder's cry of dismay on discovering the robbery, and to having rushed into the room, where she found matters as described by the last witness. Inspector Bradstreet, B division, gave evidence as to the arrest of Horner, who strug-gled frantically, and protested his innocence in the strongest terms. Evidence of a previous conviction for robbery having been given against the prisoner, the magistrate refused to deal summarily with the offence, but referred it to the Assizes. Horner, who had shown signs of intense emotion during the proceedings, fainted away at the conclusion and was carried out of court."

"Hum! So much for the police-court," said Holmes thoughtfully, tossing aside the paper. "The question for us now to solve is the sequence of events leading from a rifled jewel-case at one end to the crop of a goose in Tottenham Court Road at the other. You see, Watson, our little deductions have suddenly assumed a much more important and less innocent aspect. Here is the stone; the stone came from the goose, and the goose came from Mr. Henry Baker, the gentleman with the bad hat and all the other characteristics with which I have bored you. So now we must set ourselves very seriously to finding this gentleman and ascertaining what part he has played in this little mystery. To do this, we must try the simplest means first, and these lie undoubtedly in an advertisement in all the evening papers. If this fail, I shall have recourse to other methods."

"What will you say?"

"Give me a pencil and that slip of paper. Now, then: 'Found at the corner of Goodge Street, a goose and a black felt hat. Mr. Henry Baker can have the same by applying at 6:30 this evening at 221B, Baker Street.' That is clear and concise."

"Very. But will he see it?"

"Well, he is sure to keep an eye on the papers, since, to a poor man, the loss was a heavy one. He was clearly so scared by his mischance in breaking the window and by the approach of Peterson that he thought of nothing but flight, but since then he must have bitterly regretted the impulse which caused him to drop his bird. Then, again, the intro-duction of his name will cause him to see it, for everyone who knows him will direct his attention to it. Here you are, Peterson, run down to the advertis-ing agency and have this put in the evening papers."

"In which, sir?"

"Oh, in the *Globe, Star, Pall Mall, St. James's Gazette, Evening News, Standard, Echo,* and any others that occur to you."

"Very well, sir. And this stone?"

"Ah, yes, I shall keep the stone. Thank you. And, I say, Peterson, just buy a goose on your way back and leave it here with me, for we must have one to give to this gentleman in place of the one which your family is now devouring."

When the commissionaire had gone, Holmes took up the stone and held it against the light. "It's a bonny thing," said he. "Just see how it glints and sparkles. Of course it is a nucleus and focus of crime. Every good stone is. They are the devil's pet baits. In the larger and older jewels every facet may stand for a bloody deed. This stone is not yet twenty years old. It was found in the banks of the Amoy River in southern China and is remarkable in having every characteristic of the carbuncle, save that it is blue in shade instead of ruby red. In spite of its youth, it has already a sinister history. There have been two murders, a vitriol-throwing, a suicide, and several robberies brought about for the sake of this forty-grain weight of crystallised charcoal. Who would think that so pretty a toy would be a purveyor to the gallows and the prison? I'll lock it up in my strong box now and drop a line to the Countess to say that we have it."

"Do you think that this man Horner is innocent?"

"I cannot tell."

"Well, then, do you imagine that this other one, Henry Baker, had anything to do with the matter?"

"It is, I think, much more likely that Henry Baker is an absolutely innocent man, who had no idea that the bird which he was carrying was of considerably more value than if it were made of solid gold. That, however, I shall determine by a very simple test if we have an answer to our advertisement."

"And you can do nothing until then?"

"Nothing."

"In that case I shall continue my professional round. But I shall come back in the evening at the hour you have mentioned, for I should like to see the solution of so tangled a business."

"Very glad to see you. I dine at seven. There is a woodcock, I believe. By the way, in view of recent occurrences, perhaps I ought to ask Mrs. Hudson to examine its crop."

I had been delayed at a case, and it was a little after half-past six when I found myself in Baker Street once more. As I approached the house I saw a tall man in a Scotch bonnet with a coat which was buttoned up to his chin waiting outside in the bright semicircle which was thrown from the fanlight. Just as I arrived the door was opened, and we were shown up together to Holmes's room.

"Mr. Henry Baker, I believe," said he, rising from his armchair and greeting his visitor with the easy air of geniality which he could so readily assume. "Pray take this chair by the fire, Mr. Baker. It is a cold night, and I observe that your circulation is more adapted for summer than for winter. Ah, Watson, you have just come at the right time. Is that your hat, Mr. Baker?"

"Yes, sir, that is undoubtedly my hat."

He was a large man with rounded shoulders, a massive head, and a broad, intelligent face, sloping down to a pointed beard of grizzled brown. A touch of red in nose and cheeks, with a slight tremor of his extended hand, recalled Holmes's surmise as to his habits. His rusty black frock-coat was buttoned right up in front, with the collar turned up, and his lank wrists protruded from his sleeves without a sign of cuff or shirt. He spoke in a slow staccato fashion, choosing his words with care, and gave the impression generally of a man of learning and letters who had had ill-usage at the hands of fortune.

"We have retained these things for some days," said Holmes, "because we expected to see an advertisement from you giving your address. I am at a loss to know now why you did not advertise."

Our visitor gave a rather shamefaced laugh. "Shillings have not been so plentiful with me as they once were," he remarked. "I had no doubt that the gang of roughs who assaulted me had carried off both my hat and the bird. I did not care to spend more money in a hopeless attempt at recovering them."

"Very naturally. By the way, about the bird, we were compelled to eat it."

"To eat it!" Our visitor half rose from his chair in his excitement.

"Yes, it would have been of no use to anyone had we not done so. But I presume that this other goose upon the sideboard, which is about the same weight and perfectly fresh, will answer your purpose equally well?"

"Oh, certainly, certainly," answered Mr. Baker with a sigh of relief.

"Of course, we still have the feathers, legs, crop, and so on of your own bird, so if you wish—"

The man burst into a hearty laugh. "They might be useful to me as relics of my adventure," said he, "but beyond that I can hardly see what use the *disjecta membra* of my late acquaintance are going to be to me. No, sir, I think that, with your permission, I will confine my attentions to the excellent bird which I perceive upon the sideboard."

Sherlock Holmes glanced sharply across at me with a slight shrug of his shoulders.

"There is your hat, then, and there your bird," said he. "By the way, would it bore you to tell me where you got the other one from? I am somewhat of a fowl fancier, and I have seldom seen a better grown goose."

"Certainly, sir," said Baker, who had risen and tucked his newly gained property under his arm. "There are a few of us who frequent the Alpha Inn, near the Museum—we are to be found in the

Museum itself during the day, you understand. This year our good host, Windigate by name, instituted a goose club, by which, on consideration of some few pence every week, we were each to receive a bird at Christmas. My pence were duly paid, and the rest is familiar to you. I am much indebted to you, sir, for a Scotch bonnet is fitted neither to my years nor my gravity." With a comical pomposity of manner he bowed solemnly to both of us and strode off upon his way.

"So much for Mr. Henry Baker," said Holmes when he had closed the door behind him. "It is quite certain that he knows nothing whatever about the matter. Are you hungry, Watson?"

"Not particularly."

"Then I suggest that we turn our dinner into a supper and follow up this clue while it is still hot."

"By all means."

It was a bitter night, so we drew on our ulsters and wrapped cravats about our throats. Outside, the stars were shining coldly in a cloudless sky, and the breath of the passers-by blew out into smoke like so many pistol shots. Our footfalls rang out crisply and loudly as we swung through the doctors' quarter, Wimpole Street, Harley Street, and so through Wigmore Street into Oxford Street. In a quarter of an hour we were in Bloomsbury at the Alpha Inn, which is a small public-house at the corner of one of the streets which runs down into Holborn. Holmes pushed open the door of the private bar and ordered two glasses of beer from the ruddy-faced, white-aproned landlord.

"Your beer should be excellent if it is as good as your geese," said he.

"My geese!" The man seemed surprised.

"Yes. I was speaking only half an hour ago to Mr. Henry Baker, who was a member of your goose club."

"Ah! yes, I see. But you see, sir, them's not *our* geese."

"Indeed! Whose, then?"

"Well, I got the two dozen from a salesman in Covent Garden."

"Indeed? I know some of them. Which was it?"

"Breckinridge is his name."

"Ah! I don't know him. Well, here's your good health landlord, and prosperity to your house. Good-night."

"Now for Mr. Breckinridge," he continued, buttoning up his coat as we came out into the frosty air. "Remember, Watson, that though we have so homely a thing as a goose at one end of this chain, we have at the other a man who will certainly get seven years' penal servitude unless we can establish his innocence. It is possible that our inquiry may but confirm his guilt; but, in any case, we have a line of investigation which has been missed by the police, and which a singular chance has placed in our hands. Let us follow it out to the bitter end. Faces to the south, then, and quick march!"

We passed across Holborn, down Endell Street, and so through a zigzag of slums to Covent Garden Market. One of the largest stalls bore the name of Breckinridge upon it, and the proprietor a horsey-looking man, with a sharp face and trim side-whiskers was helping a boy to put up the shutters.

"Good-evening. It's a cold night," said Holmes.

The salesman nodded and shot a questioning glance at my companion.

"Sold out of geese, I see," continued Holmes, pointing at the bare slabs of marble.

"Let you have five hundred to-morrow morning."

"That's no good."

"Well, there are some on the stall with the gas-flare."

"Ah, but I was recommended to you."

"Who by?"

"The landlord of the Alpha."

"Oh, yes; I sent him a couple of dozen."

"Fine birds they were, too. Now where did you get them from?"

To my surprise the question provoked a burst of anger from the salesman.

"Now, then, mister," said he, with his head cocked and his arms akimbo, "what are you driving at? Let's have it straight, now."

"It is straight enough. I should like to know who sold you the geese which you supplied to the Alpha."

"Well, then, I shan't tell you. So now!"

"Oh, it is a matter of no importance; but I don't know why you should be so warm over such a trifle."

"Warm! You'd be as warm, maybe, if you were as pestered as I am. When I pay good money for a good article there should be an end of the business; but it's 'Where are the geese?' and 'Who did you sell the geese to?' and 'What will you take for the geese?' One would think they were the only geese in the world, to hear the fuss that is made over them."

"Well, I have no connection with any other people who have been making inquiries," said Holmes carelessly. "If you won't tell us the bet is off, that is all. But I'm always ready to back my opinion on a matter of fowls, and I have a fiver on it that the bird I ate is country bred."

"Well, then, you've lost your fiver, for it's town bred," snapped the salesman.

"It's nothing of the kind."

"I say it is."

"I don't believe it."

"D'you think you know more about fowls than I, who have handled them ever since I was a nipper? I tell you, all those birds that went to the Alpha were town bred."

"You'll never persuade me to believe that."

"Will you bet, then?"

"It's merely taking your money, for I know that I am right. But I'll have a sovereign on with you, just to teach you not to be obstinate."

The salesman chuckled grimly. "Bring me the books, Bill," said he.

The small boy brought round a small thin volume and a great greasy-backed one, laying them out together beneath the hanging lamp.

"Now then, Mr. Cocksure," said the salesman, "I thought that I was out of geese, but before I finish you'll find that there is still one left in my shop. You see this little book?"

"Well?"

"That's the list of the folk from whom I buy. D'you see? Well, then, here on this page are the country folk, and the numbers after their names are where their accounts are in the big ledger. Now, then! You see this other page in red ink? Well, that is a list of my town suppliers. Now, look at that third name. Just read it out to me."

"Mrs. Oakshott, 117, Brixton Road—249," read Holmes.

"Quite so. Now turn that up in the ledger."

Holmes turned to the page indicated. "Here you are, 'Mrs. Oakshott, 117, Brixton Road, egg and poultry supplier.'"

"Now, then, what's the last entry?"

"'December 22nd. Twenty-four geese at 7s. 6d.'"

"Quite so. There you are. And underneath?"

"'Sold to Mr. Windigate of the Alpha, at 12s.'"

"What have you to say now?"

Sherlock Holmes looked deeply chagrined. He drew a sovereign from his pocket and threw it down upon the slab, turning away with the air of a man whose disgust is too deep for words. A few yards off he stopped under a lamp-post and laughed in the hearty, noiseless fashion which was peculiar to him.

"When you see a man with whiskers of that cut and the 'Pink 'un' protruding out of his pocket, you can always draw him by a bet," said he. "I daresay that if I had put £100 down in front of him, that man would not have given me such complete information as was drawn from him by the idea that he was doing me on a wager. Well, Watson, we are, I fancy, nearing the end of our quest, and the only point which remains to be determined is whether we should go on to this Mrs. Oakshott to-night, or whether we should reserve it for to-morrow. It is clear from what that surly fellow said that there are others besides ourselves who are anxious about the matter, and I should—"

His remarks were suddenly cut short by a loud hubbub which broke out from the stall which we had just left. Turning round we saw a little rat-faced fellow standing in the centre of the circle of yellow light which was thrown by the swinging lamp, while Breckinridge, the salesman, framed in the door of his stall, was shaking his fists fiercely at the cringing figure.

"I've had enough of you and your geese," he shouted. "I wish you were all at the devil together. If you come pestering me any more with your silly talk I'll set the dog at you. You bring Mrs. Oakshott here and I'll answer her, but what have you to do with it? Did I buy the geese off you?"

"No; but one of them was mine all the same," whined the little man.

"Well, then, ask Mrs. Oakshott for it."

"She told me to ask you."

"Well, you can ask the King of Proosia, for all I care. I've had enough of it. Get out of this!" He rushed fiercely forward, and the inquirer flitted away into the darkness.

"Ha! this may save us a visit to Brixton Road,"

whispered Holmes. "Come with me, and we will see
what is to be made of this fellow." Striding through
the scattered knots of people who lounged round the
flaring stalls, my companion speedily overtook the
little man and touched him upon the shoulder. He
sprang round, and I could see in the gas-light that
every vestige of colour had been driven from his face.

"Who are you, then? What do you want?" he
asked in a quavering voice.

"You will excuse me," said Holmes blandly, "but
I could not help overhearing the questions which
you put to the salesman just now. I think that I could
be of assistance to you."

"You? Who are you? How could you know anything of the matter?"

"My name is Sherlock Holmes. It is my business
to know what other people don't know."

"But you can know nothing of this!"

"Excuse me, I know everything of it. You are
endeavouring to trace some geese which were sold
by Mrs. Oakshott, of Brixton Road, to a salesman
named Breckinridge, by him in turn to Mr. Windigate, of the Alpha, and by him to his club, of which
Mr. Henry Baker is a member."

"Oh, sir, you are the very man whom I have longed
to meet," cried the little fellow with outstretched

hands and quivering fingers. "I can hardly explain to you how interested I am in this matter."

Sherlock Holmes hailed a four-wheeler which was passing. "In that case we had better discuss it in a cosy room rather than in this wind-swept market-place," said he. "But pray tell me, before we go farther, who it is that I have the pleasure of assisting."

The man hesitated for an instant. "My name is John Robinson," he answered with a sidelong glance.

"No, no; the real name," said Holmes sweetly. "It is always awkward doing business with an alias."

A flush sprang to the white cheeks of the stranger. "Well then," said he, "my real name is James Ryder."

"Precisely so. Head attendant at the Hotel Cosmopolitan. Pray step into the cab, and I shall soon be able to tell you everything which you would wish to know."

The little man stood glancing from one to the other of us with half-frightened, half-hopeful eyes, as one who is not sure whether he is on the verge of a windfall or of a catastrophe. Then he stepped into the cab, and in half an hour we were back in the sitting-room at Baker Street. Nothing had been said during our drive, but the high, thin breathing of our new companion, and the claspings and unclaspings of his hands, spoke of the nervous tension within him.

"Here we are!" said Holmes cheerily as we filed into the room. "The fire looks very seasonable in this weather. You look cold, Mr. Ryder. Pray take the basket-chair. I will just put on my slippers before we settle this little matter of yours. Now, then! You want to know what became of those geese?"

"Yes, sir."

"Or rather, I fancy, of that goose. It was one bird, I imagine in which you were interested—white, with a black bar across the tail."

Ryder quivered with emotion. "Oh, sir," he cried, "can you tell me where it went to?"

"It came here."

"Here?"

"Yes, and a most remarkable bird it proved. I don't wonder that you should take an interest in it. It laid an egg after it was dead—the bonniest, brightest little blue egg that ever was seen. I have it here in my museum."

Our visitor staggered to his feet and clutched the mantelpiece with his right hand. Holmes unlocked his strong-box and held up the blue carbuncle, which shone out like a star, with a cold, brilliant, many-pointed radiance. Ryder stood glaring with a drawn face, uncertain whether to claim or to disown it.

"The game's up, Ryder," said Holmes quietly.

"Hold up, man, or you'll be into the fire! Give him an arm back into his chair, Watson. He's not got blood enough to go in for felony with impunity. Give him a dash of brandy. So! Now he looks a little more human. What a shrimp it is, to be sure!"

For a moment he had staggered and nearly fallen, but the brandy brought a tinge of colour into his cheeks, and he sat staring with frightened eyes at his accuser.

"I have almost every link in my hands, and all the proofs which I could possibly need, so there is little which you need tell me. Still, that little may as well be cleared up to make the case complete. You had heard, Ryder, of this blue stone of the Countess of Morcar's?"

"It was Catherine Cusack who told me of it," said he in a crackling voice.

"I see—her ladyship's waiting-maid. Well, the temptation of sudden wealth so easily acquired was too much for you, as it has been for better men before you; but you were not very scrupulous in the means you used. It seems to me, Ryder, that there is the making of a very pretty villain in you. You knew that this man Horner, the plumber, had been concerned in some such matter before, and that suspicion would rest the more readily upon him. What did you do, then? You made some small job in my lady's room—you and your confederate Cusack—and you managed that he should be the man sent for. Then, when he had left, you rifled the jewel-case, raised the alarm, and had this unfortunate man arrested. You then—"

Ryder threw himself down suddenly upon the rug and clutched at my companion's knees. "For God's sake, have mercy!" he shrieked. "Think of my father! Of my mother! It would break their hearts. I never went wrong before! I never will again. I swear it. I'll swear it on a Bible. Oh, don't bring it into court! For Christ's sake, don't!"

"Get back into your chair!" said Holmes sternly. "It is very well to cringe and crawl now, but you thought little enough of this poor Horner in the dock for a crime of which he knew nothing."

"I will fly, Mr. Holmes. I will leave the country, sir. Then the charge against him will break down."

"Hum! We will talk about that. And now let us hear a true account of the next act. How came the stone into the goose, and how came the goose into the open market? Tell us the truth, for there lies your only hope of safety."

Ryder passed his tongue over his parched lips. "I will tell you it just as it happened, sir," said he. "When Horner had been arrested, it seemed to me that it would be best for me to get away with the stone at once, for I did not know at what moment the police might not take it into their heads to search me and my room. There was no place about the hotel where it would be safe. I went out, as if on some commission, and I made for my sister's house. She had married a man named Oakshott, and lived in Brixton Road, where she fattened fowls for the market. All the way there every man I met seemed to me to be a policeman or a detective; and, for all that it was a cold night, the sweat was pouring down my face before I came to the Brixton Road. My sister asked me what was the matter, and why I was so pale; but I told her that I had been upset by the jewel robbery at the hotel. Then I went into the back yard and smoked a pipe and wondered what it would be best to do.

"I had a friend once called Maudsley, who went to the bad, and has just been serving his time in Pentonville. One day he had met me, and fell into talk about the ways of thieves, and how they could get rid of what they stole. I knew that he would be true to me, for I knew one or two things about him; so I made up my mind to go right on to Kilburn, where he lived, and take him into my confidence. He would show me how to turn the stone into money. But how to get to him in safety? I thought of the agonies I had gone through in coming from the hotel. I might at any moment be seized and searched, and there would be the stone in my waistcoat pocket. I was leaning against the wall at the time and looking at the geese which were waddling about round my feet, and suddenly an idea came into my head which showed me how I could beat the best detective that ever lived.

"My sister had told me some weeks before that I might have the pick of her geese for a Christmas present, and I knew that she was always as good as her word. I would take my goose now, and in it I would carry my stone to Kilburn. There was a little shed in the yard, and behind this I drove one of the birds—a fine big one, white, with a barred tail. I caught it, and prying its bill open, I thrust the stone down its throat as far as my finger could reach. The bird gave a gulp, and I felt the stone pass along its gullet and down into its crop. But the creature flapped and struggled, and out came my sister to know what was the matter. As I turned to speak to her the brute broke loose and fluttered off among the others.

"'Whatever were you doing with that bird, Jem?' says she.

"'Well,' said I, 'you said you'd give me one for Christmas, and I was feeling which was the fattest.'

"'Oh,' says she, 'we've set yours aside for

32

you—Jem's bird, we call it. It's the big white one over yonder. There's twenty-six of them, which makes one for you, and one for us, and two dozen for the market.'

"'Thank you, Maggie,' says I; 'but if it is all the same to you, I'd rather have that one I was handling just now.'

"'The other is a good three pound heavier,' said she, 'and we fattened it expressly for you.'

"'Never mind. I'll have the other, and I'll take it now,' said I.

"'Oh, just as you like,' said she, a little huffed. 'Which is it you want, then?'

"'That white one with the barred tail, right in the middle of the flock.'

"'Oh, very well. Kill it and take it with you.'

"Well, I did what she said, Mr. Holmes, and I carried the bird all the way to Kilburn. I told my pal what I had done, for he was a man that it was easy to tell a thing like that to. He laughed until he choked, and we got a knife and opened the goose. My heart turned to water, for there was no sign of the stone, and I knew that some terrible mistake had occurred. I left the bird, rushed back to my sister's, and hurried into the back yard. There was not a bird to be seen there.

"'Where are they all, Maggie?' I cried.

"'Gone to the dealer's, Jem.'

"'Which dealer's?'

"'Breckinridge, of Covent Garden.'

"'But was there another with a barred tail?' I asked, 'the same as the one I chose?'

"'Yes, Jem; there were two barred-tailed ones, and I could never tell them apart.'

"Well, then, of course I saw it all, and I ran off as hard as my feet would carry me to this man Breckinridge; but he had sold the lot at once, and not one word would he tell me as to where they had gone. You heard him yourselves to-night. Well, he has always answered me like that. My sister thinks that I am going mad. Sometimes I think that I am myself. And now—and now I am myself a branded thief, without ever having touched the wealth for which I sold my character. God help me! God help me!" He burst into convulsive sobbing, with his face buried in his hands.

There was a long silence, broken only by his heavy breathing and by the measured tapping of Sherlock Holmes's finger-tips upon the edge of the table. Then my friend rose and threw open the door.

"Get out!" said he.

"What, sir! Oh, Heaven bless you!"

"No more words. Get out!"

And no more words were needed. There was a

34

rush, a clatter upon the stairs, the bang of a door, and the crisp rattle of running footfalls from the street.

"After all, Watson," said Holmes, reaching up his hand for his clay pipe, "I am not retained by the police to supply their deficiencies. If Horner were in danger it would be another thing; but this fellow will not appear against him, and the case must collapse. I suppose that I am commuting a felony, but it is just possible that I am saving a soul. This fellow will not go wrong again; he is too terribly frightened. Send him to gaol now, and you make him a gaol-bird for life. Besides, it is the season of forgiveness. Chance has put in our way a most singular and whimsical problem, and its solution is its own reward. If you will have the goodness to touch the bell, Doctor, we will begin another investigation, in which, also a bird will be the chief feature."

Boxing Unclever

"The true spirit of Christmas," said Sir Adrian Tremayne, fingering the stem of the small glass of port which was all he was allowed, "is not to be found in the gluttony and ostentation which that charlatan and sentimentalist Charles Dickens encouraged." He looked disparagingly round at the remains of the dinner still encumbering the long table. "Not in turkey and plum pudding, still less in crackers and expensive gifts. No—a thousand times!" His voice was thrilling, but was then lowered to a whisper, and it carried as it once had carried through the theatres of the nation. "The true spirit of Christmas lies of course in reconciliation."

"Reconciliation—very true," said the Reverend Sykes.

"Why else, in the Christmas story, do we find simple shepherds and rich kings worshipping together in the stable?"

"I don't think they actually—" began the Reverend Fortescue, but he was waved aside.

"To show that man is one, of one nature, in the

37

eyes of God. This reconciliation of opposites is the one true heart of the Christmas message. That was the plan that, at every Christmastide, was acted upon by myself and my dear wife Alice, now no longer with us. Or indeed with anyone. Christmas Day we would spend quietly and simply, with just ourselves for company once the children had grown up and made their own lives. On Boxing Day we would invite a lot of people round to Herriton Hall, and in particular people with whom there had been some breech, with whom we needed to be reconciled." He paused, reaching for reserves in that treacle and molasses voice that had thrilled audiences up and down the country.

"That was what we did that memorable Christmas of 1936. Ten . . . years . . . ago."

There were many nods around the table, both from those who had heard the story before, and from those who were hearing it for the first time.

"Christmas Day was quiet—even, it must be confessed, a little dull," Sir Adrian resumed. "We listened to the new King's broadcast, and wondered at his conquest of his unfortunate speech impediment. It is always good to reflect on those who do not have one's own natural advantages. I confess the day was for me mainly notable for a sense of anticipation. I thought with joy of the beautiful work of reconciliation that was to be undertaken on the next day. And of the other work . . ."

There was a regrettable snigger from one or two quarters of the table.

"Reconciliation has its limits," suggested Martin Lovejoy.

"Regrettably it does," acknowledged Sir Adrian, with a courteous bow in Martin's direction. "We are but human, after all. I could only hope that the Christian work of reconciliation in all cases but one would plead for me at the Judgement Seat against that one where . . . Ah well, who knows? Does not the Bible speak of there being only one unforgivable sin?"

The three reverend gentlemen present all seemed to want to talk at once, which enabled Sir Adrian to sweep ahead with his story. "The first to arrive that Boxing morning was Angela Montfort, closely followed by Daniel West, the critic. Indeed, I think it probable that they in fact arrived *together*, because there was no sign of transport for Angela. West's reviews of her recent performances had made me wonder—so mindlessly enthusiastic were they— whether Something was Going On. Something usually was, with Angela, and the idea that the English critic is incorruptible is pure stardust. My quarrel with Angela, however, had nothing to do with Sex. It was her ludicrous and constant upstag-ing of me during the national tour of *Private Lives*, for which I had taken over the Coward role, and gave a performance which many thought—but, no matter. Old triumphs, old triumphs."

It was given a weary intonation worthy of Pros-pero's farewell to his Art.

"And West's offence?" asked Martin Lovejoy innocently. He was the most theatrically sophisti-cated of them, and he knew.

"A review in his provincial newspaper of my Mal-volio," said Sir Adrian shortly, "which was hurtful in the extreme."

"Was that the one which spoke of your 'shrunken shanks'?" asked Peter Carbury, who was the only person present who read the *Manchester Guardian*.

"A deliberate effect of costuming!" said Sir Adrian fiercely. "A very clever design by my dear friend Binkie Mather. Typical of a critic's ignorance and malice that he could not see that."

He took a sip of port to restore his equanimity, and while he did so Peter winked at Martin and Martin winked at Peter.

"Angela gushed, of course," resumed Sir Adrian, "as I led her into the drawing-room. 'So wonderful to be back at dear old Herriton again'—that kind of thing. West looked around with a cynical expression on his face. He had been there before, when I had been under the illusion that he was one of the more perceptive of the up-and-coming critics, and I knew he coveted the house, with its magnificent views over the Sussex Downs. I suspected that he found the idea of the gentleman actor rather ridiculous, but the idea of the gentleman critic not ridiculous at all. The gentleman's code allows dabbling. West had a large independent income, which is no guarantee of sound judgement. His cynical expression was assumed, but I was relentlessly courteous to them both, and it was while I was mixing them cocktails that Alice—dear Alice—led in Frank Mandeville."

"Her lover," said Peter Carbury.

"My dear boy, do not show your provinciality and vulgarity," said Sir Adrian severely. "In the theatre we take such things in our stride. Let us say merely that in the past he had been her *cavalier servente*."

"Her *what*?" demanded Stephen Coates in an aggrieved voice. He had an oft-proclaimed and very British hatred of pretension.

"An Italian term," explained Sir Adrian kindly, "for a man who serves a lady as a sort of additional husband. There is a long tradition of such people in Italy."

"They are usually a lot younger," said Peter Carbury. "As in this case."

"Younger," conceded Sir Adrian. "Though hardly a *lot* younger. Frank Mandeville had been playing juvenile leads for so long he could have taken a Ph.D. in juvenility. Alice's . . . patronage of him was short and long over, and when she led him in it was clear to me from the expression on her face that she was mystified as to what had once attracted her. When I saw his hair, slicked back with so much oil that it must have felt like being pleasured by a garage mechanic, I felt similarly mystified."

"It must have been a jolly party," commented Stephen Coates. Sir Adrian smiled at him, to signify to all that Stephen was not the sort of young man who could be expected to understand the ways of polite, still less theatrical, society.

"I must confess that when Frank bounced in Angela did say, 'What is this?' and looked suspiciously from Alice to me and back. But we had taken—*I* had taken—the precaution of inviting a number of local nonentities—the headmaster of a good school, an impoverished squire and his dreary wife, at least two vicars, and other such good people—and as they now began arriving they, so to speak, defused suspicion."

"Suspicion?" asked Mike, who had never heard the story before and was far from bright. Sir Adrian

waved his hand with an airy grandness gained playing aristocrats of the old school.

"It was not until things were well under way that
Richard Mallatrat and his wife arrived."

"The greatest Hamlet of his generation," put in
Peter Carbury, with malicious intent.

"I cannot think of fainter praise," responded Sir
Adrian loftily. "The art of Shakespearean acting is
dead. If the newspapers are to be believed the Theatre today is dominated by young Olivier, who can
no more speak the Bard than he can underplay a
role."

"You and Mallatrat were rivals for the part,
weren't you?" Carbury asked. Sir Adrian, after a
pause, allowed the point.

"At the Old Vic. No money to speak of, but a
great deal of prestige. I certainly wanted the part
badly."

"To revive your career?" suggested the Reverend
Sykes. He received a look of concentrated hatred.

"My career has never needed revival! To show
the younger generation how it should be done! To
set standards for people who had lost the true art
of acting. Instead of which Mallatrat was given the
role and had in it a showy success, lacking totally
the quality of *thought*, which is essential to the role,
and quite without too the *music* which . . . another

more experienced actor would have brought to it."
He bent forward malevolently, eyes glinting. *"And I
was offered the role of Polonius."*

"It's a good role," said the Reverend Fortescue,
probably to rub salt in the wound. He was ignored.

"That was his malice, of course. He organized
that, put the management up to it, then told the
story to all his friends. I never played the Old Vic
again. I had to disappoint my legion of fans, but
there are some insults not to be brooked."

"You did try to get even through his wife, didn't
you?" asked Martin Lovejoy, who was all too well
informed in that sort of area.

"A mere newspaper story. Gloria Davere was
not then his wife, though as good as, and she was
not the trumpery Hollywood 'star' she has since
become. Certainly we had—what is this new film
called?—a brief encounter. I have told you the morality of the theatre is not the morality of Leamington
Spa or Catford. We happened to meet on Crewe
Station one Saturday night, after theatre engage-
ments elsewhere. I confess—sordid though it may
sound—that for me it was no more than a means of
passing the time, stranded as we were by the vagar-
ies of the London, Midland, and Scottish Railway.
But the thought did occur to me that I would be
teaching this gauche young thing more gracious

ways—introducing her to the lovemaking of an earlier generation, when romance still reigned, and a
lady was treated with chivalry and respect."

"I believe she told the *News of the World* it was like
fucking Old Father Time," said Carbury to Martin
Lovejoy, but so *sotto* was his *voce* that Sir Adrian was
able to roll on regardless.

"She later, of course, talked, and spitefully, but
the idea that our encounter had anything in it of
revenge on my part is sheer moonshine. On her
part, perhaps, in view of the talk she put around,
but as to myself, I plead innocent of any such sordid
emotion."

"So that was the cast-list assembled, was it?"
asked the Reverend Sykes.

"Nearly, nearly," said Sir Adrian, with the unhur-
ried stance of the habitual narrator, which in the
case of this story he certainly was. "Thus far the
party seemed to be going well. The attractions of
Richard Mallatrat and his flashy wife to the nonentities was something I had anticipated: they crowded
around them, larding them with gushing compliments and expressions of admiration for this or that
trumpery performance on stage or screen. Everyone,
it seemed, had seen a Gloria Davere talkie or Richard Mallatrat as Hamlet, or Romeo, or Richard II. I
knew it would be nauseating, and nauseating it was.

Angela Montfort, for one, was immensely put out, with no knot of admirers to feed her self-love. She contented herself with swapping barbs with Frank Mandeville, who was of course enraged by the attention paid to Richard Mallatrat."

"Hardly a Shakespearean actor, though, this Frank Mandeville," commented Peter Carbury.

"Hardly an actor at all," amended Sir Adrian. "But logic does not come into theatrical feuds and jealousies. Mandeville playing Hamlet would hardly have passed muster on a wet Tuesday in Bolton, but that did not stop him grinding his teeth at the popularity of Richard Mallatrat."

"He wasn't the only one," whispered Stephen Coates.

"And so it was time for a second round of drinks. I decided on that as I saw toiling up the drive the figure of my dear old dresser Jack Roden. My once-dear old dresser. I poured out a variety of drinks including some already-mixed cocktails, two kinds of sherry, some gins and tonic, and two glasses of neat whisky. There was only one person in the room with the appalling taste to drink neat whisky before luncheon. Pouring two glasses gave that person a fifty-fifty chance of survival. Depending on how the tray was presented. With my back to the guests I dropped the hyoscine into one of the whisky glasses."

"Who was the whisky-drinker?" asked Roland, knowing the question would not be answered.

"The one with the worst taste," said Sir Adrian dismissively. "Then I went off to open the front door. Jack shuffled in, muttering something about the dreadful train and bus service you got over Christmas. He was a pathetic sight. The man who had been seduced away from me by Richard Mallatrat, and then dumped because he was not up to the contemporary demands of the job, could hardly any longer keep himself clean and neat, let alone anyone else. I threw the bottle of hyoscine as far as I could manage into the shrubbery, then ushered him with conspicuous kindness in to the drawing-room, solicitously introducing him to people he didn't know and people he did. 'But you two are old friends,' I remember saying when I led him up the scoundrel Mallatrat. Even that bounder had the grace to smile a mite queasily. Out of the corner of my eye I was pleased to see that some of the guests had already helped themselves from the tray."

"Why were you pleased?"

"It meant that others than myself had been up the tray. And it would obviously be theatrical people—the nonentities wouldn't dare."

"It doesn't sound the happiest of parties," commented Lovejoy.

47

"Doesn't it? Oh, but theatre people can relax anywhere, particularly if there are admirers present. Once some of the nonentities felt they should tear themselves away from the star duo of Mallatrat and Davere, then Angela got her share of attention, and Alice as hostess had her little knot—she had left the stage long before, of course, though she was still by nature a stage person. No, it was far from an unhappy party."

"Until the fatality," suggested the Reverend Fortescue.

"Until the fatality," agreed Sir Adrian. "Though even that . . ."

"Did not dampen spirits?"

"Not entirely. Poison is slow, of course. You can have a quick, dramatic effect with cyanide—even I have acted on occasion in thrillers, and know that—but most of them take their time. People thought at first it was an upset tummy. Alice said she hoped that was all it was. She of course was not in on my plans. I've never found women entirely reliable, have you?"

He looked around the table. None of his listeners had found women entirely reliable.

"So it wasn't she who took the tray round?" asked Simon. "Was it one of your servants?"

"No, indeed. The servants had been set to

preparing lunch, and that was *all* they did. As a gentleman I had an instinctive aversion to involving faithful retainers in . . . a matter of this kind."

"I assume you didn't take it round yourself, though?"

"I did not. I tapped poor old Jack Roden on the shoulder—he was deep in rambling reminiscence with Daniel West (viewpoints from well away from the footlights)—and I asked him if he could help by taking round fresh drinks. That had always been my plan, though I confess that when I saw how doddering and uncertain he had become I very nearly changed it, fearing he would drop everything on the floor. But I placed the tray in his hands exactly as I wanted it, so that the poisoned whisky would be closest to hand when he got to the victim."

"And—to state the obvious—the victim took it," suggested the Reverend Fortescue.

"He took it. That was the signal for the toast. I cleared my throat and all fell silent. I flatter myself I know how to enforce silence. I had thought hard about the toast, and even today I think it rather beautiful. 'My friends,' I said. 'To friends old and new, to renewal and reconciliation, to the true spirit of Christmas.' There was much warm assent to my words, and glasses were raised. We all drank to Christmas, and the victim drank his down."

"He wasn't a sipper?" enquired Stephen.

"No. The victim was the sort who drank down and then had an interval before the next. I rather think myself that sipping is more social."

"How long was it before the effects were felt?"

"Oh, twenty minutes or more," said Sir Adrian, his face set in a reminiscent smile. "First just the look of queasiness, then some time later confessions of feeling ill. Alice was all solicitude. She took the victim to my study, plied him with glasses of water, nostrums from our medicine cupboard. He was sweating badly, and his vision was impaired. Finally she came in and suggested that I ring Dr. Cameron from the village. He was *not* happy at being fetched out on Boxing Day, particularly as he had not been invited to the party."

"Because he might have spotted what was wrong with him and saved him in time?"

"Precisely. Fortunately Dr. Cameron was the old-fashioned type of doctor, now rare, who went everywhere on foot. By the time he arrived, all Scottish tetchiness and wounded self-esteem, there was nothing to be done. Then it was questions, suspicions, and eventually demands that the police be called in. It made for an exciting if somewhat uneasy atmosphere—not a Boxing Day, I fancy, that anyone present will forget."

"And the police were quick to fix the blame, were they?" asked Mike. Sir Adrian sighed a Chekhovian sigh.

"Faster, I confess, than even I could have feared. The village bobby was an unknown quantity to me, being new to the district. I had counted on a thick-headed rural flatfoot of the usual kind, but even my first impression told me that he was unusually bright. He telephoned at once for a superior from Mordwick, the nearest town, but before he arrived with the usual team so familiar to us from detective fiction, the local man had established the main sequence of events, and could set out clearly for the investigating inspector's benefit all the relevant facts."

"But those facts would have left many people open to suspicion," suggested Peter Carbury.

"Oh, of course. Practically all the theatre people had been near the tray, except the victim, and all of them might be thought to bear malice to the victim. It was, alas, my wife Alice who narrowed things down so disastrously—quite inadvertently, of course." Sir Adrian was unaware that the foot of the Reverend Sykes touched the foot of the Reverend Fortescue at this point. They knew a thing or two about human nature, those clerics. And not just their own sins of the flesh. "Yes, Alice was apparently already on friendly terms with our new constable." The feet touched again. "And when she was chatting to him quite informally after a somewhat fraught lunch, she happened to mention at some point that she had been standing near the window and imagined she saw something flying through the air."

"The bottle?"

"The bottle. That did it. The grounds were searched, the bottle was found, and its content analysed. Then there could be no doubt."

"No doubt?" asked Mike, not the brightest person there.

"Because the hyoscine had been put in the second round of drinks, and the only person who had left the room to go to the door had been myself—to let in Jack Roden. Roden could not have done it because the bottle was empty and thrown away by the time he got into the drawing-room. It could only be me. I was arrested and charged, and Theatre was the poorer."

They all shook their heads, conscious they had reached the penultimate point in Sir Adrian's narrative.

"Come along all," said Archie by the door, on cue and jangling his keys. "Time you were making a move. We've got Christmas dinner to go to as well, you know."

"But tell us," said Mike who, apart from being stupid, hadn't heard the story before, "who the victim was."

Sir Adrian turned and surveyed them, standing around the table and the debris of their meal. He was now well into the run of this particular performance: there had been ten Christmases since a concerted chorus of Thespians had persuaded the new King not to celebrate his coronation with a theatrical knight on the scaffold. His head came forward and his stance came to resemble his long-ago performance as Richard III.

"You have to ask?" he rasped. "Who else could it be but the *critic*?" How he spat it out! "Who else could it be but the man who had libelled my legs?"

As he turned and led the shuffle back to the cells all eyes were fixed on the shrunken thighs and calves of one who had once been to tights what Betty Grable now was to silk stockings.

MARJORIE BOWEN

Cambric Tea

The situation was bizarre; the accurately trained mind of Bevis Holroyd was impressed foremost by this; that the opening of a door would turn it into tragedy.

"I am afraid I can't stay," he had said pleasantly, humouring a sick man; he was too young and had not been long enough completely successful to have a professional manner but a certain balanced tolerance just showed in his attitute to this prostrate creature.

"I've got a good many claims on my time," he added, "and I'm afraid it would be impossible. And it isn't the least necessary, you know. You're quite all right. I'll come back after Christmas if you really think it worth while."

The patient opened one eye; he was lying flat on his back in a deep, wide-fashioned bed hung with a thick dark, silk lined tapestry; the room was dark for there were thick curtains of the same material drawn half across the windows, rigidly excluding all save a moiety of the pallid winter light; to make

55

his examination Dr. Holroyd had had to snap on the electric light that stood on the bedside table; he thought it a dreary unhealthy room, but had hardly found it worth while to say as much.

The patient opened one eye; the other lid remained fluttering feebly over an immobile orb.

He said in a voice both hoarse and feeble:

"But, doctor, I'm being poisoned."

Professional curiosity and interest masked by genial incredulity instantly quickened the doctor's attention.

"My dear sir," he smiled, "poisoned by this nasty bout of 'flu you mean, I suppose—"

"No," said the patient, faintly and wearily dropping both lids over his blank eyes, "by my wife."

"That's an ugly sort of fancy for you to get hold of," replied the doctor instantly. "Acute depression— we must see what we can do for you—"

The sick man opened both eyes now; he even slightly raised his head as he replied, not without dignity:

"I fetched you from London, Dr. Holroyd, that you might deal with my case impartially—from the local man there is no hope of that, he is entirely impressed by my wife."

Dr. Holroyd made a movement as if to protest

but a trembling sign from the patient made him quickly subsist.

"Please let me speak. *She* will come in soon and I shall have no chance. I sent for you secretly, she knows nothing about that. I had heard you very well spoken of—as an authority on this sort of thing. You made a name over the Pluntre murder case as witness for the Crown."

"I don't specialize in murder," said Dr. Holroyd, but his keen handsome face was alight with interest. "And I don't care much for this kind of case—Sir Harry."

"But you've taken it on," murmured the sick man. "You couldn't abandon me now."

"I'll get you into a nursing home," said the doctor cheerfully, "and there you'll dispel all these ideas."

"And when the nursing home has cured me I'm to come back to my wife for her to begin again?"

Dr. Holroyd bent suddenly and sharply over the sombre bed. With his right hand he deftly turned on the electric lamp and tipped back the coral silk shade so that the bleached acid light fell full over the patient lying on his back on the big fat pillows.

"Look here," said the doctor, "what you say is pretty serious."

And the two men stared at each other, the patient

examining his physician as acutely as his physician examined him.

Bevis Holroyd was still a young man with a look of peculiar energy and austere intelligence that heightened by contrast purely physical dark good looks that many men would have found sufficient passport to success; resolution, dignity and a certain masculine sweetness, serene and strong, different from feminine sweetness, marked his demeanour which was further softened by a quick humour and a sensitive judgment.

The patient, on the other hand, was a man of well past middle age, light, flabby and obese with a flaccid, fallen look about his large face which was blurred and dimmed by the colours of ill health, being one pasty livid hue that threw into unpleasant relief the grey speckled red of his scant hair.

Altogether an unpleasing man, but of a certain fame and importance that had induced the rising young doctor to come at once when hastily summoned to Strangeways Manor House; a man of a fine, renowned family, a man of repute as a scholar, an essayist who had once been a politician who was rather above politics; a man whom Dr. Holroyd only knew vaguely by reputation, but who seemed to him symbolical of all that was staid, respectable and stolid.

And this man blinked up at him and whimpered:

"My wife is poisoning me."

Dr. Holroyd sat back and snapped off the electric light.

"What makes you think so?" he asked sharply.

"To tell you that," came the laboured voice of the sick man. "I should have to tell you my story."

"Well, if you want me to take this up—"

"I sent for you to do that, doctor."

"Well, how do you think you are being poisoned?"

"Arsenic, of course."

"Oh? And how administered?"

Again the patient looked up with one eye, seeming too fatigued to open the other.

"Cambric tea," he replied.

And Dr. Holroyd echoed:

"Cambric tea!" with a soft amazement and interest.

Cambric tea had been used as the medium for arsenic in the Pluntre case and the expression had become famous; it was Bevis Holroyd who had discovered the doses in the cambric tea and who had put his finger on this pale beverage as the means of murder.

"Very possibly," continued Sir Harry, "the Pluntre case made her think of it."

"For God's sake, don't," said Dr. Holroyd; for in

that hideous affair the murderer had been a woman; and to see a woman on trial for her life, to see a woman sentenced to death, was not an experience he wished to repeat.

"Lady Strangeways," continued the sick man, "is much younger than I—I over persuaded her to marry me, she was at that time very much attracted by a man of her own age, but he was in a poor position and she was ambitious."

He paused, wiped his quivering lips on a silk handkerchief, and added faintly:

"Lately our marriage has been extremely unhappy. The man she preferred is now prosperous, successful and unmarried—she wishes to dispose of me that she may marry her first choice."

"Have you proof of any of this?"

"Yes. I know she buys arsenic. I know she reads books on poisons. I know she is eating her heart out for this other man."

"Forgive me, Sir Harry," replied the doctor, "but have you no near friend nor relation to whom you can confide your—suspicions?"

"No one," said the sick man impatiently. "I have lately come from the East and am out of touch with people. Besides I want a doctor, a doctor with skill in this sort of thing. I thought from the first of the Pluntre case and of you."

Bevis Holroyd sat back quietly; it was then that he thought of the situation as bizarre; the queerness of the whole thing was vividly before him, like a twisted figure on a gem—a carving at once writhing and immobile.

"Perhaps," continued Sir Harry wearily, "you are married, doctor?"

"No." Dr. Holroyd slightly smiled; his story was something like the sick man's story but taken from another angle; when he was very poor and unknown he had loved a girl who had preferred a wealthy man; she had gone out to India, ten years ago, and he had never seen her since; he remembered this, with sharp distinctness, and in the same breath he remembered that he still loved this girl; it was, after all, a common-place story.

Then his mind swung to the severe professional aspect of the case; he had thought that his patient, an unhealthy type of man, was struggling with a bad attack of influenza and the resultant depression and weakness, but then he had never thought, of course, of poison, nor looked nor tested for poison.

The man might be lunatic, he might be deceived, he might be speaking the truth; the fact that he was a mean, unpleasant beast ought not to weigh in the matter; Dr. Holroyd had some enjoyable Christmas holidays in prospect and now he was beginning to

feel that he ought to give these up to stay and inves-
tigate this case; for he could readily see that it was
one in which the local doctor would be quite useless.

"You must have a nurse," he said, rising.

But the sick man shook his head.

"I don't wish to expose my wife more than need
be," he grumbled. "Can't you manage the affair
yourself?"

As this was the first hint of decent feeling he
had shown, Bevis Holroyd forgave him his brusque
rudeness.

"Well, I'll stay the night anyhow," he conceded.

And then the situation changed, with the opening
of a door, from the bizarre to the tragic.

This door opened in the far end of the room
and admitted a bloom of bluish winter light from
some uncurtained, high windowed corridor; the chill
impression was as if invisible snow had entered the
shaded, dun, close apartment.

And against this background appeared a woman
in a smoke coloured dress with some long lace about
the shoulders and a high comb; she held a little tray
carrying jugs and a glass of crystal in which the cold
light splintered.

Dr. Holroyd stood in his usual attitude of
attentive courtesy, and then, as the patient, feebly
twisting his gross head from the fat pillow, said:

"My wife—doctor—" he recognized in Lady Strangeways the girl to whom he had once been engaged in marriage, the woman he still loved.

"This is Doctor Holroyd," added Sir Harry. "Is that cambric tea you have there?"

She inclined her head to the stranger by her husband's bed as if she had never seen him before, and he, taking his cue, and for many other reasons, was silent.

"Yes, this is your cambric tea," she said to her husband. "You like it just now, don't you? How do you find Sir Harry, Dr. Holroyd?"

There were two jugs on the tray; one of crystal half full of cold milk, and one of white porcelain full of hot water; Lady Strangeways proceeded to mix these fluids in equal proportions and gave the resultant drink to her husband, helping him first to sit up in bed.

"I think that Sir Harry has a nasty turn of influenza," answered the doctor mechanically. "He wants me to stay. I've promised till the morning, anyhow."

"That will be a pleasure and a relief," said Lady Strangeways gravely. "My husband has been ill some time and seems so much worse than he need—for influenza."

The patient, feebly sipping his cambric tea, grinned queerly at the doctor.

"So much worse—you see, doctor!" he muttered.

"It is good of you to stay," continued Lady Strangeways equally. "I will see about your room, you must be as comfortable as possible."

She left as she had come, a shadow-coloured figure retreating to a chill light.

The sick man held up his glass as if he gave a toast.

"You see! Cambric tea!"

And Bevis Holroyd was thinking: does she not want to know me? Does he know what we once were to each other? How comes she to be married to this man—her husband's name was Custiss—and the horror of the situation shook the calm that was his both from character and training; he went to the window and looked out on the bleached park; light, slow snow was falling, a dreary dance over the frozen grass and before the grey corpses that paled, one behind the other, to the distance shrouded in colourless mist.

The thin voice of Harry Strangeways recalled him to the bed.

"Would you like to take a look at this, doctor?" He held out the half-drunk glass of milk and water.

"I've no means of making a test here," said Dr. Holroyd, troubled. "I brought a few things, nothing like that."

"You are not so far from Harley Street," said Sir Harry. "My car can fetch everything you want by this afternoon—or perhaps you would like to go yourself?"

"Yes," replied Bevis Holroyd sternly. "I would rather go myself."

His trained mind had been rapidly covering the main aspects of his problem and he had instantly seen that it was better for Lady Strangeways to have this case in his hands. He was sure there was some hideous, fantastic hallucination on the part of Sir Harry, but it was better for Lady Strangeways to leave the matter in the hands of one who was friendly towards her. He rapidly found and washed a medicine bottle from among the sick room para- phernalia and poured it full of the cambric tea, casting away the remainder.

"Why did you drink any?" he asked sharply.

"I don't want her to think that I guess," whis- pered Sir Harry. "Do you know, doctor, I have a lot of her love letters—written by—"

Dr. Holroyd cut him short.

"I couldn't listen to this sort of thing behind Lady Strangeways's back," he said quickly. "That is between you and her. My job is to get you well. I'll try and do that."

And he considered, with a faint disgust, how

repulsive this man looked sitting up with pendant jowl and drooping cheeks and discoloured, pouchy eyes sunk in pads of unhealthy flesh and above the spiky crown of Judas-coloured hair.

Perhaps a woman, chained to this man, living with him, blocked and thwarted by him, might be wrought upon to—

Dr. Holroyd shuddered inwardly and refused to continue his reflection.

As he was leaving the gaunt sombre house about which there was something definitely blank and unfriendly, a shrine in which the sacred flames had flickered out so long ago that the lamps were blank and cold, he met Lady Strangeways.

She was in the wide entrance hall standing by the wood fire that but faintly dispersed the gloom of the winter morning and left untouched the shadows in the rafters of the open roof.

Now he would not, whether she wished or no, deny her; he stopped before her, blocking out her poor remnant of light.

"Mollie," he said gently, "I don't quite understand—you married a man named Custiss in India."

"Yes. Harry had to take this name when he inherited this place. We've been home three years from the East, but lived so quietly here that I don't suppose anyone has heard of us."

She stood between him and the firelight, a shadow among the shadows; she was much changed; in her thinness and pallor, in her restless eyes and nervous mouth he could read signs of discontent, even of unhappiness.

"I never heard of you," said Dr. Holroyd truthfully. "I didn't want to. I liked to keep my dreams."

Her hair was yet the lovely cedar wood hue, silver, soft and gracious; her figure had those fluid lines of grace that he believed he had never seen equalled.

"Tell me," she added abruptly, "what is the matter with my husband? He has been ailing like this for a year or so."

With a horrid lurch of his heart that was usually so steady, Dr. Holroyd remembered the bottle of milk and water in his pocket.

"Why do you give him that cambric tea?" he counter questioned.

"He will have it—he insists that I make it for him—"

"Mollie," said Dr. Holroyd quickly, "you decided against me, ten years ago, but that is no reason why we should not be friends now—tell me, frankly, are you happy with this man?"

"You have seen him," she replied slowly. "He

seemed different ten years ago. I honestly was attracted by his scholarship and his learning as well as—other things."

Bevis Holroyd needed to ask no more; she was wretched, imprisoned in a mistake as a fly in amber; and those love letters? Was there another man?

As he stood silent, with a dark reflective look on her weary brooding face, she spoke again:

"You are staying?"

"Oh yes," he said, he was staying, there was nothing else for him to do.

"It is Christmas week," she reminded him wistfully. "It will be very dull, perhaps painful, for you."

"I think I ought to stay."

Sir Harry's car was announced; Bevis Holroyd, gliding over frozen roads to London, was absorbed with this sudden problem that, like a mountain out of a plain, had suddenly risen to confront him out of his level life.

The sight of Mollie (he could not think of her by that sick man's name) had roused in him tender memories and poignant emotions and the position in which he found her and his own juxtaposition to her and her husband had the same devastating effect on him as a mine sprung beneath the feet of an unwary traveller.

London was deep in the whirl of a snow storm

and the light that penetrated over the grey roof tops to the ugly slip of a laboratory at the back of his consulting rooms was chill and forbidding.

Bevis Holroyd put the bottle of milk on a marble slab and sat back in the easy chair watching that dreary chase of snow flakes across the dingy London pane.

He was thinking of past springs, of violets long dead, of roses long since dust, of hours that had slipped away like lengths of golden silk rolled up, of the long ago when he had loved Mollie and Mollie had seemed to love him; then he thought of that man in the big bed who had said:

"My wife is poisoning me."

Late that afternoon Dr. Holroyd, with his suit case and a professional bag, returned to Strangeways Manor House in Sir Harry's car; the bottle of cambric tea had gone to a friend, a noted analyst; somehow Doctor Holroyd had not felt able to do this task himself; he was very fortunate, he felt, in securing this old solitary and his promise to do the work before Christmas.

As he arrived at Strangeways Manor House which stood isolated and well away from a public high road where a lonely spur of the weald of Kent drove into the Sussex marshes, it was in a blizzard of snow that effaced the landscape and gave the murky outlines of the house an air of unreality, and Bevis Holroyd experienced that sensation he had so often heard of and read about, but which so far his cool mind had dismissed as a fiction.

He did really feel as if he was in an evil dream; as the snow changed the values of the scene, altering distances and shapes, so this meeting with Mollie, under these circumstances, had suddenly changed the life of Bevis Holroyd.

He had so resolutely and so definitely put this woman out of his life and mind, deliberately refusing to make enquiries about her, letting all knowledge of her cease with the letter in which she had written from India and announced her marriage.

And now, after ten years, she had crossed his path in this ghastly manner, as a woman her husband accused of attempted murder.

The sick man's words of a former lover disturbed him profoundly; was it himself who was referred to? Yet the love letters must be from another man for he had not corresponded with Mollie since her marriage, not for ten years.

He had never felt any bitterness towards Mollie for her desertion of a poor, struggling doctor, and he had always believed in the integral nobility of her character under the timidity of conventionality; but the fact remained that she had played him false—what if that *had* been "the little rift within the lute" that had now indeed silenced the music!

With a sense of bitter depression he entered the gloomy old house; how different was this from the pleasant ordinary Christmas he had been rather looking forward to, the jolly homely atmosphere of good fare, dancing, and friends!

When he had telephoned to these friends excusing himself his regret had been genuine and the cordial "bad luck!" had had a poignant echo in his own heart; bad luck indeed, bad luck—

She was waiting for him in the hall that a pale young man was decorating with boughs of prickly stiff holly that stuck stiffly behind the dark heavy pictures.

He was introduced as the secretary and said gloomily:

"Sir Harry wished everything to go on as usual, though I am afraid he is very ill indeed."

Yes, the patient had been seized by another violent attack of illness during Dr. Holroyd's absence; the young man went at once upstairs and found Sir Harry in a deep sleep and a rather nervous local doctor in attendance.

An exhaustive discussion of the case with this doctor threw no light on anything, and Dr. Holroyd, leaving in charge an extremely sensible looking housekeeper who was Sir Harry's preferred nurse, returned, worried and irritated, to the hall where Lady Strangeways now sat alone before the big fire.

She offered him a belated but fresh cup of tea.

"Why did you come?" she asked as if she roused herself from deep reverie.

"Why? Because your husband sent for me."

"He says you offered to come; he has told everyone in the house that."

"But I never heard of the man before to-day."

"You had heard of me. He seems to think that you came here to help me."

"He cannot be saying that," returned Dr. Holroyd sternly, and he wondered desperately if Mollie was lying, if she had invented this to drive him out of the house.

"Do you want me here?" he demanded.

"I don't know," she replied dully and confirmed his suspicions; probably there was another man and she wished him out of the way; but he could not go, out of pity towards her he could not go.

"Does he know we once knew each other?" he asked.

"No," she replied faintly, "therefore it seems such a curious chance that he should have sent for you, of all men!"

"It would have been more curious," he responded

grimly, "if I had heard that you were here with a sick husband and had thrust myself in to doctor him! Strangeways must be crazy to spread such a tale and if he doesn't know we are old friends it becomes nonsense!"

"I often think that Harry is crazy," said Lady Strangeways wearily; she took a rose silk lined work basket, full of pretty trifles, on her knee, and began winding a skein of rose-coloured silk; she looked so frail, so sad, so lifeless that the heart of Bevis Holroyd was torn with bitter pity.

"Now I am here I want to help you," he said earnestly. "I am staying for that, to help you—"

She looked up at him with a wistful appeal in her fair face.

"I'm worried," she said simply. "I've lost some letters I valued very much—I think they have been stolen."

Dr. Holroyd drew back; the love letters; the letters the husband had found, that were causing all his ugly suspicions.

"My poor Mollie!" he exclaimed impulsively. "What sort of a coil have you got yourself into!"

As if this note of pity was unendurable, she rose impulsively, scattering the contents of her work basket, dropping the skein of silk, and hastened away down the dark hall.

73

Bevis Holroyd stooped mechanically to pick up the hurled objects and saw among them a small white packet, folded, but opened at one end; this packet seemed to have fallen out of a needle case of gold silk.

Bevis Holroyd had pounced on it and thrust it in his pocket just as the pale secretary returned with his thin arms most incongruously full of mistletoe.

"This will be a dreary Christmas for you, Dr. Holroyd," he said with the air of one who forces himself to make conversation. "No doubt you had some pleasant plans in view—we are all so pleased that Lady Strangeways had a friend to come and look after Sir Harry during the holidays."

"Who told you I was a friend?" asked Dr. Holroyd brusquely. "I certainly knew Lady Strangeways before she was married—"

The pale young man cut in crisply:

"Oh, Lady Strangeways told me so herself."

Bevis Holroyd was bewildered; why did she tell the secretary what she did not tell her husband?—both the indiscretion and the reserve seemed equally foolish.

Languidly hanging up his sprays and bunches of mistletoe the pallid young man, whose name was Garth Deane, continued his aimless remarks.

"This is really not a very cheerful house, Dr.

Holroyd—I'm interested in Sir Harry's oriental
work or I should not remain. Such a very unhappy
marriage! I often think," he added regardless of
Bevis Holroyd's darkling glance, "that it would be
very unpleasant indeed for Lady Strangeways if anything happened to Sir Harry."

"Whatever do you mean, sir?" asked the doctor
angrily.

The secretary was not at all discomposed.

"Well, one lives in the house, one has nothing
much to do—and one notices."

Perhaps, thought the young man in anguish, the
sick husband had been talking to this creature, perhaps the creature *had* really noticed something.

"I'll go up to my patient," said Bevis Holroyd
briefly, not daring to anger one who might be an
important witness in this mystery that was at present
so unfathomable.

Mr. Deane gave a sickly grin over the lovely pale
leaves and berries he was holding.

"I'm afraid he is very bad, doctor."

As Bevis Holroyd left the room he passed Lady
Strangeways; she looked blurred, like a pastel
drawing that has been shaken; the fingers she kept
locked on her bosom; she had flung a silver fur over
her shoulders that accentuated her ethereal look of
blonde, pearl and amber hues.

"I've come back for my work basket," she said. "Will you go up to my husband? He is ill again—"

"Have you been giving him anything?" asked Dr. Holroyd as quietly as he could.

"Only some cambric tea, he insisted on that."

"Don't give him anything—leave him alone. He is in my charge now, do you understand?"

She gazed up at him with frightened eyes that had been newly washed by tears.

"Why are you so unkind to me?" she quivered.

She looked so ready to fall that he could not resist the temptation to put his hand protectingly on her arm, so that, as she stood in the low doorway leading to the stairs, he appeared to be supporting her drooping weight.

"Have I not said that I am here to help you, Mollie?"

The secretary slipped out from the shadows behind them, his arms still full of winter evergreens.

"There is too much foliage," he smiled, and the smile told that he had seen and heard.

Bevis Holroyd went angrily upstairs; he felt as if an invisible net was being dragged closely round him, something which, from being a cobweb, would become a cable; this air of mystery, of horror in the big house, this sly secretary, these watchful-looking servants, the nervous village doctor ready to credit

76

anything, the lovely agitated woman who was the woman he had long so romantically loved, and the sinister sick man with his diabolic accusations, a man Bevis Holroyd had, from the first moment, hated—all these people in these dark surroundings affected the young man with a miasma of apprehension, gloom and dread.

After a few hours of it he was nearer to losing his nerve than he had ever been; that must be because of Mollie, poor darling Mollie caught into all this nightmare.

And outside the bells were ringing across the snow, practising for Christmas Day; the sound of them was to Bevis Holroyd what the sounds of the real world are when breaking into a sleeper's thick dreams.

The patient sat up in bed, fondling the glass of odious cambric tea.

"Why do you take the stuff?" demanded the doctor angrily.

"She won't let me off, she thrusts it on me," whispered Sir Harry.

Bevis Holroyd noticed, not for the first time since he had come into the fell atmosphere of this dark house that enclosed the piteous figure of the woman he loved, that husband and wife were telling different tales; on one side lay a burden of careful lying.

"Did she—" continued the sick man, "speak to you of her lost letters?"

The young doctor looked at him sternly.

"Why should Lady Strangeways make a confidante of me?" he asked. "Do you know that she was a friend of mine ten years ago before she married you?"

"Was she? How curious! But you met like strangers."

"The light in this room is very dim—"

"Well, never mind about that, whether you knew her or not—" Sir Harry gasped out in a sudden snarl. "The woman is a murderess, and you'll have to bear witness to it—I've got her letters, here under my pillow, and Garth Deane is watching her—"

"Ah, a spy! I'll have no part in this, Sir Harry. You'll call another doctor—"

"No, it's your case, you'll make the best of it— My God, I'm dying, I think—"

He fell back in such a convulsion of pain that Bevis Holroyd forgot everything in administering to him. The rest of that day and all that night the young doctor was shut up with his patient, assisted by the secretary and the housekeeper.

And when, in the pallid light of Christmas Eve morning, he went downstairs to find Lady Strangeways, he knew that the sick man was suffering from arsenic poison, that the packet taken from Mollie's work box was arsenic, and it was only an added horror when he was called to the telephone to learn that a stiff dose of the poison had been found in the specimen of cambric tea.

He believed that he could save the husband and thereby the wife also, but he did not think he could close the sick man's mouth; the deadly hatred of Sir Harry was leading up to an accusation of attempted murder; of that he was sure, and there was the man Deane to back him up.

He sent for Mollie, who had not been near her husband all night, and when she came, pale, distracted, huddled in her white fur, he said grimly:

"Look here, Mollie, I promised that I'd help you and I mean to, though it isn't going to be as easy as I thought, but you have got to be frank with me."

"But I have nothing to conceal—"

"The name of the other man—"

"The other man?"

"The man who wrote those letters your husband has under his pillow."

"Oh, Harry has them!" she cried in pain. "That man Deane stole them then! Bevis, they are your letters of the olden days that I have always cherished."

"*My* letters!"

"Yes, do you think that there has ever been anyone else?"

"But he says—Mollie, there is a trap or trick here, some one is lying furiously. Your husband is being poisoned."

"Poisoned?"

"By arsenic given in that cambric tea. And he knows it. And he accuses you."

She stared at him in blank incredulity, then she slipped forward in her chair and clutched the big arm.

"Oh, God," she muttered in panic terror. "He always swore that he'd be revenged on me—because he knew that I never cared for him—"

But Bevis Holroyd recoiled; he did not dare listen, he did not dare believe.

"I've warned you," he said, "for the sake of the old days, Mollie—"

A light step behind them and they were aware of the secretary creeping out of the embrowning shadows.

"A cold Christmas," he said, rubbing his hands together. "A really cold, seasonable Christmas. We are almost snowed in—and Sir Harry would like to see you, Dr. Holroyd."

"I have only just left him—"

Bevis Holroyd looked at the despairing figure

of the woman, crouching in her chair; he was distracted, overwrought, near to losing his nerve.

"He wants particularly to see you," cringed the secretary.

Mollie looked back at Bevis Holroyd, her lips moved twice in vain before she could say: "Go to him."

The doctor went slowly upstairs and the secretary followed.

Sir Harry was now flat on his back, staring at the dark tapestry curtains of his bed.

"I'm dying," he announced as the doctor bent over him.

"Nonsense. I am not going to allow you to die."

"You won't be able to help yourself. I've brought you here to see me die."

"What do you mean?"

"I've a surprise for you too, a Christmas present. These letters now, these love letters of my wife's— what name do you think is on them?"

"Your mind is giving way, Sir Harry."

"Not at all—come nearer, Deane—the name is Bevis Holroyd."

"Then they are letters ten years old. Letters written before your wife met you."

The sick man grinned with infinite malice.

"Maybe. But there are no dates on them and

the envelopes are all destroyed. And I, as a dying man, shall swear to their recent date—I, as a foully murdered man."

"You are wandering in your mind," said Bevis Holroyd quietly. "I refuse to listen to you any further."

"You shall listen to me. I brought you here to listen to me. I've got you. Here's my will, Deane's got that, in which I denounced you both, there are your letters, every one thinks that *she* put you in charge of the case, every one knows that you know all about arsenic in cambric tea through the Pluntre case, and every one will know that I died of arsenic poisoning."

The doctor allowed him to talk himself out; indeed it would have been difficult to check the ferocity of his malicious energy.

The plot was ingenious, the invention of a slightly insane, jealous recluse who hated his wife and hated the man she had never ceased to love; Bevis Holroyd could see the nets very skilfully drawn round him; but the main issue of the mystery remained untouched; who *was* administering the arsenic?

The young man glanced across the sombre bed to the dark figure of the secretary.

"What is your place in all this farrago, Mr. Deane?" he asked sternly.

"I'm Sir Harry's friend," answered the other

Cambric Tea

stubbornly, "and I'll bring witness any time against Lady Strangeways. I've tried to circumvent her—"

"Stop," cried the doctor. "You think that Lady Strangeways is poisoning her husband and that I am her accomplice?"

The sick man, who had been looking with bitter malice from one to another, whispered hoarsely:

"That is what you think, isn't it, Deane?"

"I'll say what I think at the proper time," said the secretary obstinately.

"No doubt you are being well paid for your share in this."

"I've remembered his services in my will," smiled Sir Harry grimly. "You can adjust your differences then, Dr. Holroyd, when I'm dead, *poisoned, murdered*. It will be a pretty story, a nice scandal, you and she in the house together, the letters, the cambric tea!"

An expression of ferocity dominated him, then he made an effort to dominate this and to speak in his usual suave stilted manner.

"You must admit that we shall all have a very Happy Christmas, doctor."

Bevis Holroyd was looking at the secretary, who stood at the other side of the bed, cringing, yet somehow in the attitude of a man ready to pounce; Dr. Holroyd wondered if this was the murderer.

83

"Why," he asked quietly to gain time, "did you hatch this plan to ruin a man you had never seen before?"

"I always hated you," replied the sick man faintly. "Mollie never forgot you, you see, and she never allowed *me* to forget that she never forgot you. And then I found those letters she had cherished."

"You are a very wicked man," said the doctor dryly, "but it will all come to nothing, for I am not going to allow you to die."

"You won't be able to help yourself," replied the patient. "I'm dying, I tell you. I shall die on Christmas Day."

He turned his head towards the secretary and added:

"Send my wife up to me."

"No," interrupted Dr. Holroyd strongly. "She shall not come near you again."

Sir Harry Strangeways ignored this.

"Send her up," he repeated.

"I will bring her, sir."

The secretary left, with a movement suggestive of flight, and Bevis Holroyd stood rigid, waiting, thinking, looking at the ugly man who now had closed his eyes and lay as if insensible. He was certainly very ill, dying perhaps, and he certainly had been poisoned by arsenic given in cambric tea, and, as certainly, a terrible scandal and a terrible danger would threaten with his death; the letters were *not* dated, the marriage was notoriously unhappy, and he, Bevis Holroyd, was associated in every one's mind with a murder case in which this form of poison, given in this manner, had been used.

Drops of moisture stood out on the doctor's forehead; sure that if he could clear himself it would be very difficult for Mollie to do so; how could even he himself in his soul swear to her innocence!

Of course he must get the woman out of the house at once, he must have another doctor from town, nurses—but could this be done in time; if the patient died on his hands would he not be only bringing witnesses to his own discomfiture? And the right people, his own friends, were difficult to get hold of now, at Christmas time.

He longed to go in search of Mollie—she must at least be got away, but how, without a scandal, without a suspicion?

He longed to have the matter out with this odious secretary, but he dared not leave his patient.

Lady Strangeways returned with Garth Deane and seated herself, mute, shadowy, with eyes full of panic, on the other side of the sombre bed.

"Is he going to live?" she presently whispered

as she watched Bevis Holroyd ministering to her unconscious husband.

"We must see that he does," he answered grimly.

All through that Christmas Eve and the bitter night to the stark dawn when the church bells broke ghastly on their wan senses did they tend the sick man who only came to his senses to grin at them in malice.

Once Bevis Holroyd asked the pallid woman:

"What was that white packet you had in your work box?"

And she replied:

"I never had such a packet."

And he:

"I must believe you."

But he did not send for the other doctors and nurses, he did not dare.

The Christmas bells seemed to rouse the sick man from his deadly swoon.

"You can't save me," he said with indescribable malice. "I shall die and put you both in the dock—"

Mollie Strangeways sank down beside the bed and began to cry, and Garth Deane, who by his master's express desire had been in and out of the room all night, stopped and looked at her with a peculiar expression. Sir Harry looked at her also.

"Don't cry," he gasped, "this is Christmas Day.

86

We ought all to be happy—bring me my cambric tea—do you hear?"

She rose mechanically and left the room to take in the tray with the fresh milk and water that the housekeeper had placed softly on the table outside the door; for all through the nightmare vigil, the sick man's cry had been for "cambric tea."

As he sat up in bed feebly sipping the vapid and odious drink the tortured woman's nerves slipped her control.

"I can't endure those bells, I wish they would stop those bells!" she cried and ran out of the room.

Bevis Holroyd instantly followed her; and now as suddenly as it had sprung on him, the fell little drama disappeared, fled like a poison cloud out of the compass of his life.

Mollie was leaning against the closed window, her sick head resting against the mullions; through the casement showed, surprisingly, sunlight on the pure snow and blue sky behind the withered trees.

"Listen, Mollie," said the young man resolutely. "I'm sure he'll live if you are careful—you mustn't lose heart—"

The sick room door opened and the secretary slipped out.

He nervously approached the two in the window place.

"I can't stand this any longer," he said through dry lips. "I didn't know he meant to go so far, he is doing it himself, you know; he's got the stuff hidden in his bed, he puts it into the cambric tea, he's willing to die to spite you two, but I can't stand it any longer."

"You've been abetting this!" cried the doctor.

"Not abetting," smiled the secretary wanly. "Just standing by. I found out by chance—and then he forced me to be silent—I had his will, you know, and I've destroyed it."

With this the strange creature glided downstairs.

The doctor sprang at once to Sir Harry's room; the sick man was sitting up in the sombre bed and with a last effort was scattering a grain of powder into the glass of cambric tea.

With a look of baffled horror he saw Bevis Holroyd but the drink had already slipped down his throat; he fell back and hid his face, baulked at the last of his diabolic revenge.

When Bevis Holroyd left the dead man's chamber he found Mollie still leaning in the window; she was free, the sun was shining, it was Christmas Day.

NICHOLAS OLDE

The Invisible Weapon

Before the snow had time to melt the great frost was upon us; and, in a few days, every pond and dyke was covered with half a foot of ice.

Hern and I were spending a week in a village in Lincolnshire, and, at the sight of the frozen fen, we sent to Peterborough for skates in keen anticipation of some happy days upon the ice.

'And now,' said Hern, 'as our skates will not be here until tomorrow, we had better take this opportunity of going to see Grumby Castle. I had not intended to go until later in the week, but, as neither of us wants to lose a day's skating, let us take advantage of Lord Grumby's permission immediately. The castle, as I told you, is being thoroughly overhauled to be ready for his occupation in the spring.'

Thus it was that, that same morning, we turned our backs upon the fen and trudged through the powdery snow into the undulating country towards the west until at last we came within sight of that historic pile and passed through the lodge gates and up the stately avenue. When we reached the great entrance door Hern took out Lord Grumby's letter to show to the caretaker – but it was not a caretaker that opened to our knock. It was a policeman.

The policeman looked at the letter and shook his head.

'I'll ask the inspector anyhow,' he said, and disappeared with the letter in his hand.

The inspector arrived on the doorstep a minute later.

'You are not Mr Rowland Hern, the detective, are you?' he asked.

'The same, inspector,' said Hern. 'I didn't know that I was known so far afield.'

'Good gracious, yes!' said the inspector. 'We've all heard of you. There's nothing strange in that. But that you should be here this morning is a very strange coincidence indeed.'

'Why so?' asked Hern.

'Because,' said the inspector, 'there is a problem to be solved in this castle that is just after your own heart. A most mysterious thing has happened here. Please come inside.'

We followed him through a vestibule littered with builders' paraphernalia and he led us up the wide stairway.

'A murder has been committed in this castle – not two hours since,' said the inspector. 'There is

only one man who could have done it – and he
could not have done it.'

'It certainly does seem to be a bit of a puzzle
when put like that,' said Hern. 'Are you sure that it
is not a riddle, like "When is a door not a door?"'

We had reached the top of the stairs.

'I will tell you the whole story from start to – well,
to the present moment,' said the inspector. 'You
see this door on the left? It is the door of the ante-
room to the great ballroom; and the ante-room is
vital to this mystery for two reasons. In the first
place, it is, for the time being, absolutely the only
way by which the ballroom can be entered. The door
at the other end has been bricked up in accordance
with his lordship's scheme of reconstruction, and the
proposed new doorway has not yet been knocked
through the wall: (that is one occasion when a door is
not a door),' he added with a smile; 'and even the fire-
places have been removed and the chimneys blocked
since a new heating system has rendered them super-
fluous. In the second place,' he continued, 'the work
in the ballroom itself being practically finished, this
ante-room has been, for the time being, appropri-
ated as an office by the contractors. Consequently it
is occupied all day by draughtsmen and clerks and
others, and no one can enter or leave the ballroom
during office hours unseen.

'Among other alterations and improvements that have been carried out is, as I have said, the installation of a heating apparatus; and there appears to have been a good deal of trouble over this.

'It has been installed by a local engineer named Henry Whelk, and the working of it under tests has been so unsatisfactory that his lordship insisted, some time since, on calling in a consulting engineer, a man named Blanco Persimmon.

'Henry Whelk has, from the first, very much resented the "interference", as he calls it, of this man; and the relations between the two have been, for some weeks, strained almost to the breaking-point.

'A few days ago the contractor received a letter from Mr Persimmon saying that he would be here this morning and would make a further test of the apparatus. He asked them to inform Whelk and to see to the firing of the boiler.

'Persimmon arrived first and went into the ball-room to inspect the radiators. He was there, talking to one of the clerks, when Whelk arrived and the clerk returned at once to the ante-room and shut the ballroom door behind him.

'Five minutes later Whelk came out and told the clerks to have the cock turned on that allows the hot water to circulate in that branch of the system, and to see that the ballroom door was not opened until Mr Persimmon came out, as he was going to test the temperature. He spoke with his usual resentment of the consultant and told the clerks that the latter had imagined that he could see a crack in one of the radiators which he thought would leak under pressure, and that that was his real reason for having the ballroom branch of the heating system connected up.

'In the meantime he took a seat in the anteroom with the intention of waiting there to hear Persimmon's report when he came out. Mr Hern,' said the inspector gravely, 'Persimmon never did come out.'

'Do you mean that he is still there?' asked Hern.

'He is still there,' said the inspector. 'He will be there until the ambulance comes to take him to the mortuary.'

'Has a doctor seen the body?' asked Hern.

'Yes,' said the inspector. 'He left five minutes before you came. He went by a field path, so you did not meet him in the avenue.

'Persimmon died of a fracture at the base of the skull caused by a violent blow delivered with some very heavy weapon. But we cannot find any weapon at all.

'Of course the clerks detained Whelk when, Persimmon failing to appear, they discovered the body.

They kept Whelk here until our arrival, and he is now detained at the police station. We have searched him, at his own suggestion; but nothing heavier than a cigarette-holder was found upon his person.'

'What about his boots?' asked Hern.

'Well, he has shoes on,' said the inspector, 'and very light shoes too – unusually light for snowy weather. They could not possibly have struck the terrible blow that broke poor Persimmon's skull and smashed the flesh to a pulp. Whelk had an attaché-case too. I have it here still, and it contains nothing but papers.'

'I suppose,' said Hern, 'that you have made sure that there is no weapon concealed about the body of Persimmon?'

'Yes,' said the inspector. 'I considered that possibility and have made quite sure.'

'Could not a weapon have been thrown out of one of the windows?' asked Hern.

'It could have been,' answered the inspector, 'but it wasn't. That is certain because no one could open them without leaving finger-marks. The insides of the sashes have only just been painted, and the paint is still wet; while the hooks for lifting them have not yet been fixed.

'I have examined every inch of every sash system-atically and thoroughly, and no finger has touched them. They are very heavy sashes too, and it would require considerable force to raise them without the hooks. No. It is a puzzle. And, although I feel that I must detain him, I cannot believe that Whelk can be the culprit. Would a guilty man wait there, actually abusing his victim before witnesses, until his crime was discovered? Impossible! Again, could he have inflicted that ghastly wound with a cigarette-holder? Quite impossible! But then the whole thing is quite impossible from beginning to end.'

'May I go into the ballroom?' said Hern.

'Certainly,' said the inspector.

He led the way through the ante-room, where three or four scared clerks were simulating industry at desks and drawing-boards, and we entered the great ballroom.

'Here is poor Persimmon's body,' said the inspector; and we saw the sprawling corpse, with its terribly battered skull, face down, upon the floor near one of the radiators.

'So the radiator did leak after all,' said Hern, pointing to a pool of water beside it.

'Yes,' said the inspector. 'But it does not seem to have leaked since I had the apparatus disconnected. The room was like an oven when I came in.'

Hern went all round the great bare hall examining

everything – floor, walls and windows. Then he looked closely at the radiators.

'There is no part of these that he could detach?' he asked. 'No pipes or valves?'

'Certainly not, unless he had a wrench,' said the inspector; 'and he hadn't got a wrench.'

'Could anyone have come through the windows from outside?' asked Hern.

'They could be reached by a ladder,' said the inspector; 'but the snow beneath them is untrodden.'

'Well,' said Hern; 'there doesn't seem to be anything here to help us. May I have a look at Whelk's case and papers?'

'Certainly,' said the inspector. 'Come into the ante-room. I've locked them in a cupboard.'

We followed him and he fetched a fair-sized attaché-case, laid it on a table and opened it.

Hern took out the papers and examined the inside of the case.

'A botanical specimen!' he exclaimed, picking up a tiny blade of grass. 'Did he carry botanical specimens about in his case? It seems a bit damp inside,' he added; 'especially at the side furthest from the handle. But let's have a look at the papers. Hullo! What's this?'

'It seems to be nothing but some notes for his business diary,' said the inspector.

Feb. 12. Letter from Jones. Mr Filbert called re
estimate.

Feb. 13. Office closed.

Feb. 14. Letter from Perkins & Fisher re Grumby
Castle.

Feb. 15. Letter from Smith & Co. Wrote Messrs.
Caraway re repairs to boiler. Visit Grumby Castle and
meet Persimmon 10.30 A.M.

'February the 15th is today.'

'Yes,' said Hern. 'The ink seems to have run a bit,
doesn't it? Whereabouts does Whelk live?'

'He lives in Market Grumby,' said the inspector.
His house is not far from where he is now – the
police-station. Market Grumby lies over there –
north of the castle. That footpath that goes off at
right angles from the avenue leads to the Market
Grumby road.'

Hern put everything back carefully into the
case – even the blade of grass – and handed it back
to the inspector.

'When do you expect the ambulance?' he asked.

'It should be here in a few minutes,' said the
inspector. 'I must wait, of course, until it comes.'

'Well,' said Hern. 'I suppose, when the body has
gone, there will be no harm in mopping up that

mess in there? There is a certain amount of blood as well as that pool of water.'

'No harm at all,' said the inspector.

'Well then,' said Hern. 'Please have it done. And, if it is not asking too much, could you oblige me by having the hot water turned on once more and waiting until I come back. I shall not be away for long; and I think that it may help in the solution of your problem.'

'Certainly,' said the inspector.

Hern and I went out again into the snowy drive and found, without difficulty, the path that led towards Market Grumby, for, in spite of the covering snow, it was clearly marked by footprints.

We walked along until we saw the opening into the road. A cottage stood on one side of the path, close to the road; and on the other side was a pond.

This was covered, like every pond, with a thick covering of ice, but in one spot, opposite the cottage, the ice had been broken with a pick and here an old man was dipping a bucket.

The water in the hole looked black against the gleaming ice and the sun glinted on the edges of the fragments loosened and thrown aside by the pick.

'Took a bit of trouble to break it, I expect,' said Hern to the old man.

'Took me half an hour,' grumbled the old fellow; 'it's that thick.'

'Is that the way to Market Grumby?' asked Hern, pointing to the road.

'That's it,' said the other, and went into the cottage with his bucket.

The snow in the few yards between the cottage and the hole in the ice was trodden hard by the hobnailed boots of the old man, but Hern pointed out to me that another set of footprints, of a much less bucolic type, could be seen beside them.

'Let us go back,' he said, 'and see how the inspector is getting on with the heating apparatus.'

'I've had it on for half an hour now,' said the inspector when we got back to the ante-room. 'The ambulance came soon after you went out.'

'Well,' said Hern. 'Let us see how that leak is going on'; and he opened the door of the ballroom.

'Good heavens,' cried the inspector. 'It's not leaking now.'

'It never did leak,' said Hern.

'What is the meaning of it all?' asked the inspector.

'You remember,' said Hern, 'that you came to the conclusion that if Whelk had been guilty he would have got away before his crime had been discovered.

'Well, my conclusion is different. In fact, I think

that, if he had been innocent, he would not have waited.'

'Why so?' asked the inspector.

'I will tell you,' said Hern. 'Whelk had to stay or he would certainly have been hanged. He hated Persimmon and had every reason for *taking* his life. If he had gone away you would have said that he had hidden the weapon that killed Persimmon.

'Don't you see that his only chance was to stay until you had searched him and found that he had no weapon? Was not that a clear proof of his innocence?'

'But there must have been some weapon,' exclaimed the worried inspector. 'Where is the weapon?'

'There was a weapon,' said Hern, 'and you and I saw it lying beside the corpse.'

'I saw no weapon,' said the inspector.

'Do you remember,' said Hern, 'that your first account of the problem made me think of a certain old riddle? Well, the answer to this problem is the answer to a new riddle: "When is a weapon not a weapon?"'

'I give it up,' said the inspector promptly.

'The answer to that riddle,' said Hern, 'is "when it melts".'

The inspector gasped.

'I will tell you,' said Hern, 'what happened. There is a pond close to the Market Grumby road, and Whelk passed this as he was coming here this morning to meet his enemy. The thick ice on that pond has been broken so that a bucket may be dipped, and chunks of broken ice lie all around the hole. Whelk saw these, and a terrible thought came into his wicked head. Everything fitted perfectly. He had found a weapon that would do its foul work and disappear. He picked up the biggest block of ice that would go inside his case. I dare say that it weighed twenty pounds. He waited until his enemy stooped to examine a radiator, and then he opened his case and brought down his twenty-pound sledge-hammer on the victim's skull.

'Then he put his weapon against the radiator, had the heat turned on, told his story about a leak, and waited calmly until a search should prove his innocence.

'But by the very quality for which he chose his weapon, that weapon has betrayed him in the end. For that jagged chunk of ice began to melt before its time – very slightly, it is true, but just enough to damp the side of the case on which it rested, to make the ink run on his papers and to set loose one tiny blade of grass that had frozen on to it as it lay

beside the pond. A very tiny blade but big enough
to slay the murderer.

'If you will go to the pond, inspector, you will
find footsteps leading to it which are not the cot-
tager's footsteps; and, if you compare them with the
shoes that Henry Whelk is wearing, you will find
that they tally.

'And, if they do not tally, then you may ask your
friends a new riddle.'

'What is that?' asked the officer.

'"When is a detective not a detective?"' replied
my friend; 'and the answer will be "When he is
Rowland Hern."'

Margery Allingham

Murder Under the Mistletoe

'Murder under the Mistletoe—and the man who must have done it couldn't have done it. That's my Christmas and I don't feel merry thank you very much all the same.' Superintendent Stanislaus Oates favoured his old friend Mr Albert Campion with a pained smile and sat down in the chair indicated.

It was the afternoon of Christmas Day and Mr Campion, only a trifle more owlish than usual behind his horn rims, had been fetched down from the children's party which he was attending at his brother-in-law's house in Knightsbridge to meet the Superintendent, who had moved heaven and earth to find him.

'What do you want?' Mr Campion inquired facetiously. 'A little armchair miracle?'

'I don't care if you do it swinging from a trapeze. I just want a reasonable explanation.' Oates was rattled. His dyspeptic face with the perpetually sad expression was slightly flushed and not with festivity. He plunged into his story.

'About eleven last night a crook called Sampson

was found shot dead in the back of a car in a garage under a small drinking club in Alcatraz Mews—the club is named The Humdinger. A large bunch of mistletoe which had been lying on the front seat ready to be driven home had been placed on top of the body partially hiding it—which was why it hadn't been found before. The gun, fitted with a silencer, but wiped of prints, was found under the front seat. The dead man was recognized at once by the owner of the car who is also the owner of the club. He was the owner's current boy friend. She is quite a well-known West End character called "Girl-ski". What did you say?'

'I said "Oo-er," murmured Mr Campion. 'One of the Eumenides, no doubt?'

'No.' Oates spoke innocently. 'She's not a Greek. Don't worry about her. Just keep your mind on the facts. She knows, as we do, that the only person who wanted to kill Sampson is a nasty little snake called Kroll. He has been out of circulation for the best of reasons. Sampson turned Queen's evidence against him in a matter concerning a conspiracy to rob Her Majesty's mails and when he was released last Tuesday Kroll came out breathing retribution.'

'Not the Christmas spirit,' said Mr Campion inanely.

'That is exactly what *we* thought,' Oates agreed.

'So about five o'clock yesterday afternoon two of our chaps, hearing that Kroll was at The Humdinger, where he might have been expected to make trouble, dropped along there and brought him in for questioning and he's been in custody ever since.

'Well, now. We have at least a dozen reasonably sober witnesses to prove that Kroll did not meet Sampson at the Club. Sampson had been there earlier in the afternoon but he left about a quarter to four saying he'd got to do some Christmas shopping but promising to return. Fifteen minutes or so later Kroll came in and stayed there in full view of Girlski and the customers until our men turned up and collected him. *Now* what do you say?'

'Too easy!' Mr Campion was suspicious. 'Kroll killed Sampson just before he came in himself. The two met in the dusk outside the club. Kroll forced Sampson into the garage and possibly into the car and shot him. With the way the traffic has been lately, he'd hardly have attracted attention had he used a mortar, let alone a gun with a silencer. He wiped the weapon, chucked it in the car, threw the mistletoe over the corpse, and went up to Girlski to renew old acquaintance and establish an alibi. Your chaps, arriving when they did, must have appeared welcome.'

Oates nodded. 'We thought that. *That is what*

happened. That is why this morning's development has set me gibbering. We now have two unimpeachable witnesses who swear that the dead man was in Chipperwood West at six last evening delivering some Christmas purchases he had made on behalf of a neighbour. That is *a whole hour* after Kroll was pulled in.

'The assumption is that Sampson returned to Alcatraz Mews sometime later in the evening and was killed by someone else—which we know is not true. Unfortunately the Chipperwood West witnesses are not the kind of people we are going to shake. One of them is a friend of yours. She asked our Inspector if he knew you because you were "so good at crime and all that nonsense".'

'Good Heavens!' Mr Campion spoke piously as the explanation of the Superintendent's unlikely visitation was made plain to him. 'I don't think I know Chipperwood West.'

'It's a suburb which is becoming fashionable. Have you ever heard of Lady Larradine?'

'Old Lady 'ell?' Mr Campion let the joke of his salad days escape without its being noticed by either of them. 'I don't believe it. She must be dead by this time!'

'There's a type of woman who never dies before you do,' said Oates with apparent sincerity. 'She's quite a dragon, I understand from our Inspector. However, she isn't the actual witness. There are two of them. Brigadier Brose is one. Ever heard of *him*?'

'I don't think I have.'

'My information is that you'd remember him if you'd met him. Well, we'll find out. I'm taking you with me, Campion. I hope you don't mind?'

'My sister will hate it. I'm due to be Santa Claus in about an hour.'

'I can't help that.' Oates was adamant. 'If a bunch of silly crooks want to get spiteful at the festive season, someone must do the homework. Come and play Santa Claus with me. It's your last chance. I'm retiring in the summer.'

Oates continued in the same vein as he and Mr Campion sat in the back of a police car threading their way through the deserted Christmas streets where the lamps were growing bright in the dusk.

'I've had bad luck lately,' the Superintendent said seriously. 'Too much. It won't help my memoirs if I go out in a blaze of no-enthusiasm.'

'You're thinking of the Phaeton Robbery,' Mr Campion suggested. 'What are you calling the memoirs? *Man-eaters of the Yard*?'

Oates's mild old eyes brightened, but not greatly. 'Something of the kind,' he admitted. 'But no one could be blamed for not solving that blessed Phaeton business. Everyone concerned was bonkers. A silly old musical star, for thirty years the widow of an eccentric Duke, steps out into her London garden one autumn morning leaving the street door wide open and all her most valuable jewellery collected from strong-rooms all over the country lying in a brown paper parcel on her bureau in the first room off the hall. Her excuse was that she was just going to take it to the Bond Street auctioneers and was carrying it herself for safety! The thief was equally mental to lift it.'

'It wasn't saleable?'

'Saleable! It couldn't even be broken up. The stuff is just about as well-known as the Crown Jewels. Great big enamels which the old Duke had collected at great expense. No fence would stay in the same room with them, yet, of course, they are worth the Earth as every newspaper has told us at length ever since they were pinched!'

'He didn't get anything else either, did he?'

'He was a madman.' Oates dismissed him with contempt. 'All he gained was the old lady's house-keeping money for a couple of months which was in her hand-bag—about a hundred and fifty quid—and the other two items which were on the same shelf, a soapstone monkey and plated paperknife. He simply wandered in, took the first things he happened to see and wandered out again. Any sneak thief, tramp, or casual snapper-upper could have done it and who gets blamed? *Me!*'

He looked so woebegone that Mr Campion hastily changed the subject. 'Where are we going?' he inquired. 'To call on her ladyship? Do I understand that at the age of one hundred and forty-six or whatever it is she is cohabiting with a Brig? Which war?'

'I can't tell you.' Oates was literal as usual. 'It could be the South African. They're all in a nice residential hotel—the sort of place that is very popular with the older members of the landed gentry just now.'

'When you say landed, you mean as in fish?'

'Roughly, yes. Elderly people living on capital. About forty of them. This place used to be called *The Haven* and has now been taken over by two ex-society widows and renamed *The CCraven*—with two Cs. It's a select hotel-cum-Old-Duck's Home for Mother's Friends. You know the sort of place?'

'I can envisage it. Don't say your murdered chum from The Humdinger lived there too?'

'No, he lived in a more modest place whose garden backs on *The CCraven*'s grounds. The Brigadier and one of the other residents, a Mr Charlie Taunton, who has become a bosom friend of his, were in the habit of talking to Sampson over the wall. Taunton is a lazy man who seldom goes out and has little money but he very much wanted to get some gifts for his fellow guests—something in the nature of little jokes from the chain stores, I understand; but he dreaded the exertion of shopping for them and Sampson appears to have offered to get him some little items wholesale and to deliver them by six o'clock on Christmas Eve—in time for him to package them up and hand them to Lady Larradine who was dressing the tree at seven.'

'And you say Sampson actually did this?' Mr Champion sounded bewildered.

'Both old gentlemen—the Brigadier and Taunton—swear to it. They insist they went down to the wall at six and Sampson handed the parcel over as arranged. My Inspector is an experienced man and he doesn't think we'll be able to shake either of them.'

'That leaves Kroll with a complete alibi. How did these Chipperwood witnesses hear of Sampson's death?'

'Routine. The local police called at Sampson's home address this morning to report the death, only to discover the place closed. The land-lady and her family are away for the holiday and Sampson himself was due to spend it with Girlski. The police stamped about a bit, making sure of all this, and in the course of their investigations they were seen and hailed by the two old boys in the adjoining garden. The two were shocked to hear that their kind acquaintance was dead and volunteered the information that he had been with them at six.'

Mr Campion looked blank. 'Perhaps they don't keep the same hours as anybody else,' he suggested. 'Old people can be highly eccentric.'

Oates shook his head. 'We thought of that. My Inspector, who came down the moment the local police reported, insists that they are perfectly normal and quite positive. Moreover, they had the purchases. He saw the packages already on the tree. Lady Larradine pointed them out to him when she asked after you. She'll be delighted to see you, Campion.'

'I can hardly wait!'

'You don't have to,' said Oates grimly as they pulled up before a huge Edwardian villa. 'It's all yours.'

'My dear Boy! You haven't aged any more than I have!'

Lady Larradine's tremendous voice—one of her chief terrors, Mr Campion recollected—echoed over the crowded first-floor room where she received them. There she stood in an outmoded but glittering

evening gown looking, as always, exactly like a
spray-flecked seal.

'I *knew* you'd come,' she bellowed. 'As soon as
you got my oblique little S.O.S. How do you like our
little hideout? Isn't it *fun*! Moira Spryg-Fysher and
Janice Poole-Poole wanted something to do, so we
all put our pennies in it and here we are!'

'Almost too marvellous,' murmured Mr Campion in all sincerity. 'We really want a word with
Brigadier Brose and Mr Taunton.'

'Of course you do and so you shall! We're all
waiting for the Christmas tree. Everybody will be
there for that in about ten minutes in the drawing
room. My dear, when *we* came they were calling it
the Residents' Lounge!'

Superintendent Oates remained grave. He was
startled to discover that the dragon was not only
fierce but also wily. The news that her apparently
casual mention of Mr Campion to the Inspector had
been a ruse to get hold of him shocked the innocent
Superintendent. He retaliated by insisting that he
must see the witnesses at once.

Lady Larradine silenced him with a friendly roar.
'My dear man, you can't! They've gone for a walk.
I always turn men out of the house after Christmas luncheon. They'll soon be back. The Brigadier
won't miss his Tree! Ah. Here's Fiona. This is Janice

Poole-Poole's daughter, Albert. Isn't she a pretty girl?'

Mr Campion saw Miss Poole-Poole with relief, knowing of old that Oates was susceptible to the type. The newcomer was young and lovely and even her beehive hair and the fact that she appeared to have painted herself with two black eyes failed to spoil the exquisite smile she bestowed on the helpless officer.

'Fabulous to have you really here,' she said and sounded as if she meant it. While he was still recovering, Lady Larradine led Oates to the window.

'You can't see it because it's pitch-dark,' she said, 'but out there, down in the garden, there's a wall and it was over it that the Brigadier and Mr Taunton spoke to Mr Sampson at six o'clock last night. No one liked the man Sampson—I think Mr Taunton was almost afraid of him. Certainly he seems to have died very untidily!'

'But he *did* buy Mr Taunton's Christmas gifts for him?'

The dragon lifted a webby eyelid.

'You have already been told that. At six last night Mr Taunton and the Brigadier went to meet him to get the box. I got them into their mufflers so I know! I had the packing paper ready, too, for Mr Taunton

to take up to his room . . . Rather a small one on
the third floor.'

She lowered her voice to reduce it to the volume
of distant traffic. 'Not many pennies, but a dear
little man!'

'Did you *see* these presents, Ma'am?'

'Not before they were wrapped! That would have
spoiled the surprise!'

'I shall have to see them.' There was a mulish
note in the Superintendent's voice which the lady
was too experienced to ignore.

'I've thought how to do that without upsetting
anybody,' she said briskly. 'The Brigadier and I will
cut the presents from the Tree and Fiona will be
handing them round. All Mr Taunton's little gifts are
in the very distinctive black and gold paper I bought
from Millie's Boutique and so, Fiona, you must give
every package in black and gold paper not to the
person to whom it is addressed but to the Superintendent. Can you do that, dear?'

Miss Poole-Poole seemed to feel the task difficult
but not impossible and the trusting smile she gave
Oates cut short his objections like the sun melting
frost.

'Splendid!' The dragon's roar was hearty. 'Give
me your arm, Superintendent. You shall take me
down.'

As the procession reached the hall, it ran into the Brigadier himself. He was a large, pink man, affable enough, but of a martial type and he bristled at the Superintendent. 'Extraordinary time to do your business—middle of Christmas Day!' he said after acknowledging the introductions.

Oates inquired if he had enjoyed his walk.

'Talk?' said the Brigadier. 'I've not been talking. I've been asleep in the card room. Where's old Taunton?'

'He went for a walk, Athole dear,' bellowed the dragon gaily.

'So he did. You sent him! Poor feller.'

As the old soldier led the way to the open door of the drawing room, it occurred to both the Superintendent and Mr Campion that the secret of Lady Larradine's undoubted attraction for the Brigadier lay in the fact that he could hear *her* if no one else. The discovery cast a new light altogether on the story of the encounter with Sampson in the garden.

Meanwhile, they had entered the drawing room and the party had begun. As Mr Campion glanced at the company, ranged in a full circle round a magnificent tree loaded with gifts and sparkling like a waterfall, he saw face after familiar face. They were elder acquaintances of the dizzy 1930s whom he had mourned as gone forever, when he thought of them at all. Yet here they all were, not only alive but released by great age from many of the restraints of convention.

He noticed that every type of headgear from night-cap to tiara was being sported with fine individualistic enthusiasm. But Lady Larradine gave him little time to look about. She proceeded with her task immediately.

Each guest had been provided with a small invalid table beside his armchair, and Oates, reluctant but wax in Fiona's hands, was no exception. The Superintendent found himself seated between a mountain in flannel and a wraith in mauve mink, waiting his turn with the same beady-eyed avidity.

Christmas Tree procedure at *The CCraven* proved to be well organized. The dragon did little work herself. Armed with a swagger stick, she merely prodded parcel after parcel hanging amid the boughs while the task of detaching them was performed by the Brigadier who handed them to Fiona.

Either to add to the excitement or perhaps to muffle any unfortunate comment on gifts received by the uninhibited company, jolly Christmas music was played throughout, and under cover of the noise Mr Campion was able to tackle his hostess.

'Where is Taunton!' he whispered.

'Such a nice little man. Most presentable, but just a little teeny-weeny bit dishonest.'

Lady Larradine ignored the question in his eyes and continued to put him in the picture at great speed, while supervising the Tree at the same time. 'Fifty-seven convictions, I believe, but only small ones. I only got it all out of him last week. Shattering! He'd been so *useful*, amusing the Brigadier. When he came, he looked like a lost soul with no luggage, but after no time at all he settled in perfectly.'

She paused and stabbed at a ball of coloured cellophane with her stick before returning to her startled guest.

'Albert, I am terribly afraid that it was poor Mr Taunton who took that dreadful jewelry of Maisie Phaeton's. It appears to have been entirely her fault. He was merely wandering past her house, feeling in need of care and attention. The door was wide open and Mr Taunton suddenly found himself inside, picking up a few odds and ends. When he discovered from all that fuss in the newspapers what he had got hold of—how well-known it was, I mean—he was quite horrified and had to hide. And where better place than here with us where he never had to go out?'

'Where indeed!' Mr Campion dared not glance across the room at the Superintendent unwrapping his black and gold parcels. 'Where is he now? Poor Mr Taunton, I mean.'

'Of course I hadn't the faintest idea what was worrying the man until he confessed,' the dragon went on stonily. 'Then I realized that something would have to be done at once to protect everybody. The wretch had hidden all that frightful stuff in our toolshed for three months, not daring to keep it in the house; and to make matters worse, the impossible person at the end of the garden, Mr Sampson, had recognized him and *would* keep speaking. Apparently people in the—er—underworld all know each other just like those of us in—er—other closed circles do.'

Mr Campion, whose hair was standing on end, had a moment of inspiration. 'This absurd rigmarole about Taunton getting Sampson to buy him some Christmas gifts wholesale was *your* idea!' he said accusingly.

The dragon stared. 'It seemed the best way of getting Maisie's jewelry back to her without any *one* person being involved,' she said frankly. 'I knew we should all recognize the things the moment we saw them and I was certain that after a lot of argument we should decide to pack them up and send

hem round to her. But, if there *were* any repercus-
ions, we should *all* be in it—quite a formidable
array, dear Boy—and the blame could be traced to
Mr Sampson if absolutely necessary. You see, the
Brigadier is convinced that Sampson *was* there last
night. Mr Taunton very cleverly left him on the lawn
and went behind the toolshed and came back with
the box.'

'How completely immoral!' Mr Campion couldn't
restrain himself.

The dragon had the grace to look embarrassed.

'I don't think the Sampson angle would ever have
arisen,' she said. 'But if it had, Sampson was quite
a terrible person. Almost a black-mailer. Utterly
dishonest and inconsiderate. Think how he has
spoiled everything and endangered us all by getting
himself killed on the *one* afternoon when we said he
was here, so that the police were brought in. Just the
one thing I was trying to avoid. When the Inspector
appeared this morning I was so upset I thought
of you!'

In his not unnatural alarm Mr Campion so far
forgot himself as to touch her sleeve. 'Where is
Taunton now?'

The dragon threshed her train. 'Really, Boy!
What a fidget you are! If you must know, I gave him
his Christmas present—every penny I had in cash

for he was broke again, he told me—and sent him
for a nice long walk after lunch. Having seen the
Inspector here this morning he was glad to go.'

She paused and a granite gleam came into her
hooded eyes. 'If that Superintendent friend of yours
has the stupidity to try to find him once Maisie has
her monstrosities back, none of us will be able to
identify him, I'm afraid. And there's another thing.
If the Brigadier should be *forced* to give evidence, I
am sure he will stick to his guns about Mr Sampson
being down in the garden here at six o'clock last
night. That would mean that the man Kroll would
have to go unpunished for his revenge murder,
wouldn't it? Sampson was a terrible person—but *no
one* should have killed him.'

Mr Campion was silenced. He glanced fearfully
across the room.

The Superintendent was seated at his table
wearing the strained yet slap-happy expression of a
man with concussion. On his left was a pile of black
and gilt wrappings, on his right a rajah's ransom in
somewhat specialized form.

From where he stood, Mr Campion could see
two examples amid the rest—a breastplate in gold,
pearl, and enamel in the shape of a unicorn and an
item which looked like a plover's egg in tourmaline

encased in a ducal coronet. There was also a soap-stone monkey and a solid-silver paperknife.

Much later that evening Mr Campion and the Superintendent drove quietly back to headquarters. Oates had a large cardboard box on his knee. He clasped it tenderly.

He had been silent for a long time when a thought occurred to him. 'Why did they take him into the house in the first place?' he said. 'An elderly crook looking lost! And no luggage!'

Mr Campion's pale eyes flickered behind his spectacles.

'Don't forget the Duchess' house-keeping money,' he murmured. 'I should think he offered one of the widows who really run that place the first three months' payment in cash, wouldn't you? That must be an impressive phenomenon in that sort of business, I fancy.'

Oates caught his breath and fell silent once more. Presently he burst out again.

'Those people! That woman!' he exploded. 'When they were younger they led me a pretty dance—losing things or getting themselves swindled. But now they're old they take the blessed biscuit! Do you see how she's tied my hands, Campion?'

Mr Campion tried not to grin.

'Snapdragons are just permissible at Christmas,'

he said. 'Handled with extreme caution they burn very few fingers, it seems to me.'

Mr Campion tapped the cardboard box. 'And some of them provide a few plums for retiring coppers, don't they, Superintendent?'

Happy Christmas

While caught up in the maelstrom of Christmas shoppers in the big department store, buffeted, crushed and elbowed by desperate purchasers, Edna Burrows began to feel claustrophobic. Perhaps it wasn't such a good idea after all, coming out late on Christmas Eve to visit the shops, but she'd acted on a whim. With the prospect of a lonely Christmas spent on her own, she had just wanted some company, some contact with humanity before she closed her door on the world for the duration of the festive season. Now she wasn't so sure she wanted any interaction with these inconsiderate, selfish demons whose only thoughts were to grab something from the shelves and barge their way to the tills, taking no notice of who they might shove out of the way in the process.

In desperation, Edna headed for the exit and squeezed her way out into the cold chill of a late December afternoon. *If that is humanity*, she mused, *you can keep it.* Doggedly, she made her way to the bus station and caught a number 43, which dropped her quite near to where she lived: Thornhill Avenue, a row of narrow terraced dwellings that had seen better days. As she approached home, she noticed a figure standing by the streetlamp adjacent to her house. It was a tall man, who was standing absolutely still and looking directly at number 12: her house. She felt her tummy tighten with apprehension. Who was this man? Why was he gazing at her house?

Moving closer, she could now see that the man was wearing a uniform: a police uniform. He turned to face her as she approached.

'Evening, madam,' he said in a friendly tone. He had a strong face, with a neat moustache and kind eyes. 'Do you live here?'

Edna nodded. 'Yes. Is there something wrong?'

'We're doing a house check down here, Mrs . . . ?'

'Burrows.'

'Yes, Mrs Burrows. I'm afraid one of the patients at Colston House has escaped . . .'

'Colston House, the mental place?'

The policeman nodded. 'The psychiatric hospital, yes. Apparently he used to live around here at one time and the doctors think he may well be headed back to his old stomping ground.'

Edna shivered. 'Oh dear.'

'I'm afraid he's very dangerous. So we're

checking all the houses in the area to make sure he hasn't sort of . . . y'know, got himself inside one of them, if you see what I mean.'

'Oh dear,' Edna repeated.

'I've been to all the properties on Thornhill apart from yours. So, Mrs Burrows, if you wouldn't mind letting me have a quick look round in your house, just checking to be on the safe side, like.'

'You want to go inside my house . . . now?'

He gave her a firm nod. 'Yes, if you don't mind. I'll just have a quick shufty. It won't take me long. Better safe than sorry, eh?'

'I suppose so,' said Edna, leading the way up the path and opening the door. Switching on the lights in the hall, she beckoned the policeman inside.

'Would you like a cup of tea?' she asked.

'That's very kind, but I'm OK, thanks.' He pulled a large torch from his jacket pocket. 'I'll just take a quick look upstairs and then finish off down here. I'm sure everything will be all right, but, as I say, better safe than sorry. I'll be out of your hair in less than ten minutes. I expect you've got plans, with it being Christmas Eve'.

Edna gave him a wan smile. As she made her way to the kitchen, she could hear the policeman's heavy footsteps clumping up the stairs. She filled the kettle at the sink and plugged it in. 'Plans for Christmas Eve,' she murmured and added a bitter laugh.

Having brewed the tea, she moved into the small sitting room, switched on the electric fire and drew the curtains. Moments later the policeman entered. 'All safe and sound,' he grinned. 'Nothing to worry about.'

He didn't notice the door behind swing open and a figure advance on him at speed. A figure with a knife in his hand. The figure plunged the blade into the neck of the policeman, who emitted a gurgling groan as he sank to his knees, eyes wide with shock and blood spewing from his mouth.

The man with the knife gazed down at the inert figure with a grin of satisfaction and then he turned his attention to Edna. 'Hello, Mum, I'm back,' he said. 'Happy Christmas.'

PETER LOVESEY

The Case of the Dead Wait

A Christmas at home wasn't ever in Laura Thyme's plans. Where was home? She'd hurled a large stone through the front window of her last one. Her two-timing cradle-snatcher of a husband Nick had blighted all the nice memories of that place. She tried to think of herself these days as a free spirit. *Tried*, because deep inside she hadn't entirely got the man out of her system. He still had the capacity to hurt.

Well, she was sure of one thing. She wouldn't dump herself on either of her grown-up children. They would have plans of their own, and quite right, too. If Matthew or Helena looked forward to pulling anything on Christmas Day it wasn't a cracker with their mum. They really were free spirits, long past the stage when Laura made it her business to know who they were sleeping with.

As for Rosemary – her gardening oppo, Dr Rosemary Boxer, the ex-academic with the happy knack of finding wealthy clients with ailing plants – she'd be the perfect company for a festive lunch, but she had an elderly mum living alone. Last weekend Rosemary had called to wish Laura a merrier time than she was expecting for herself.

The result: Laura was house-sitting.

She was alone in The Withers, a large Jacobean house in Wiltshire. Two of her oldest and richest friends, Jane and Michael Eadington, were having three weeks in the Canaries. A call at the end of November had set it up. 'We're in such trouble, Laura. You know we've got these silly orchids that are Mike's latest hobby? Our daughter Maeve – the model – was going to look after them and now she's got a chance to do a series of shows with Calvin Klein in New York. Could you, would you, *will* you, please, be our fairy godmother?'

Sorted.

Even after discovering that the house had another resident – Wilbur, the rescue greyhound.

She'd driven the Land Rover down there on Christmas Eve. For all its mechanical uncertainties the ancient four by four was ideal transport for the country. She overheated only once, and the car didn't overheat at all. She was just in time to see the Eadingtons off. A quick introduction to the orchids, six trays of them in the conservatory under banks of fluorescent tubing. Hurried instructions about the central heating, persuading Wilbur to wear a coat for

winter walks and what to do in a power failure. Firm
orders not to be in the least concerned if anything
broke or went wrong. 'It's all replaceable, darling.
We're just so pleased to have you here. Treat it like
your own home. Raid the freezer, watch the DVDs,
drink the wine in the cellar, have an orgy if you want.'

For a few minutes after they'd driven up the lane
Laura wondered if she'd done the right thing. The
house seemed bigger than she remembered from
the last visit. She'd never once set foot upstairs. The
orchids were in flower, but didn't look pleased at
being handed over to her care. Winter was supposed
to be the flowering season, but some of them were
wilting. Mike had talked about misting and humid-
ity levels and feeding. She didn't want any casualties.
She returned to the vast space the Eadingtons used
as the living room.

A sudden movement at the window gave her a
wicked shock. The greyhound had emerged from
behind the curtain, where he'd been sitting on the
sill. Yes, a greyhound on a window sill. It was that
kind of room, that kind of window, that kind of
curtain. 'I'm in charge now, Wilbur,' she told him,
wagging a finger, 'and if the two of us are going to
survive you'd better not play any more tricks like
that.'

Treat the place like your home, they'd said, so

she took out her Christmas cards and started setting them up. The cards triggered mixed feelings. It was good to hear from old friends, but it could hurt when the envelopes came addressed to Nick and Laura with messages along the lines of 'How are you two getting along? Give us a call and let's all meet up in 2005.'

Wilbur jumped back on his sill and knocked down most of the cards.

'Making some kind of point, are we?' Laura said. But she moved them to the grand piano.

When the doorbell rang a moment later, the rest of the cards dropped out of her hand. It was a chiming bell and her charming friends had set it to the opening bar of 'God Rest Ye, Merry Gentlemen', which can be pretty startling when you don't expect it. Wilbur barked, so she had to shut him in the conservatory first.

A tall – six-foot-tall, at least – thin-faced woman with deep-set, accusing eyes was on the doorstep with a plate covered with a cloth. 'And who the devil are you?' she said.

Laura did her best to explain, but it didn't make much impact.

'Where's young Maeve? She ought to be looking after the house,' the woman said.

'Yes, but she's dashed off to New York. A last-minute change of plans.'

'What do I do with these, then? I made them for the family.' She lifted the cloth briefly to reveal a batch of underdone mince pies.

'I don't know,' Laura said, adding with tact, 'They smell delicious. I'm sorry, but you didn't say who you are.'

'Gertrude Appleton from next door. We always exchange mince pies at Yuletide. Have you made yours?'

'I just arrived.'

That didn't count with Gertrude Appleton. She clicked her tongue and looked ready to stamp her foot as well. 'I must have one of yours, or I'll get bad luck for a year.'

'Why?'

'It's Wiltshire custom, isn't it? You eat a pie on each of the twelve days of Christmas, and every one has to be baked by a different friend. Then if the Lord is merciful you'll survive to see another Christmas. Bless my soul, there isn't anyone else I can ask.'

'You'd better step inside a moment,' Laura said, not wanting to panic this woman and playing for time while she thought about ways to resolve the problem.

'No, I won't come in,' Gertrude Appleton said,

and those fierce eyes were suddenly red at the edges and starting to water. 'I don't know you from Adam. Couldn't call thee a friend.'

'Let's be friends. Why not? It's the season for it,' Laura said, dredging deep to sound convivial. 'Listen, Gertrude, why don't I do some baking right now and make some pies for you?'

'But you won't have mincemeat.'

'I'm positive all the ingredients must be in the kitchen. Jane adores cooking, as you know.'

Gertrude raised her chin in a self-righteous way. 'Mine was made with the puddings four weeks ago, the week after Stir-up Sunday.'

'Stirrup what?'

'Stir-up Sunday. Haven't you heard of that? The last Sunday before Advent. That's when you make your puddings and mince, after the collect for the day; "Stir up, we beseech thee, O Lord, the wills of thy people."'

This was getting more and more weird.

'In that case, Jane may have made hers already,' Laura said. 'I'll check. One way or another, you'll get a mince pie from me, Gertrude. Depend upon it.'

'Take these, then.' Gertrude thrust the plate towards her. 'You'll need some for the waits.'

Laura had a mental picture of old-fashioned

kitchen scales, with her mince pie being weighed against Gertrude's and found wanting.

'The carollers. They come round every Christmas Eve, and they always want a bite to eat and mulled wine, too, the boozy lot. I must be off. I have seasonal jobs to do. There's greenfly and aphids in the greenhouse.'

'You're a gardener?' Laura said with interest.

'Ha!' She tossed her head. 'Am I a gardener? I wouldn't bother to go on without my garden. It's the saving of me.'

'I do some gardening, too. What are you going to do about the aphids – spray them?'

Gertrude looked shocked. 'I don't hold with chemicals. No, I'll smoke the varmints out, like I always do.'

'Fumigation? Effective, I expect, though I've never tried it,' Laura said.

'I've got these magical smoke things, like little strips of brown paper. Had them for years. Just close up all the windows and seal the cracks and set light to the strips. Let it blaze for a while, and then I stamp it out so they can smoulder. Soon as the smoke appears I'm out of there quicker than hell would scorch a feather and shut the door behind me. When I go in again, there's not a greenfly left to say it ever happened.'

Laura refrained from mentioning that the magical smoke things undoubtedly contained chemicals of some kind. 'Good luck with it, then. And I won't forget the mince pies. Which direction do you live?'

She was glad to have a task, although she could think of better ones than this. After closing the door she carried the plate to Jane's enormous kitchen, plonked it on the table and checked the walk-in larder for jars of mincemeat.

No joy. If you were planning to spend Christmas in Lanzarote, she reflected, you wouldn't feel obliged to make mincemeat. Even on Stir-up Sunday.

She checked the freezer. Well stocked, but not with seasonal items.

She thought of the supermarket in Bradford on Avon. A bought mince pie wouldn't suffice of course. Those eyes like calculators would spot a Mr Kipling at fifty paces. The pastry, at the very least, would have to look homemade.

Then Laura had her inspiration. She'd save herself the toil, tears and sweat by recycling some of Gertrude's own mince pies and simply making new lids for them. She picked a sharp knife and prised the lid off one. A neat dissection. The trick would be to spread a little jam over the mincemeat to seal the replacement.

She found all the ingredients she needed and switched on the oven.

When the phone on the wall rang she was up to her elbows in flour.

'You'll just have to leave a message after the tone,' she said to it.

'This is Calvin Klein's office in New York. Mr Klein was hoping to speak to Maeve about the trip. We'll call back.'

Laura said, 'Calvin Klein! I could be speaking to Calvin Klein and I'm sifting ruddy pastry?'

She was adding the egg yolk and water when the phone went again. This time she grabbed it with a floury hand. In a come-hitherish tone she said, 'Hi, how can I be of service?'

'Laura?'

She knew that voice and it wasn't Calvin Klein's. 'You! I thought you were someone else. Oh, never mind. It's good to hear from you.'

'It's a miracle,' Rosemary said. 'I used one of those directory enquiry numbers and I'm sure it was someone in Calcutta, but she seemed to know the Eadingtons. You're installed in deepest Wilts, then?'

'In deepest sums it up. I haven't been here an hour and I'm already making pastry for the locals. What's with you?'

'A change of plans, actually. Mother forgot to tell

me. When I got here she was all packed up to leave. You know she does competitions? She won a trip for two to the Bahamas, courtesy of Cadbury's, or Kellogg's, or someone.'

'How marvellous! But what are you going to wear? I bet you didn't pack your bikini.'

'Oh, she isn't taking me,' Rosemary said as if that went without saying. 'You know what mother's like. She's taking some old gent called Mr Pinkerton from the Tai Chi group. I'm high and dry, Laura. I was wondering if – well – if there's a spare bed in this stately pile you're looking after.'

Laura took a step back and there was a yelp from Wilbur, who had got too close. 'That wasn't me. Do I have a spare bed? Dozens. That's brilliant.'

'I could get a train to Bath tonight.'

'You've made my Christmas. I'll be waiting on the platform.'

She had fitted the fresh lids on those pies, twelve of them, and very appetizing they looked. She'd used a beaten egg glaze that gave them a lovely amber finish to leave no doubt that they were different from Gertrude Appleton's insipid-looking offerings. Rosemary was due on a late train at 10.50, so it was likely that the carollers would get their treats. Would eleven pies be enough? She needed to put one aside, of course, for Gertrude, to help her survival plan. If twelve or more carollers came, Laura told herself, it was a sure bet that some wouldn't want another pie if they'd been eating them all around the village. The mulled wine simmering in a saucepan was another matter.

About eight-thirty, Wilbur howled and Laura heard muted singing. She shut Wilbur in the kitchen and opened the front door. She needn't have worried about the catering. A mere four men stood under a lantern. Three wore cardboard and tinsel crowns and were giving an uneven rendering of 'We Three Kings'. The fourth, holding up the lantern, was the vicar unless his collar was from a carnival shop, like the crowns. He looked too young to be a clergyman. Just like policemen, Laura thought.

When they started on the solo verses, Melchior's reedy voice almost faded away. For a fat man he was producing a very thin sound. Caspar, with 'Frankincense to offer have I' was marginally better, and Balthazar, 'Myrrh is mine, its bitter perfume', lost the tune altogether. She was thankful when they got to the last chorus. She popped a two-pound coin into the box and invited them inside.

'Muddy feet,' said the vicar. 'We'd better not.'

Melchior had already taken a step forward and needed restraining by his companions. Too much

PETER LOVESEY

mulled wine already, Laura suspected. But she still
fetched the tray from the kitchen with the jug of
wine and the pies.

'I may have over-catered here. I was expecting
more of you,' she said as she invited them to help
themselves. The man who'd sung the part of Caspar
handed round the plate of mince pies, but it was
obvious that they'd eaten well already. Only Melchior took one. The wine was more popular.

'We would have had two shepherds as well,' Balthazar said, 'but one didn't show up and the other
dropped out at Long Farm.'

'It's quite a trek,' the vicar said.

'He was legless,' Balthazar said.

'You don't live here, do you?' Caspar asked
Laura. 'You're not a burglar, by any chance?'

'Giving us mulled wine and the finest mince pie
I've had all night? You must be joking,' Melchior
said to his friend.

A slightly dodgy mince pie, Laura almost confessed. They seemed likeable men, even if their
singing wasn't up to much. She introduced herself
and explained about the house-sitting. They told her
their names but she soon forgot them. They were the
vicar and Caspar, Melchior and Balthazar tonight,
and she'd probably never see them again, so why
think of them as anything else?

'What do you do when you're not house-sitting?' the tuneless one, Balthazar, asked.

'Gardening, mainly.'

'So do I. Not a lot of gardening to be done this time of year,' little Caspar said.

'You're wrong about that,' Laura said. 'There are no end of jobs. I'll be out there tomorrow.'

'Cutting some holly and mistletoe?' the vicar said.

'Good suggestion. The house could do with some, as you see.'

'Christmas roses? You've got some in the front.'

'If you mean the *helleborus niger*, they're not such good specimens. The ones you buy in florists come so much taller and whiter, thanks to forcing,' Laura said, thinking Rosemary would have been proud of that bit of expertise.

'Nasty things. Poisonous,' Melchior said, slurring his words even more.

'Mistletoe berries are poisonous, too,' Balthazar said.

The vicar decided not to go down that route. 'We'd better drink up, gentlemen. Three more houses and a long walk to go.'

'Have you been to Gertrude Appleton?' Laura asked.

'The house afore you. Stingy old mucker,' Melchior said.

'That's a bit unseasonal, isn't it?' the vicar said.

'We all know Gertrude,' Caspar said. 'Before we get a glass or a bite to eat from her, we have to promise to take *her* a mince pie after Christmas.'

'And if we forget, she'll come hammering on our doors,' Balthazar said.

Laura was about to explain that it was a superstition, but stopped herself. These villagers didn't miss a thing. They'd know all about Gertrude.

'Thanks for these, good lady,' Caspar said as he returned the plate, with ten of the eleven pies remaining. 'Sorry we couldn't all do justice to them.'

Melchior said without warning, 'I need to sit down. I'm feeling dizzy.'

'You'd better come in,' Laura offered. 'I was wondering about you.'

'And it's not the wine,' said Balthazar. 'He's a teetotaller.'

Laura gave Balthazar a second look, but he seemed to be speaking in all seriousness. She noticed Melchior didn't have a glass in his hand.

'Would you mind, Mrs Thyme?' the vicar said. 'I don't think he's capable of continuing.' He picked the crown off the fat man's head. 'I'll have to be Melchior now.' Judged by the speed of the change he'd wanted a starring role all evening.

Laura took a grip on Melchior's arm and steered

him inside to an armchair. Then she said something she was to regret. 'Why don't you gentlemen finish your round and come back for him?'

'He farms just up the lane,' Caspar said, and Laura thought she detected a suggestion that they might not, after all, return for their companion. 'Blackberry Farm. It can't be more than three hundred yards.'

They waved goodnight.

After closing the door, Laura glanced at her watch. There was still ample time before she needed to collect Rosemary.

Melchior had slumped in the chair and was snoring softly.

'Strong coffee for you,' Laura said.

He made a sound she chose to take as appreciation. It could have been a belch.

In the kitchen, Wilbur was round her feet. She found the store of dog food and opened a tin. She said, 'Consider yourself lucky, Wilbur. I've got other demands on my time.'

When she took the coffee to Melchior his snoring was heavier and his chin was buried in his chest. This wasn't good. She didn't want this overweight man settling into a deep sleep and being immovable just when she needed to drive to Bath. She checked the time again. She really ought to be leaving in less than an hour. She wasn't certain how long it would take to drive to the station.

'Coffee?'

No response.

'Have some coffee. It'll brighten you up.'

Wishful thinking. He didn't make a murmur that wasn't a snore.

In a louder voice she said, 'I made the coffee.'

This was becoming a predicament. She'd have to touch the man's face or hands to get a response, but she'd only just met him. Didn't even know his real name. How do I get myself into situations like this? she thought.

She put down the coffee and stood with her arms folded wondering how to deal with this. Wilbur came in and sniffed at the mud on the boots.

Fresh air, she decided. She flung open a couple of windows and an icy blast of December ripped through the room.

Wilbur streaked upstairs, but Melchior didn't move a muscle.

'Come on, man!' Laura said. She found the remote and switched on the television. Nine Lessons and Carols at full volume. Switched the channel to the Three Tenors.

No result.

In frustration Laura brought her two hands

together and slapped her own face quite hard. She'd
have to overcome her innate decorum and give him
a prod. Alone with a strange bloke in someone else's
house, but it had to be done.

First she switched off the three of them belting
out 'Nessun Dorma'. Her nerves couldn't take it.

Tentatively she put out a finger and touched the
back of Melchior's right hand, resting on the arm
of the chair. It remained quite still. She placed the
whole of her hand across it and squeezed.

There was a slight reaction, a twitch of the eyelids, but they didn't open. Laura leaned closer and
blew on them. Nothing.

She drew a deep breath and patted his fat face.

He made a sound, no more than 'Mm' – but a
definite response.

'Wake up, please,' she said. 'I don't want you
asleep.'

A triumph. The eyes opened and stared at her.

'It's no good,' she told him. 'You can't sit here for
ever. Let's see if you can walk to the car and I'll drive
you home. Blackberry Farm, isn't it?'

At the mention of his address, Melchior made
a definite effort to move. He rocked forward and
groaned. Laura thrust her hand under his armpit and
encouraged the movement. Out of sheer determin-
ation she got him to his feet. He was still unsteady,

but she wrapped his arm around her shoulders and hung on to it and kept him upright.

'The car's outside. Come on. Start walking.'

It was slow progress and a huge physical effort, but she kept him on the move, talking all the time in the hope that it would keep him conscious. Getting down the two small steps at the front door was hard enough, but the real challenge was hoisting him onto the passenger seat of the Land Rover.

She swung the door open with her free hand. 'I'm going to need your help here, Melchior. One giant leap for mankind.'

He moaned a little, maybe at Laura's attempt to be cheerful.

To encourage him, she curled her hand under his knee and lifted his right leg up to the level of the vehicle floor. It felt horribly limp. She found places for his hands to grip. 'On the count of three,' she said, 'and I'll probably end up with a slipped disc. One, two, three!'

If he made some gesture towards the performance it wasn't obvious. Laura found herself making a superhuman effort. Dignity abandoned, she put her shoulder under his rump and inched him upwards. All those hours of heavy gardening paid off. He got one buttock onto the seat and she rammed him like a front-row forward until he was in a position where she could snap the safety belt across.

She ran back to the house and closed the windows and door. Wilbur was inside, but did she have the key? She hoped so.

The Land Rover, bless its antiquated ignition system, started first time.

Blackberry Farm. Which way? Her passenger was in no condition to say. Laura swung right and hoped. The lanes were unlit, of course. Her full beam probed the hedgerows ahead. Can't be more than three hundred yards, Caspar had said. She'd gone that distance already. She continued for another two minutes, then found a gate entrance. Nothing so helpful as a sign. She reversed into the space and retraced her route. Maybe she should have turned left coming out of The Withers.

Then she saw the board for Blackberry Farm fixed to a drystone wall. Drove into the yard and sounded the horn. She'd need help getting Melchior down. It would be useful if he had a couple of hefty sons.

From one of the farm buildings came a wisp of a woman wearing overalls and wellies. She was about Melchior's age, Laura judged. Two sheep dogs came with her, barking.

'I've brought the farmer home,' Laura said,

competing to be heard. 'He's rather tired. Is there anyone who can help get him down?'

The little lady spread her hands. 'There's only me, my love.'

Laura got out and opened the passenger door. 'We'll have to manage together then. Is he your husband?'

'Yes, and I don't like the look of 'un,' the little lady said. 'Douglas, you gawpus, what's the matter with 'ee?'

Laura looked. Her passenger had taken a definite turn for the worse. He was making jerky movements with his head and left leg. Change of plan. 'I think we should get your husband to a doctor fast,' she said. 'Jump aboard.'

'I can't come with 'ee,' the farmer's wife said. 'I've got a cow in calf.'

'But I'm a stranger here. I don't know where to take him,' Laura almost wailed.

'Horse piddle.'

'What?'

'Royal United, Bath. Agzy-dennal Emergissy.'

Laura understood now. 'Which way?'

'Left out of the yard and straight up the lane till you reach the A36. You'll pick up the horse piddle signs when you get close to the city.'

'Can you call them and say I'm on the way with a man having convulsions?'

'After I've seen to the cow.'

Laura swung the Land Rover towards the gate, scattering the dogs, and started up the lane. 'Don't worry,' she said to Melchior, or Douglas, 'you'll be getting help very soon.' The only response was a vomiting sound.

'Please! Not in the Land Rover,' she muttered.

She was forced to concentrate on the drive, trusting in the Lord that she wouldn't meet anything as she belted along the lane. Passing points seemed to be unknown in this part of Wiltshire. The beam picked out the scampering shape of a badger up ahead. It saved itself by veering off to the left.

Then she spotted headlights descending a hill and guessed she was close to the main road. Right or left? She'd have to make a guess. Her instinct said right.

Forced to stop at the intersection, she glanced at her passenger. His face was still twitching and looked a dreadful colour in the passing lights. This was much more serious than over-indulgence in mulled wine.

Now was when she could do with an emergency light and siren. Out on the A36, with a long run into Bath – and a sign told her she *had* taken the right direction – she was overtaking like some teenage joyrider in a stolen Merc. Other drivers flashed their lights at her and one idiot got competitive and tried to force her to stay in the wrong lane. But there came a point when she was high on the downs and the city lights appeared below her. At any other time she would have been enchanted by the view. All she could think was where is the hospital?

At the first traffic lights she wound down the window and asked. Of course it had to be on the opposite side of the city. Another hair-raising burn-up through the streets and she found seriously helpful signs at last.

A&E. She drew up behind an ambulance. Someone was rolling a stretcher on wheels towards the Land Rover. The farmer's wife must have alerted them. The passenger door was opened.

'Is this the man with convulsions?'

Laura took this to be one of those inane questions people ask in times of crisis. Of course he had convulsions. He'd been convulsing all the way to the hospital.

But when she turned to look at him, he'd gone still.

They checked his heart. The doctor shook his head. They unstrapped Melchior and transferred him to the stretcher and raced it inside.

Nothing had been said to Laura. She could only

conclude that she'd brought in a man who was dead. Maybe they'd revive him. She moved the Land Rover away from the entrance and went in to find out.

She was twenty minutes late collecting Rosemary. It was such a relief to see her.

'I'm so sorry.'

'My dear, you look drained. Whatever has happened?'

Rosemary insisted on taking the wheel and Laura told her story as they headed out of the city.

'So couldn't they revive him?' Rosemary said.

'What's the phrase? Dead on arrival. They worked on him, but it was no use.'

'What was it – heart?'

'No one would say. They'll do an autopsy, I suppose. I told them all I could. It seemed to happen very suddenly. He said he felt dizzy and asked to sit down. I thought it was the mulled wine, but it turned out he hadn't had a drop all evening. He's TT. Then he fell asleep, a really deep sleep. I got him into the car – I don't know how – he was pretty far gone – and his wife noticed the convulsions, which was when I knew he needed medical help.'

'Dizziness, anaesthesia and convulsions. Was he vomiting?'

'Trying to, anyway.'

'It sounds more like poisoning to me,' Rosemary said.

'Poisoning?'

'Did he eat anything?'

'One of the mince pies I handed out. That's all.'

'That's all right then,' Rosemary said. 'No problem with that, if you were the cook.'

Laura clapped her hand to her mouth.

Rosemary said, 'What's wrong?'

'I did something dreadful. I may have killed him.'

'Hold on.' Rosemary pulled into a layby and turned off the engine. 'Laura, get a grip and tell me just what you're talking about.'

Laura's voice shook as she explained what she had done with Gertrude Appleton's pies. 'If there was anything in them I'll never forgive myself.'

From a distant field came the triple bark of a dog-fox, answered by a vixen sounding eerily like a woman screaming. Rosemary shivered. 'We'll face this together.'

It was close to midnight when they drove up the lane to The Withers. Christmas morning, almost.

In an effort to lighten the mood, Rosemary said, 'If you look in that bag at your feet you'll find I packed a bottle of bubbly. Let's open it as soon as we get in, shall we?'

'You're a star,' Laura said. 'Some Christmas

cheer in spite of everything.' But her voice trailed away.

A police car was on the drive.

'Is one of you ladies Mrs Laura Thyme?' the officer asked. 'You're about to see in Christmas at the police station.'

It was the day after Boxing Day, and still Laura was troubled by guilt.

'What upset me most was the way that detective put his hand on my head and pressed down when I got in their car, just like they do with murderers.'

'That didn't mean a thing,' Rosemary said.

'Well, he didn't do it to you.' Laura's voice shook a little. 'Is it possible those pies were poisoned?'

'Possible, I suppose.'

'Think of what goes into mincemeat – all those rich flavours, the fruits, the spice, the peel. You could add almost any poison and it wouldn't be obvious.'

'If they were poisoned, we've still got eleven of them sitting in the fridge.'

'Ten. I handed the singers a plate with eleven and ten came back. The farmer took one and ate it. That's certain.'

'There are eleven in the fridge. I counted,' Rosemary said in her precise way.

Laura snapped her fingers. 'You're right. I kept

one back for Gertrude, the neighbour. She asked specially.'

'Gertrude,' said Rosemary. 'She's the one the police should be questioning. I wonder if she'd eat that pie if you offered it. She wouldn't know it's one of hers with a new lid.'

'I don't want another death on my hands.'

'This is all supposition anyway,' Rosemary said. 'We'll probably find the poor man died of natural causes.'

'Listen, if Gertrude is a poisoner, those pies were meant for my friends Jane, Michael and Maeve. Was she in dispute with them? You know what neighbours can be like.'

'Neighbourly, in most cases.'

'What could she have used?'

'You said she's a gardener. You and I know that a garden is full of plants capable of poisoning people.'

'Christmas roses!' Laura said. 'We've got some in the front.'

'Let's not leap to any conclusions,' Rosemary said, trying to remain calm. 'Besides, your carol singers had been round most of the village eating mince pies and drinking wine before they got to you. If he was poisoned, it could have been someone else's pie that did it.'

Laura refused to think of anyone else except

Gertrude as responsible. 'I'd dearly like to know if she was having a feud with Jane and family.'

'Why don't we ask someone?'

'In a village? Who do you ask?'

'The vicar. He ought to be discreet.'

The vicarage was ten minutes away, at the end of a footpath across the frost-covered fields. If nothing else, they'd be exercising Wilbur the greyhound. With difficulty they got him into his coat.

They passed Gertrude's garden on the way. Laura grabbed Rosemary's arm. 'Look, she's got a patch of Christmas roses.'

'She's also got white bryony in her hedge and a poinsettia in her window, both of them potential killers, but it doesn't make her a murderer,' Rosemary said to curb Laura's imagination. 'She may have mistletoe inside the house. Death cap toadstools growing in her compost. I see she has a greenhouse. There could be an oleander in there.'

But Laura was unstoppable. 'I didn't tell you about the greenhouse. She told me she was fumigating it for pests, and I don't know what she was using, but it sounded primitive and hazardous as well. Would you believe burning shreds of paper that she had to stamp on to produce the smoke?'

Rosemary winced. 'Out of the ark, by the sound of it. Well, out of some dark shed. Old gardeners used flakes of nicotine. Highly dangerous, of course, and illegal now. What's wrong with a spray?'

Laura tapped the side of her nose. 'Chemicals.'

'Fumes are eco-friendly, are they? Isn't that the vicarage ahead?'

They shouted to Wilbur, who must have scented fox or rabbit. He raced back, tail going like a mainspring, and got no reward for obedience. He was put on the lead and no doubt decided it's a dog's life.

The vicarage was surrounded by a ten-foot yew hedge that Rosemary mentioned was another source of deadly poison. Laura gave her a long look. 'You wouldn't be winding me up, would you?'

She smiled. 'Encouraging a sense of proportion.'

The vicar, in a Bath Rugby Club sweatshirt, was relaxing after his Christmas duties. He sounded genuinely disturbed about the death of Melchior, and guilt-stricken, also. 'If I'd had any idea he was so ill, I wouldn't have asked you to take him in,' he said to Laura. 'You acted splendidly, getting him to hospital.'

'I couldn't tell the police much about him,' Laura said. 'Didn't even know his surname.'

'Boon. Douglas Boon. His family have farmed here for generations. Blackberry Farm is the last of the old farms. I suppose his wife inherits. There aren't any children. She'll have to sell up, I should think.'

'What do you mean by the last of the old farms?'

'Traditional. Cattle and sheep. Everyone's switching to flowers and bulbs since that foot and mouth epidemic. We didn't have an outbreak here, thank the Lord, but other farmers didn't want the risk and sold up. Much of the land has been put under glass by Ben Black, known to you as Balthazar.'

'The tall man?' Laura said.

'A giant in the nursery garden business and a very astute businessman. Lay chairman of the Parochial Church Council as well, so I have to work closely with him. He's from London originally. To the locals, he's an incomer, but he gives them a living.'

'So he'll be interested in Blackberry Farm if it comes on the market?' Rosemary said.

'No question.' The vicar sighed. 'I happen to know he made Douglas a handsome offer last week, far more than it's worth, and I heard that Douglas was willing at last to sell.'

'Every man has his price,' Laura remarked.

'Yes, and it is also said that gold goes in at any gate except the gate of heaven. As it turns out, Ben will get the farm for a fraction of that offer if Kitty Boon wants to sell.' He looked wistful. 'I'll be sorry if the cows go. They hold up the traffic when they're being driven along the lane for milking, but rows of daffodils wouldn't be the same at all.'

Laura had a vision of rows of daffies holding up the traffic.

'Do you mind if I ask about someone else?' she said. 'On Christmas Eve Gertrude Appleton called with some mince pies.'

'Gertrude?' The vicar had a special smile for this member of his flock. 'That's one of her many superstitions. Something about exchanging pies to avoid bad luck. False worship really. I don't approve, but we all indulge her because she's such a formidable lady.'

'Harmless?'

'We have to hope so.'

'Is she on good terms with my friends, Jane and Michael Eadington?'

'As far as I know.'

'No boundary disputes? Complaints about the greyhound? Excessive noise?'

'I've never heard of any. Why do you ask?'

Rosemary said quickly, 'It's a joke. Those pies she brought round aren't the most appetising.'

The vicar smiled. 'Now I understand. Did you try one?'

She shook her head. 'It's the look of them, paler than Hamlet's father.'

His eyes twinkled at that. 'I'm afraid not one of the carollers could face one the other night.'

'And will you indulge her, as you put it, and exchange mince pies?'

He smiled. 'The annual batch of pies for Gertrude is one more parochial duty for me. I don't have a wife to cook for me, unfortunately.'

'Your pies are delicious, I'm sure,' Laura said, liking this young clergyman.

Rosemary said in her no-nonsense voice, 'The third of the Three Kings was Caspar, right?'

'Little Colin Price the other night,' the vicar said. 'He's my tenor, at the other end of the scale from Ben Black.'

'As a singer, do you mean?'

'I was thinking of his situation. Colin's up against it financially. He was a dairy farmer like Douglas, but less efficient. He lost a big contract with the Milk Marketing Board a couple of years ago and Douglas bought him out. He's reduced to work as a jobbing gardener these days.'

Laura exchanged a wry smile with Rosemary. 'There are worse ways to make a living.'

'True. But I have to object when he does it on Sundays sometimes and misses Morning Service. Colin just smiles and quotes those lines "One is nearer God's heart in a garden than anywhere else on earth." That isn't scripture, I tell him, it's a bit of doggerel.'

The vicar came out to see them off and Rosemary admired the yew hedge and asked if he clipped it himself.

'Every twig,' he said. 'Can't afford a gardener on my stipend. Some people seem to have the idea that yew is slow-growing. From experience I can tell you that's a myth.'

'What do you do with the clippings – burn them?'

'No, I bag them up and send them away to be used in cancer treatment.'

'For the taxol in them,' Rosemary said. 'Very public-spirited.'

'I must admit they pay me as well,' the vicar said with a fleeting smile at Laura.

Their return across the frost-white fields was spoiled by a blue police light snaking through the lanes. Laura said, 'I just *know* it's going to stop at The Withers.'

She was right.

When they got there the inspector was looking smug. 'You might be thinking the forensics lab was closed over Christmas, but I happen to know one scientist who is a perfect Scrooge, can't stand the parties and the eating and only too grateful to earn double overtime. It's bad news for you, I'm afraid,

Mrs Thyme. The late Douglas Boon was poisoned. My scientist found significant amounts of taxin in his body.'

'Toxin?' Laura said.

'Taxin. It comes from the yew,' Rosemary murmured. 'Just like taxol, only this is no help to anyone, not to be taken in any form.'

'You're well informed,' the inspector said.

'I'm a plant biologist.'

'And Mrs Thyme? Are you also an expert?'

'Only an amateur,' Laura said.

About as amateur as a million-pound-a-week footballer, if the inspector's look was anything to go by. 'I've got a warrant to search this house.'

'Here? What are you looking for?' Rosemary asked.

'We know from the stomach contents that the last food Mr Boon ingested was a mince pie. In your statement of Christmas Eve, Mrs Thyme, you admitted administering a pie to the deceased.'

'*Administering?*' said Rosemary. 'She handed round a plate of pies, that's all.'

'And we'd like to have them examined, if they aren't already destroyed.'

This was a defining moment for Laura. Should she confess to changing the lids on Gertrude's pies? She glanced towards Rosemary, who nodded back.

'Inspector,' she said, 'there's something I ought to tell you, something I didn't mention last time.'

The inspector raised both hands as if a wall was about to collapse. 'Don't say another word. I'm going to issue an official caution and you're going to accompany me to the police station.'

'Oh, what nonsense,' Rosemary said. 'The pies were made by someone else, and that's all there is to it.'

'Don't put ideas in her head, Miss Boxer. She's in enough trouble already.'

As Laura got into the police car, Wilbur whimpered. The hand pressing down on the back of Laura's head felt like an executioner's this time. They kept her waiting more than an hour while the house was searched. The plate of mince pies, wrapped now in a polythene evidence bag, was carried from the kitchen in triumph.

Rosemary watched in silence, sickened and infuriated by this turn of events. She could see Laura's troubled face through the rear window of the patrol car as they drove away. She thought about following in the Land Rover, and then decided they wouldn't let her near the interview room. She'd be more useful finding out precisely what had been going on in this sinister village.

*

By asking around, she tracked Colin Price (the little man Laura knew as Caspar) to the garden behind the village hall. He was up a ladder pruning a huge rambler rose. The clippings were going into a trailer he'd wheeled across the lawn.

'What's that – an albertine?' Rosemary asked, seeing how the new shoots sprouted from well up the old stems.

'Spot on.'

'Late pruning, then?'

'It's a matter of getting round to these jobs,' he said. 'I can only do so much. It's mostly grass-cutting through the summer and well into autumn. Other jobs have to wait.'

She introduced herself and mentioned that she was Laura Thyme's friend. 'Laura had the unpleasant job of driving poor Mr Boon to hospital on Christmas Eve. You met her earlier, of course.'

'That's correct,' he said. 'And now she's been picked up by the police, I hear.'

'Word travels fast,' Rosemary said.

'Fields have eyes, and woods have ears, as the saying goes.' He got down from his ladder. 'But all of us can see a police car with the light flashing. What do you want to ask me?'

'It's about the man who died, Douglas Boon.

161

Could anyone have predicted that he'd take one of the mince pies my friend offered round?'

He shrugged. 'Doug liked his food. Everyone knew that. I've rarely seen him let a plate of pies go by.'

'So he had one at every house that evening?'

'Every one except Miss Appleton's.'

'Gertrude's? Was there a reason for that?'

A slow smile. 'Have you met the lady?'

'No.'

'Have you sampled her cooking?'

'No.'

'If you had, you'd understand.' He closed the pruning shears in a way that punctuated the remark.

She said, 'I thought you all exchanged pies with her.'

'We do, but we don't have to eat them. My wife always makes a batch and I prefer hers any day.'

Rosemary ventured into even more uncertain territory. 'Did Douglas have any enemies around here?'

He mused on that for a moment. 'None that I heard of.'

'His dairy farm was the last in the village, I heard. What will happen to it now?'

'Kitty isn't capable of running it alone. Likely it'll be bought for peanuts by Ben Black and turned into another nursery. That's the trend.'

'Sad to see the old farms disappearing,' Rosemary said. 'It happened to yours, I was told.'

'Bad management on my part,' Colin said without hesitation. 'I've no one to blame but myself. Doug acquired the herd and my three fields.'

'Would you buy them back if they came on the market?'

'I'm in no position to. Ben is the only winner here.'

She asked where Ben was to be found.

'This time of day? I wouldn't know. Last I saw of him was yesterday morning.'

She decided instead to call on the village Lucretia Borgia.

The cottage could have done with some new thatching, but otherwise it looked well maintained. Gertrude Appleton must have seen Rosemary coming because the door opened before she reached it.

Tall, certainly. She had to dip her head to look out of her door.

And she was holding a meat cleaver.

'What brings you here?' she asked Rosemary. The eyes fitted Laura's description of them as about as sympathetic as wet pebbles.

'I'm staying next door.'

'You think I don't know that? What do you want?'

A little Christmas cheer wouldn't come amiss,

Rosemary thought. 'My friend Laura has been taken to the police station for questioning about the death of Mr Boon.'

'So?'

'So she can't keep her promise to bring you a mince pie. We had some left, but the police have seized them.'

Those cheerless eyes widened a little. 'She baked me a pie?'

Rosemary sidestepped that one. 'She was saying it mattered to you, something about good luck for next year.'

Gertrude's face lightened up and she lowered the cleaver to her side. 'Did she really?'

'She said you generously made her a present of some pies of your own, and advised her that the carol singers were coming round.'

Abruptly, the whole look reverted to deep hostility. 'Was it one of my pies she fed to Douglas Boon?'

'I believe it was.'

'And now they're saying he was poisoned? Are you accusing me?' Suddenly the cleaver was in front of her chest again.

Rosemary swayed out of range. 'Absolutely not.'

'You said the police seized some pies. Were any of mine among them?'

'Actually, yes.'

Gertrude took in a sharp breath. 'I've made pies for twenty years and more, and never a word of complaint.'

'So we've got to find out how some taxin – that's from a yew bush or a tree, the seeds, the foliage or the stems – found its way into that pie, which apparently killed him.'

'One of mine? How could it?'

'Can you remember making the mincemeat? Did anyone come by while you were mixing the fruit?'

'Not a living soul.'

'Could anyone have interfered with it since?'

'Impossible. This isn't open house to strangers, you know. No one crosses my threshold.'

That much Rosemary was willing to believe. 'You don't have a yew bush in your garden, I suppose?'

'I wouldn't. It's the tree of death. It kills horses, cattle, more animals than any other plant.'

'Yes, but this was deliberate. Human deaths from taxin are rare. Someone added seeds of yew, or some part of it, to the mincemeat Douglas Boon consumed on Christmas Eve. Don't you see, Gertrude? We've got to discover how this happened. I'm certain Laura is innocent.'

'They'll pin this on me,' she said. 'That's what they'll do, and everyone in the village will say the old witch deserves it.'

'Will you do something for Laura's sake? For your own sake?' Rosemary said. 'Will you think about everything connected with the making of the mincemeat? The chopping of the fruit, the source of all the ingredients, sultanas, currants, raisins, peel, nuts – whatever went into it. Go over it in your mind. Did anyone else contribute anything?'

'No.'

'Please take time to think it over.'

Gertrude sniffed, stepped back and closed the door.

Late that afternoon, Wilbur's barking brought Rosemary to the front door before Laura emerged from the police car that returned her to The Withers.

'What a relief,' Rosemary said. 'Have they finished with you?'

'I wouldn't count on it,' Laura said as she scratched behind Wilbur's ears. He'd given her a delightful, if slobbery, welcome.

Over a fortifying cup of tea, she told her tale. She had been interviewed three times and kept in a room that wasn't quite a cell, but felt like one. She'd told the detectives everything she knew and provided a written statement. 'I'm sure they would have charged me with murder if it wasn't for Gertrude's pies. They had them analysed and got the results back this afternoon.'

'Poisoned?'

'No.' Laura smiled. 'They were harmless, all of them.'

Rosemary pressed her fingers to her lips. 'I find that hard to believe.'

'So did the inspector. You should have seen his face when he told me I was free to leave.'

'That's amazing. Gertrude is innocent.'

'And so am I.' Laura glanced across the room. 'What's he eating? Wilbur, what have you got in your mouth? No, Wilbur, no!' She dashed across and forced open the dog's jaws. A small piece of mince-meat fell into her palm. 'Rosemary, look. There are crumbs on the carpet. I think he's had a mince pie.'

Rosemary was already at her side fingering the pastry crumbs. 'It can't have come from inside the house. The police spent over an hour searching the place.'

'The garden, then,' Laura said. 'He must have found it in the garden.'

They went to the front door. 'Let him show us,' Rosemary said. 'Find it, Wilbur. Good dog.'

Wilbur knew what was wanted. He went straight to a lavender bush and lifted it with his nose. A brownish conical thing was exposed.

'A death cap,' Rosemary said.

'Do you mind?' Laura said. 'That's pastry. That's one of my lids.' She picked it up and turned it over. 'How on earth did this get here?'

The question hung in the air unanswered. Wilbur's co-operation could only go so far.

'Should we get him to a vet?' Laura said.

'Let's give him water first.'

Rosemary filled his bowl and brought it to him. He lapped it obediently.

'He doesn't seem to be suffering,' Laura said. 'The onset was rapid with Douglas Boon.'

'Taxin is one of the quickest of all the plant poisons,' Rosemary said. 'I doubt if we'd get him to a vet in time.'

'He looks all right.'

Wilbur licked her hand and wagged his tail.

'I think he wants some more.'

An hour later, he was still all right.

Rosemary and Laura allowed themselves the luxury of fresh tea. They didn't get to drink it because Wilbur unexpectedly barked several times and ran to the door. Someone was outside holding a flashlight.

Laura looked out. The evening had drawn in and she had difficulty seeing who it was.

The voice was familiar. 'You'd better call the

police,' Gertrude Appleton said. 'I've gone and killed another man.'

'This can't be true,' Laura said. 'You're in the clear. Your pies were analysed today and there's nothing toxic in them.'

With a stare like the condemned woman in a silent movie, Gertrude said, 'Follow me,' and started towards the gate.

Laura looked at Rosemary. They'd been in dangerous situations before. Rosemary shrugged. At least Gertrude wasn't wielding that cleaver. They went after her.

She paused at her garden gate and turned the flashlight beam on Rosemary and Laura to check that they were behind her. Then she led them to her greenhouse and unlocked the door.

The place would have been creepy even in daylight, with a huge overhanging vine that still had some of its leaves, brown and contorted. Other skeletal plants in pots had been brought in for the winter. Gertrude edged around a raised flowerbed in the centre and directed the flashlight at a dark shape on the floor.

A man's body.

'I killed him,' Gertrude said with a stricken sigh. 'I never looked here when I smoked out the pests on Christmas Eve. I just put down the stuff and set light to it.'

'He is dead, I suppose?' Laura said.

Rosemary leaned over for a closer look. 'Well dead, I would say.'

Gertrude was still reliving the experience. 'I made sure it was smouldering and got out, locking the door behind me. Opened it an hour ago and found him. I can only suppose he was drunk and crept in here to sleep it off.' She paused. 'Will I go to prison?'

'Let me have the flashlight,' Laura said. She edged past Gertrude for a closer inspection. 'I can't say I know him intimately, but isn't this one of the carol singers, the tall one, Balthazar?'

'Ben Black? It is!' Gertrude said in despair. 'God forgive me. What have I done?'

'Unless I've got my facts muddled, you haven't done anything at all,' Laura said. 'You fumigated on Christmas Eve after visiting me, am I right?'

Gertrude nodded.

'That was in the afternoon? You locked the door and didn't open up until today? You left the key in the lock?'

Another nod from Gertrude.

'Think about it,' Laura said. 'Ben was alive and singing carols that same evening. He couldn't have been trapped in here. See, there's dried blood on the back of his scalp. It looks as if someone hit him over the head and dumped the body in here. Yes, we will call the police, but I don't think you're in any trouble.'

Over cocoa that night, with the dog asleep in front of a real log fire, Rosemary summed up the case. 'What we have are two impossible crimes. One man poisoned by a harmless mince pie and another bludgeoned to death in a locked greenhouse.'

'The second crime isn't impossible,' Laura said. 'The key was in the door. Obviously the killer could get in and out. They put the body in there and locked it again thinking it might not be found for some time.'

'They?'

'Could be a man or a woman. That's all I mean.'

'Then are we agreed that there's only one killer?' Rosemary said.

'Let's hope so.'

'So why was Ben Black bumped off?'

'Because he knew something about the first crime?'

'Very likely. And why did the first crime take place?'

'The death of Douglas Boon? It could have been

a mistake,' Laura said. 'Maybe he ate a poisoned pie intended for Ben Black.'

'I don't think so,' Rosemary said. 'Remember, Douglas was a gannet. He was guaranteed to take any pie that was offered except one of Gertrude's.'

'Hers were on the heavy side,' Laura recalled.

'So if we assume Douglas's death was planned and carried out in cold blood, what did Ben find out that meant he had to be murdered as well?'

'It's got to be something to do with the mince pie Wilbur found under the lavender bush,' Laura said.

'Another harmless pie?'

They were silent for some time, staring into the flames. 'Do you think that young vicar is all he seems?' Rosemary said.

Laura frowned. 'I rather like him.'

'A bad sign usually,' Rosemary said. 'Let's go and see him tomorrow.'

'Won't the police say we're interfering?'

'They're going to be ages getting to the truth, if they ever do. For them it's all about analysing DNA evidence, and we know how long that takes. A good old-fashioned face-to-face gets a quicker result.'

Overnight it snowed and they both slept late.

'It's the total silence, I think,' Laura said. 'I always get a marvellous sleep when there's a snowfall.'

'Whatever it is,' Rosemary said, 'I've had a few ideas about these deaths and I'd like to try them out on you.'

After breakfast they put on wellies and took Wilbur for his longest walk yet. He was more frisky than ever, bounding through the snow regardless of that mince pie the day before. People might spurn Gertrude's cooking, but this hound had thrived on it. Along the way, they kept a look out for yew trees, and counted five in and around the village, and three yew hedges. Over a pre-lunch drink in a quiet corner of the pub, Rosemary unfolded her theory to Laura and it made perfect sense. They knew from experience that theories are all very well, but the proof can be more elusive. They decided to go looking for it late in the afternoon.

'Are we clear about what each of us does?' Rosemary said.

'All too clear,' Laura said. 'You get the inside job while I wait out here with Wilbur and freeze.'

'He'll be fine. He loves the snow and he's got his coat on. Just stroll around as if you're exercising him.'

They had parked outside the village church.

Rosemary went in and found the vicar slotting hymn numbers into the frame above the pulpit.

'Busy, I see.'

He almost dropped the numbers. 'You startled me. I have a choir practice shortly.'

'I know. We had a walk this morning, and I saw the church notice board.'

'We meet earlier when the schools are on holiday.'

'A smaller choir now.'

'Sadly, yes. Plenty of trebles and altos, but only one tenor remaining. I'm going to miss Ben and Douglas dreadfully.'

'Would you mind if I stay and listen?'

He looked uneasy. 'I don't know what sort of voice they'll be in after Christmas. There's always a feeling of anticlimax.'

'If it's inconvenient, vicar, I'll go.' She watched this challenge him. He was supposed to welcome visitors to his church.

After a moment, he said, 'Stay, by all means. But I must go and turn up the heating. I don't insist they wear vestments for practice, but I don't like to see them in coats and scarves.'

'Of course.'

Little boys started arriving, standing around the vestry on the north side, chattering about their Christmas presents. The choirstalls gradually filled. Two women choristers appeared from the vestry and so did Colin Price. He recognised Rosemary and smiled.

The practice was due at four. Some were looking at their watches. It was already ten past. The organist played a few bars and stopped. Everyone was in place except the vicar.

There was a certain amount of coughing. Then, unexpectedly, raised voices from the direction of the vestry. The vicar was saying, 'Outrageous. I can't believe you would be so brazen.'

A female voice said, 'I'll be as brazen as I like. I've got what I came for and now it's up to the police.' It was Laura.

'We'll see about that,' the vicar said.

'Get your hands off me,' Laura said.

Rosemary got up from the pew where she was sitting and walked quickly around the pulpit to the vestry. The door was open. Inside, the vicar was grappling with Laura, pressing her against the hanging coats and scarves.

Rosemary snatched up a brass candlestick and raised it high.

Over the vicar's shoulder Laura said, 'No, Rosemary!'

Distracted, the vicar turned his head and Laura seized her chance and shoved him away. He fell into a stack of kneelers.

He shouted to Rosemary, 'Don't help her. She's a thief. I caught her going through people's clothes.'

Laura said, 'You were right, Rosemary. There were pastry crumbs in his pocket. Oh, get out of my way, vicar. I'm going to make a citizen's arrest.'

She dodged past him and ran into the main part of the church in time to see a small figure making an exit through the west door.

Rosemary, some yards behind her, called out, 'Laura, that man is dangerous.'

'So am I when roused,' Laura said.

She dashed up the aisle and out of the church to the car park. There, the runaway, Colin Price, was standing by his pick-up truck. But he'd shied away from the door because a dog was baring its teeth in the driver's seat.

'Wilbur, you're a hero,' Laura said when she'd recovered enough breath. Before going in to search the vestry, she'd noticed the door of the pick-up was unlocked, so she'd installed Wilbur in the cab as a back-up.

Colin wasn't going to risk opening that door and he knew he wouldn't get far through the snow on foot. He raised both hands in an act of surrender.

To the delight of the choirboys, the practice was abandoned, and they were sent home. In the warmth of the vestry, Colin seemed not just willing to talk, but eager. 'I've been an idiot. I should never have killed twice. It was meant to turn out differently.'

'Why kill at all?' the vicar said. He'd dusted down his clothes and was a dignified figure again.

'I hated Douglas Boon,' Colin said. 'We were rivals in the old days, both of us dairy farmers, but he was so damned successful and I was failing on the paperwork. I couldn't compete. Lost my contract and had to sell up, and of course there was all the humiliation of selling to him – and for less than it was worth. He had me over a barrel. So I was reduced to odd jobs. I'd see my beautiful herd every day when I was on my way to mow another lawn. The resentment festered. And then I learned that Ben Black had made him an offer for the land, a huge offer, and he was selling up, for millions. He could retire and live in luxury and my cows would go for slaughter. The anger boiled over.'

'But they weren't your cows any more,' the vicar pointed out. 'You'd sold them.'

'You don't understand about animals, do you?' he said. 'I raised them from calves. They were a dairy herd, not for beef.'

'So you made up your mind to kill him,' Rosemary said, 'and you chose poison as the method. The yew, because its dangers are well known to all farmers, and the mince pie because it was part of the tradition here.'

'And Boon was a glutton,' he said. 'He was certain to take it.'

'Your wife had made a set of pies, knowing Gertrude would be round at some stage,' Rosemary went on. 'You added seeds of yew to one of them and had it with you on Christmas Eve. When you got to The Withers you took the plate as if to hand it round, but you passed your poisoned pie to Douglas.'

Colin glared at her. 'How do you know that? You weren't even there.'

Laura said, 'Pastry crumbs in your pocket, the obvious place to hide the killer pie. Our dog Wilbur found a pie in the garden and ate it. He survived, so it must have been a harmless one of ours that you chucked under a bush. I checked your coat for crumbs just now. That was what all the fuss was about. The vicar thought I was a thief.'

Rosemary said to Colin, 'Thanks to Laura getting the poor man to hospital, the police were alerted. News of the poisoning went quickly around the village and at some point over Christmas, Ben Brown got suspicious enough to come and see you. He threatened to tell the police. You panicked, cracked him on the head and killed him.'

Laura said, 'And transferred the body to

Gertrude's greenhouse in your pick-up and trailer. She was under suspicion, so you thought you'd add to it. While you were in church just now I checked under the tarpaulin in the trailer. Bloodstains. The police will match them to Ben's blood group.'

Colin's shoulders sagged. All the fight had gone out of him.

In all the excitement, Laura hadn't given a thought to her main reason for being in the house. Over supper that evening, she dropped her knife and fork and said, 'The orchids. I've completely forgotten about them.'

She had visions of dead and drooping plants in their dried-up trays.

'What am I going to say to Mike?' she said as she raced to the conservatory.

But the orchids were doing fine, better than when she'd taken over. The droopy ones were standing tall.

'They benefited from being left alone,' Rosemary said. 'He's a novice at this. The roots of an orchid are covered by a spongy material that holds water.'

'Like a camel's hump?'

'Well . . . I'm saying he must have overwatered them.'

That evening Wilbur was rewarded with a supper of chopped turkey and baked ham. After he'd curled up in front of the fire, Rosemary and Laura slipped out of the front door to make a call on a neighbour

Gertrude invited them in and poured large glasses of sherry.

'I'm so grateful to you both,' she said. 'I must have had calls from half the village saying how sorry they are for all I've been through. I kept telling them you two are the heroes.'

'Far from it,' Rosemary said with modesty.

'But you are. And you, Laura, being mistaken for a thief and wrestling with the vicar.'

'That wasn't so bad.'

Rosemary said, 'He's rather dishy. She enjoyed getting into a clinch.'

They all laughed.

'And now,' Gertrude said, looking happier than they'd seen her, 'another Christmas tradition. To ensure good fortune for us all in the new year, I insist that you have a slice of my homemade Christmas cake. You can make a wish.' She went out to the kitchen.

Rosemary said in confidence, 'I'm going to wish that I survive this.'

Laura said, 'I'm so glad I wore this cardigan. It's got pockets.'

Markheim

'Yes," said the dealer, "our windfalls are of various kinds. Some customers are ignorant, and then I touch a dividend on my superior knowledge. Some are dishonest," and here he held up the candle, so that the light fell strongly on his visitor, "and in that case," he continued, "I profit by my virtue."

Markheim had but just entered from the daylight streets, and his eyes had not yet grown familiar with the mingled shine and darkness in the shop. At these pointed words, and before the near presence of the flame, he blinked painfully and looked aside.

The dealer chuckled. "You come to me on Christmas Day," he resumed "when you know that I am alone in my house, put up my shutters, and make a point of refusing business. Well, you will have to pay for that; you will have to pay for my loss of time, when I should be balancing my books; you will have to pay, besides, for a kind of manner that I remark in you today very strongly. I am the essence of discretion, and ask no awkward questions; but when a customer cannot look me in the eye, he has to pay for it."

The dealer once more chuckled; and then changing to his usual business voice, though still with a note of irony, "You can give, as usual, a clear account of how you came into the possession of the object?" he continued. "Still your uncle's cabinet? A remarkable collector, sir!"

And the little pale, round-shouldered dealer stood almost on tip-toe, looking over the top of his gold spectacles, and nodding his head with every mark of disbelief. Markheim returned his gaze with one of infinite pity, and a touch of horror.

"This time," said he, "you are in error. I have not come to sell, but to buy. I have no curios to dispose of; my uncle's cabinet is bare to the wainscot; even were it still intact, I have done well on the Stock Exchange, and should more likely add to it than otherwise, and my errand to-day is simplicity itself. I seek a Christmas present for a lady," he continued, waxing more fluent as he struck into the speech he had prepared; "and certainly I owe you every excuse for thus disturbing you upon so small a matter. But the thing was neglected yesterday; I must produce my little compliment at dinner; and, as you very well know, a rich marriage is not a thing to be neglected."

There followed a pause, during which the dealer seemed to weigh this statement incredulously. The ticking of many clocks among the curious lumber of the shop, and the faint rushing of the cabs in a near thoroughfare, filled up the interval of silence.

"Well, sir," said the dealer, "be it so. You are an old customer after all; and if, as you say, you have the chance of a good marriage, far be it from me to be an obstacle. Here is a nice thing for a lady now," he went on, "this hand glass—fifteenth century, warranted; comes from a good collection, too; but I reserve the name, in the interests of my customer, who was just like yourself, my dear sir, the nephew and sole heir of a remarkable collector."

The dealer, while he thus ran on in his dry and biting voice, had stopped to take the object from its place; and, as he had done so, a shock had passed through Markheim, a start both of hand and foot, a sudden leap of many tumultuous passions to the face. It passed as swiftly as it came, and left no trace beyond a certain trembling of the hand that now received the glass.

"A glass," he said hoarsely, and then paused, and repeated it more clearly. "A glass? For Christmas? Surely not?"

"And why not?" cried the dealer. "Why not a glass?"

Markheim was looking upon him with an indefinable expression. "You ask me why not?" he said. "Why, look here—look in it—look at yourself! Do you like to see it? No! nor—nor any man."

The little man had jumped back when Markheim had so suddenly confronted him with the mirror; but now, perceiving there was nothing worse on hand, he chuckled. "Your future lady, sir, must be pretty hard-favoured," said he.

"I ask you," said Markheim, "for a Christmas present, and you give me this—this damned reminder of years, and sins and follies—this hand-conscience? Did you mean it? Had you a thought in your mind? Tell me. It will be better for you if you do. Come, tell me about yourself. I hazard a guess now, that you are in secret a very charitable man?"

The dealer looked closely at his companion. It was very odd, Markheim did not appear to be laughing; there was something in his face like an eager sparkle of hope, but nothing of mirth.

"What are you driving at?" the dealer asked.

"Not charitable?" returned the other gloomily. "Not charitable; not pious; not scrupulous; unloving, unbeloved; a hand to get money, a safe to keep it. Is that all? Dear God, man, is that all?"

"I will tell you what it is," began the dealer, with some sharpness, and then broke off again into a chuckle. "But I see this is a love match of yours, and you have been drinking the lady's health."

"Ah!" cried Markheim, with a strange curiosity. "Ah, have you been in love? Tell me about that."

"I," cried the dealer. "I in love! I never had the time, nor have I the time to-day for all this nonsense. Will you take the glass?"

"Where is the hurry?" returned Markheim. "It is very pleasant to stand here talking; and life is so short and insecure that I would not hurry away from any pleasure—no, not even from so mild a one as this. We should rather cling, cling to what little we can get, like a man at a cliff's edge. Every second is a cliff, if you think upon it—a cliff a mile high—high enough, if we fall, to dash us out of every feature of humanity. Hence it is best to talk pleasantly. Let us talk of each other: why should we wear this mask? Let us be confidential. Who knows, we might become friends?"

"I have just one word to say to you," said the dealer. "Either make your purchase, or walk out of my shop!"

"True, true," said Markheim. "Enough fooling. To business. Show me something else."

The dealer stooped once more, this time to replace the glass upon the shelf, his thin blond hair falling over his eyes as he did so. Markheim moved a little nearer, with one hand in the pocket of his greatcoat; he drew himself up and filled his lungs; at the same time many different emotions were depicted together on his face—terror, horror, and resolve, fascination and a physical repulsion; and through a haggard lift of his upper lip, his teeth looked out.

"This, perhaps, may suit," observed the dealer: and then, as he began to re-arise, Markheim bounded from behind upon his victim. The long, skewerlike dagger flashed and fell. The dealer struggled like a hen, striking his temple on the shelf, and then tumbled on the floor in a heap.

Time had some score of small voices in that shop, some stately and slow as was becoming to their great age; others garrulous and hurried. All these told out the seconds in an intricate chorus of tickings. Then the passage of a lad's feet, heavily running on the pavement, broke in upon these smaller voices and startled Markheim into the consciousness of his surroundings.

He looked about him awfully. The candle stood on the counter, its flame solemnly wagging in a draught; and by that inconsiderable movement, the whole room was filled with noiseless bustle and kept heaving like a sea: the tall shadows nodding, the gross blots of darkness swelling and dwindling as with respiration, the faces of the portraits and the china gods changing and wavering like images in water. The inner door stood ajar, and peered into that leaguer of shadows with a long slit of daylight like a pointing finger.

From these fear-stricken rovings, Markheim's eyes returned to the body of his victim, where it lay both humped and sprawling, incredibly small and strangely meaner than in life. In these poor, miserly clothes, in that ungainly attitude, the dealer lay like so much sawdust. Markheim had feared to see it, and, lo! it was nothing. And yet, as he gazed, this bundle of old clothes and pool of blood began to find eloquent voices. There it must lie; there was none to work the cunning hinges or direct the miracle of locomotion—there it must lie till it was found. Found! ay, and then? Then would this dead flesh lift up a cry that would ring over England, and fill the world with the echoes of pursuit. Ay, dead or not, this was still the enemy.

"Time was that when the brains were out," he thought; and the first word struck into his mind. Time, now that the deed was accomplished—time, which had closed for the victim, had become instant and momentous for the slayer.

The thought was yet in his mind, when, first one and then another, with every variety of pace and voice—one deep as the bell from a cathedral turret, another ringing on its treble notes the prelude of a waltz—the clocks began to strike the hour of three in the afternoon.

The sudden outbreak of so many tongues in that dumb chamber staggered him. He began to bestir himself, going to and fro with the candle, beleaguered by moving shadows, and startled to the soul by chance reflections. In many rich mirrors, some of home designs, some from Venice or Amsterdam, he saw his face repeated and repeated, as it were an army of spies; his own eyes met and detected him; and the sound of his own steps, lightly as they fell, vexed the surrounding quiet.

And still, as he continued to fill his pockets, his mind accused him with a sickening iteration, of the thousand faults of his design. He should have chosen a more quiet hour; he should have prepared an alibi; he should not have used a knife; he should have been more cautious, and only bound and gagged the dealer, and not killed him; he should have been more bold, and killed the servant also; he should have done all things otherwise—poignant regrets, weary, incessant toiling of the mind to change what was unchangeable, to plan what was now useless, to be the architect of the irrevocable past.

Meanwhile, and behind all this activity, brute

terrors, like the scurrying of rats in a deserted attic, filled the more remote chambers of his brain with riot; the hand of the constable would fall heavy on his shoulder, and his nerves would jerk like a hooked fish; or he beheld, in galloping defile, the dock, the prison, the gallows, and the black coffin.

Terror of the people in the street sat down before his mind like a besieging army. It was impossible, he thought, but that some rumour of the struggle must have reached their ears and set on edge their curiosity; and now, in all the neighbouring houses, he divined them sitting motionless and with uplifted ear—solitary people, condemned to spend Christmas dwelling alone on memories of the past, and now startlingly recalled from that tender exercise; happy family parties, struck into silence round the table, the mother still with raised finger: every degree and age and humour, but all, by their own hearths, prying and hearkening and weaving the rope that was to hang him.

Sometimes it seemed to him he could not move too softly; the clink of the tall Bohemian goblets rang out loudly like a bell; and alarmed by the bigness of the ticking, he was tempted to stop the clocks. And then, again, with a swift transition of his terrors, the very silence of the place appeared a source of peril, and a thing to strike and freeze the passer-by; and he would step more boldly, and bustle aloud among the contents of the shop, and imitate, with elaborate bravado, the movements of a busy man at ease in his own house.

But he was now so pulled about by different alarms that, while one portion of his mind was still alert and cunning, another trembled on the brink of lunacy. One hallucination in particular took a strong hold on his credulity. The neighbour hearkening with white face beside his window, the passer-by arrested by a horrible surmise on the pavement— these could at worst suspect, they could not know; through the brick walls and shuttered windows only sounds could penetrate.

But here, within the house, was he alone? He knew he was; he had watched the servant set forth sweet-hearting, in her poor best, "out for the day" written in every ribbon and smile. Yes, he was alone, of course; and yet, in the bulk of empty house above him, he could surely hear a stir of delicate footing— he was surely conscious, inexplicably conscious of some presence. Ay, surely; to every room and corner of the house his imagination followed it; and now it was a faceless thing, and yet had eyes to see with; and again it was a shadow of himself; and yet again behold the image of the dead dealer, reinspired with cunning and hatred.

At times, with a strong effort, he would glance at the open door which still seemed to repel his eyes. The house was tall, the skylight small and dirty, the day blind with fog; and the light that filtered down to the ground story was exceedingly faint, and showed dimly on the threshold of the shop. And yet, in that strip of doubtful brightness, did there not hang wavering a shadow?

Suddenly, from the street outside, a very jovial gentleman began to beat with a staff on the shop-door, accompanying his blows with shouts and railleries in which the dealer was continually called upon by name. Markheim, smitten into ice, glanced at the dead man. But no! he lay quite still; he was fled away far beyond earshot of these blows and shoutings; he was sunk beneath seas of silence; and his name, which would once have caught his notice above the howling of a storm, had become an empty sound. And presently the jovial gentleman desisted from his knocking and departed.

Here was a broad hint to hurry what remained to be done, to get forth from this accusing neighbour-hood, to plunge into a bath of London multitudes, and to reach, on the other side of day, that haven of safety and apparent innocence—his bed. One visitor had come; at any moment another might follow and be more obstinate. To have done the deed, and yet not to reap the profit, would be too abhorrent a failure. The money, that was now Markheim's concern; and as a means to that, the keys.

He glanced over his shoulder at the open door, where the shadow was still lingering and shivering; and with no conscious repugnance of the mind, yet with a tremor of the belly, he drew near the body of his victim. The human character had quite departed. Like a suit half-stuffed with bran, the limbs lay scattered, the trunk doubled, on the floor; and yet the thing repelled him. Although so dingy and inconsiderable to the eye, he feared it might have more significance to the touch.

He took the body by the shoulders, and turned it on its back. It was strangely light and supple, and the limbs, as if they had been broken, fell into the oddest postures. The face was robbed of all expression; but it was as pale as wax, and shockingly smeared with blood about one temple. That was, for Markheim, the one displeasing circumstance. It carried him back, upon the instant, to a certain fair-day in a fishers' village: a gray day, a piping wind, a crowd upon the street, the blare of the brasses, the booming of drums, the nasal voice of a ballad singer; and a boy going to and fro, buried over head in the crowd and divided between interest and fear, until, coming out upon the chief place of concourse, he

beheld a booth and a great screen with pictures, dis-
mally designed, garishly coloured: Brownrigg with
her apprentice; the Mannings with their murdered
guest; Weare in the death-grip of Thurtell; and a
score besides of famous crimes.

The thing was as clear as an illusion; he was once
again that little boy; he was looking once again, and
with the same sense of physical revolt, at these vile
pictures; he was still stunned by the thumping of
the drums. A bar of that day's music returned upon
his memory; and at that, for the first time, a qualm
came over him, a breath of nausea, a sudden weakness of the joints, which he must instantly resist and
conquer.

He judged it more prudent to confront than to
flee from these considerations; looking the more
hardily in the dead face, bending his mind to realise
the nature and greatness of his crime. So little a
while ago that face had moved with every change of
sentiment, that pale mouth had spoken, that body
had been on fire with governable energies; and now,
by his act, that piece of life had been arrested, as
the horologist, with interjected finger, arrests the
beating of the clock. So he reasoned in vain; he
could rise to no more remorseful consciousness; the
same heart which had shuddered before the painted
effigies of crime, looked on its reality unmoved. At

best, he felt a gleam of pity for one who had been endowed in vain with all those faculties that can make the world a garden of enchantment, one who had never lived and who was now dead. But of penitence, no, not a tremor.

With that, shaking himself clear of these considerations, he found the keys and advanced towards the open door of the shop. Outside, it had begun to rain smartly; and the sound of the shower upon the roof had banished silence. Like some dripping cavern, the chambers of the house were haunted by an incessant echoing, which filled the ear and mingled with the ticking of the clocks. And, as Markheim approached the door, he seemed to hear, in answer to his own cautious tread, the steps of another foot withdrawing up the stair. The shadow still palpitated loosely on the threshold. He threw a ton's weight of resolve upon his muscles, and drew back the door.

The faint, foggy daylight glimmered dimly on the bare floor and stairs; on the bright suit of armour posted, halberd in hand, upon the landing; and on the dark wood-carvings, and framed pictures that hung against the yellow panels of the wainscot. So loud was the beating of the rain through all the house that, in Markheim's ears, it began to be distinguished into many different sounds. Footsteps and sighs, the tread of regiments marching in the distance, the chink of money in the counting, and the creaking of doors held stealthily ajar, appeared to mingle with the patter of the drops upon the cupola and the gushing of the water in the pipes.

The sense that he was not alone grew upon him to the verge of madness. On every side he was haunted and begirt by presences. He heard them moving in the upper chambers; from the shop, he heard the dead man getting to his legs; and as he began with a great effort to mount the stairs, feet fled quietly before him and followed stealthily behind. If he were but deaf, he thought, how tranquilly he would possess his soul! And then again, and hearkening with ever fresh attention, he blessed himself for that unresting sense which held the outposts and stood a trusty sentinel upon his life. His head turned continually on his neck; his eyes, which seemed starting from their orbits, scouted on every side, and on every side were half-rewarded as with the tail of something nameless vanishing. The four-and-twenty steps to the first floor were four-and-twenty agonies.

On that first story, the doors stood ajar, three of them like three ambushes, shaking his nerves like the throats of cannon. He could never again, he felt, be sufficiently immured and fortified from men's observing eyes; he longed to be home, girt in by walls, buried among bedclothes, and invisible to all but God. And at that thought he wondered a little, recollecting tales of other murderers and the fear they were said to entertain of heavenly avengers. It was not so, at least, with him. He feared the laws of nature, lest, in their callous and immutable procedure, they should preserve some damning evidence of his crime. He feared tenfold more, with a slavish, superstitious terror, some scission in the continuity of man's experience, some wilful illegality of nature. He played a game of skill, depending on the rules, calculating consequence from cause; and what if nature, as the defeated tyrant overthrew the chessboard, should break the mould of their succession?

The like had befallen Napoleon (so writers said) when the winter changed the time of its appearance. The like might befall Markheim: the solid walls might become transparent and reveal his doings like those of bees in a glass hive; the stout planks might yield under his foot like quicksands and detain him in their clutch; ay, and there were soberer accidents that might destroy him: if, for instance, the house should fall and imprison him beside the body of his victim; or the house next door should fly on fire, and the firemen invade him from all sides. These things he feared; and, in a sense, these things might be called the hands of God reached forth against sin. But about God Himself he was at ease; his act was doubtless exceptional, but so were his excuses, which God knew; it was there, and not among men, that he felt sure of justice.

When he had got safe into the drawing-room, and shut the door behind him, he was aware of a respite from alarms. The room was quite dismantled, uncarpeted besides, and strewn with packing cases and incongruous furniture; several great pier-glasses, in which he beheld himself at various angles, like an actor on a stage; many pictures, framed and unframed, standing with their faces to the wall, a fine Sheraton sideboard, a cabinet of marquetry, and a great old bed, with tapestry hangings. The windows opened to the floors; but by great good fortune the lower part of the shutters had been closed, and this concealed him from the neighbours. Here, then, Markheim drew in a packing case before the cabinet, and began to search among the keys.

It was a long business, for there were many; and it was irksome, besides; for after all there might be nothing in the cabinet, and time was on the wing. But the closeness of the occupation sobered him. With the tail of his eye he saw the door—even glanced at it from time to time directly, like a besieged commander pleased to verify the good estate of his defences. But in truth he was at peace. The rain falling in the street sounded natural and pleasant. Presently, on the other side, the notes of a piano were wakened to the music of a hymn, and the voices of many children took up the air and words. How stately, how comfortable was the melody! How fresh the youthful voices!

Markheim gave ear to it smilingly, as he sorted out the keys; and his mind was thronged with answerable ideas and images; church-going children and the pealing of the high organ; children afield, bathers by the brookside, ramblers on the brambly common, kite-flyers in the windy and cloud-navigated sky; and then, at another cadence of the hymn, back again to church, and the somnolence of summer Sundays, and the high genteel voice of the parson (which he smiled a little to recall) and the painted Jacobean tombs, and the dim lettering of the Ten Commandments in the chancel.

And as he sat thus, at once busy and absent, he was startled to his feet. A flash of ice, a flash of fire, a bursting gush of blood, went over him, and then he stood transfixed and thrilling. A step mounted the stair slowly and steadily and presently a hand was laid upon the knob, and the lock clicked, and the door opened.

Fear held Markheim in a vice. What to expect

he knew not, whether the dead man walking, or the official ministers of human justice, or some chance witness blindly stumbling in to consign him to the gallows. But when a face thrust into the aperture, glanced round the room, looked at him, nodded and smiled as if in friendly recognition, and then withdrew again, and the door closed behind it, his fear broke loose from his control in a hoarse cry. At the sound of this the visitant returned.

"Did you call me?" he asked pleasantly, and with that he entered the room and closed the door behind him.

Markheim stood and gazed at him with all his eyes. Perhaps there was a film upon his sight, but the outlines of the newcomer seemed to change and waver like those of the idols in the wavering candle-light of the shop; and at times he thought he knew him; and at times he thought he bore a likeness to himself; and always, like a lump of living terror, there lay in his bosom the conviction that this thing was not of the earth and not of God.

And yet the creature had a strange air of the commonplace, as he stood looking on Markheim with a smile; and when he added: "You are looking for the money, I believe?" it was in the tones of everyday politeness.

Markheim made no answer.

"I should warn you," resumed the other, "that the maid has left her sweetheart earlier than usual and will soon be here. If Mr. Markheim be found in this house, I need not describe to him the consequences."

"You know me?" cried the murderer.

The visitor smiled. "You have long been a favourite of mine," he said; "and I have long observed and often sought to help you."

"What are you?" cried Markheim; "the devil?"

"What I may be," returned the other, "cannot affect the service I propose to render you."

"It can," cried Markheim; "it does! Be helped by you? No, never; not by you! You do not know me yet; thank God, you do not know me!"

"I know you," replied the visitant, with a sort of kind severity or rather firmness. "I know you to the soul."

"Know me!" cried Markheim. "Who can do so? My life is but a travesty and slander on myself. I have lived to belie my nature. All men do, all men are better than this disguise that grows about and stifles them. You see each dragged away by life, like one whom bravos have seized and muffled in a cloak. If they had their own control—if you could see their faces, they would be altogether different, they would shine out for heroes and saints! I am worse than most; myself is more overlaid; my excuse is known to men and God. But, had I the time, I could disclose myself."

"To me?" inquired the visitant.

"To you before all," returned the murderer. "I supposed you were intelligent. I thought—since you exist—you could prove a reader of the heart. And yet you would propose to judge me by my acts! I was born and I have lived in a land of giants; giants have dragged me by the wrists since I was born out of my mother—the giants of circumstance. And you would judge me by my acts! But can you not look within? Can you not see within me the clear writing of conscience, never blurred by any willful sophistry, although too often disregarded? Can you not read me for a thing that surely must be common as humanity—the unwilling sinner?"

"All this is very feelingly expressed," was the reply, "but it regards me not. These points of consistency are beyond my province, and I care not in the least by what compulsion you may have been dragged away, so as you are but carried in the right direction. But time flies; the servant delays, looking in the faces of the crowd and at the pictures on the hoardings, but still she keeps moving nearer; and remember, it is as if the gallows itself was striding towards you through the Christmas streets! Shall I help you; I, who know all? Shall I tell you where to find the money?"

"For what price?" asked Markheim.

"I offer you the service for a Christmas gift," returned the other.

Markheim could not refrain from smiling with a kind of bitter triumph. "No," said he, "I will take nothing at your hands; if I were dying of thirst, and it was your hand that put the pitcher to my lips, I should find the courage to refuse. It may be credulous, but I will do nothing to commit myself to evil."

"I have no objection to a deathbed repentance," observed the visitant.

"Because you disbelieve their efficacy!" Markheim cried.

"I do not say so," returned the other; "but I look on these things from a different side, and when the life is done my interest falls. The man has lived to serve me, to spread black looks under colour of religion, or to sow tares in the wheatfield, as you do, in a course of weak compliance with desire. Now that he draws so near to his deliverance, he can add but one act of service—to repent, to die smiling, and thus to build up in confidence and hope the more timorous of my surviving followers. I am not so hard a master. Try me. Accept my help. Please yourself in life as you have done hitherto; please yourself more amply, spread your elbows at the board; and when the night begins to fall and the curtains to be drawn, I tell you, for your greater comfort, that you will find it even easy to compound your quarrel with your conscience, and to make a truckling peace with God. I came but now from such a deathbed, and the room was full of sincere mourners, listening to the man's last words; and when I looked into that face, which had been set as a flint against mercy, I found it smiling with hope."

"And do you, then, suppose me such a creature?" asked Markheim. "Do you think I have no more generous aspirations than to sin, and sin, and sin, and, at the last, sneak into heaven? My heart rises at the thought. Is this, then, your experience of mankind? Or is it because you find me with red hands that you presume such baseness? And is this crime of murder indeed so impious as to dry up the very springs of good?"

"Murder is to me no special category," replied the other. "All sins are murder, even as all life is war. I behold your race, like starving mariners on a raft, plucking crusts out of the hands of famine and feeding on each other's lives. I follow sins beyond the moment of their acting; I find in all that the last consequence is death; and to my eyes, the pretty maid who thwarts her mother with such taking graces on a question of a ball, drips no less visibly with human gore than such a murderer as yourself. Do I say that I follow sins? I follow virtues also; they differ not by the thickness of a nail, they are both scythes for the reaping angel of Death. Evil, for which I live, consists not in action but in character. The bad man is dear to me; not the bad act, whose fruits, if we could follow them far enough down the hurtling cataract of the ages, might yet be found more blessed than those of the rarest virtues. And it is not because you have killed a dealer, but because you are Markheim, that I offer to forward your escape."

"I will lay my heart open to you," answered Markheim. "This crime on which you find me is my last. On my way to it I have learned many lessons; itself is a lesson, a momentous lesson. Hitherto I have been driven with revolt to what I would not; I was a bond-slave to poverty, driven and scourged. There are robust virtues that can stand in these temptations; mine are not so: I had a thirst of pleasure. But to-day, and out of this deed, I pluck both warning and riches—both the power and a fresh resolve to be myself. I become in all things a free actor in the world; I begin to see myself all changed, hands the agents of good, this heart at peace. Something comes over me out of the past; something of what I have dreamed on Sabbath evenings to the sound of the church organ, of what I forecast when I shed tears over noble books, or talked, an innocent child, with my mother. There lies my life; I have wandered a few years, but now I see once more my city of destination."

"You are to use this money on the Stock Exchange, I think?" remarked the visitor; "and there, if I mistake not, you have already lost some thousands?"

"Ah," said Markheim, "but this time I have a sure thing."

"This time, again, you will lose," replied the visitor quietly.

"Ah, but I keep back the half!" cried Markheim.

"That also you will lose," said the other.

The sweat started upon Markheim's brow. "Well, then, what matter?" he exclaimed. "Say it be lost, say I am plunged again in poverty, shall one part of me, and that the worst, continue until the end to override the better? Evil and good run strong in me, haling me both ways. I do not love the one thing, I love all. I can conceive great deeds, renunciations, martyrdoms; and though I be fallen to such a crime as murder, pity is no stranger to my thoughts. I pity the poor; who knows their trials better than myself? I pity and help them; I prize love, I love honest laughter; there is no good thing nor true thing on earth but I love it from my heart. And are my vices only to direct my life, and my virtues without effect, like some passive lumber of the mind? Not so; good, also, is a spring of acts."

But the visitant raised his finger. "For six-and-thirty years that you have been in this world," said he, "through many changes of fortune and varieties of humour, I have watched you steadily fall. Fifteen years ago you would have started at a theft. Three years back you would have blanched at the name of murder. Is there any crime, is there any cruelty or meanness, from which you still recoil?—five years from now I shall detect you in the fact! Downward, downward, lies your way; nor can anything but death avail to stop you."

"It is true," Markheim said huskily, "I have in some degree complied with evil. But it is so with all; the very saints, in the mere exercise of living, grow less dainty, and take on the tone of their surroundings."

"I will propound to you one simple question," said the other; "and as you answer, I shall read to you your moral horoscope. You have grown in many things more lax; possibly you do right to be so; and at any account, it is the same with all men. But granting that, are you in any one particular, however trifling, more difficult to please with your own conduct, or do you go in all things with a looser rein?"

"In any one?" repeated Markheim, with an anguish of consideration. "No," he added, with despair, "in none! I have gone down in all."

"Then," said the visitor, "content yourself with what you are, for you will never change; and the words of your part on this stage are irrevocably written down."

Markheim stood for a long while silent, and indeed it was the visitor who first broke the silence. "That being so," he said, "shall I show you the money?"

"And grace?" cried Markheim.

"Have you not tried it?" returned the other. "Two or three years ago did I not see you on the platform of revival meetings, and was not your voice the loudest in the hymn?"

"It is true," said Markheim; "and I see clearly what remains for me by way of duty. I thank you for these lessons from my soul; my eyes are opened, and I behold myself at last for what I am."

At this moment, the sharp note of the door-bell rang through the house; and the visitant, as though this were some concerted signal for which he had been waiting, changed at once in his demeanour.

"The maid!" he cried. "She has returned, as I

forewarned you, and there is now before you one more difficult passage. Her master, you must say, is ill; you must let her in, with an assured but rather serious countenance—no smiles, no over-acting, and I promise you success! Once the girl within, and the door closed, the same dexterity that has already rid you of the dealer will relieve you of this last danger in your path. Thenceforward you have the whole evening—the whole night, if needful—to ransack the treasures of the house and to make good your safety. This is help that comes to you with the mask of danger. Up!" he cried; "up, friend; your life hangs trembling in the scales: up, and act!"

Markheim steadily regarded his counsellor. "If I be condemned to evil acts," he said, "there is still one door of freedom open—I can cease from action. If my life be an ill thing, I can lay it down. Though I be, as you say truly, at the beck of every small temptation, I can yet, by one decisive gesture, place myself beyond the reach of all. My love of good is damned to barrenness; it may, and let it be! But I have still my hatred of evil; and from that, to your galling disappointment, you shall see that I can draw both energy and courage."

The features of the visitor began to undergo a wonderful and lovely change: they brightened and softened with a tender triumph, and, even as they brightened, faded and dislimned. But Markheim did not pause to watch or understand the transformation. He opened the door and went downstairs very slowly, thinking to himself. His past went soberly before him; he beheld it as it was, ugly and strenuous like a dream, random as chance-medley—a scene of defeat. Life, as he thus reviewed it, tempted him no longer; but on the farther side he perceived a quiet haven for his bark.

He paused in the passage, and looked into the shop, where the candle still burned by the dead body. It was strangely silent. Thoughts of the dealer swarmed into his mind, as he stood gazing. And then the bell once more broke out into impatient clamour.

He confronted the maid upon the threshold with something like a smile.

"You had better go for the police," said he. "I have killed your master."

H. R. F. KEATING

The Case of the Seven Santas

Mrs Craggs, former cleaning lady, secure in her retirement to the remote village of Princefinger, lying somewhere between the Dartmoor cragginess of Princeton and the mild Buckinghamshire comforts of Princes Risborough, wondered silently why she had ever agreed to a visit from her co-worker of old, Mrs Milhorne.

'Yaiss,' Mrs Milhorne was saying with elegant reflectiveness, 'I do love the countryside. So peaceful and what you might call "armon-hhharmonious."'

She looked round.

'Why,' she went on, 'I don't suppose as 'ow – as hhhow you'd find anywhere in all England peacefuller than your Princefinger. Though, mind, I like a touch of class meself. That little bit of, you know, excitement.'

'Good thing you wasn't here last Christmas then,' Mrs Craggs replied. 'Dare say you'd of found it a mite too exciting.'

'Oh, I don't think so. I'd of enjoyed a real country Christmas. All the jollity.'

'Yeh, well, it was a real country Christmas all right up at the Manor. Old Mr Ebenezer, 'e really liked that sort

o' thing. The 'ole Charles Dickens bit. 'Olly, carols, plum
pudding, Santa Claus, Yule log, presents round the tree
Pity 'e 'ad to go an' get murdered right in the middle of it.

Mrs Milhorne choked.

'O' course,' Mrs Craggs resumed when her friend had
been patted on the back and was able to manage another
sip of tea, 'asked for it, old Eb did. No getting past that.
I mean, when you're a rich bachelor living all on your
ownio 'cept for a valet 'oose 'alf daft any'ow, to go bringing down fer Christmas seven different people as you've
told are coming in fer something under the will an' then
to threaten to cut some of 'em out of it . . . Signing your
death stiffticicate, that is.'

'So it was one of them as done – as was doing it?'
Mrs Milhorne breathed, pale eyes glowing.

'Well, there they was, each one of 'em due fer a cool
'undred thousand, an' there was 'e saying some of 'em
might not 'ave the right Christmas spirit . . .'

'So one of them – one of those seven did – No, I'm
wrong. There was eight. There was that valet.'

'You're counting 'im in then? That's more than what
the police did. Soon as they 'eard old Tiny Tom – that's
what I called 'im on account of 'im being so tall – as
soon as they 'eard 'e was provided for with a nice little
annuity started years before, they ruled 'im right out.'

'So it was just the seven then? Just the seven.'

★

It was Mrs Craggs who discovered the body. When she came plodding into the big, stone-flagged kitchen at the Manor on Christmas morning, stamping off her boots the snow that had fallen overnight, she was greeted by old Mr Ebenezer's ancient valet, Tiny Tom, in even more of a dither than usual.

'Oh, Mrs Craggs, Mrs Craggs,' he moaned in his dungeon-deep voice the moment he saw her. 'I can't find him. I can't find him. Not in his bed when I took him his morning tea. Not in his bathroom. Not in his bed when I went back to look again. It hadn't been slept in, Mrs Craggs. That's what I can't understand. It hadn't even been slept in.'

'Then perhaps 'e never got into it,' Mrs Craggs replied with a sharp sniff.

'Never went to bed? You mean, he – he never went to bed?'

'Yes, you daft lummox. Fell asleep in 'is chair down in what 'e calls the 'all, most likely. Decked with boughs 'o 'oily indeed.'

'He could have, Mrs Craggs. He could have. They passed the steaming bowl of punch about enough last night, the smoking bishop as Mr Ebenezer said in his very own words.'

'I'll give 'im bishop,' Mrs Craggs replied, setting off, tramp, tramp, tramp, towards the manor's lofty hall, with Tiny Tom trailing along behind her like an outsize question-mark.

But bishop Mrs Craggs was unable to give old Mr Ebenezer. He was in his chair all right, but there was a neat little bullet hole in the middle of his forehead.

There was more to the scene of the crime, too. Mr Ebenezer's corpse was buried up to the chest in Christmas crackers. Bright red and vibrant green with here and there a little glued-on picture of a robin or a reindeer, they were piled up by the hundred round his tall carved armchair. And, more, stuck on the knob at the chair's top there was a sheet of paper. It bore in neat printed letters the simple words 'Old Scratch has got his own at last.'

'Well, don't just stand there with your mouth 'anging open like a blooming codfish,' Mrs Craggs said to Tiny Tom. 'Phone for the police. There's been murder done, you know.'

But, of course, in the end it was Mrs Craggs who got herself put straight on to Inspector Hummbugg. She woke him from his bed, at the end of which dangled the stocking his faithful spouse, Martha Hummbugg née Wilkins, had filled the night before with fifty-two tins of his favourite tobacco, one for each week of the year.

'Yes,' Mrs Craggs pounded into his scarcely woken ear. 'Murdered. That's what I said. Murdered.

An' plenty o' clues fer you, too. So you'd better get 'ere just as fast as you can. An' bring yer fingerprint set. I think you're going to need it. Princefinger Manor. Princefinger Manor. Now, 'ave you got that, or 'aven't you?'

'I shall arrive in due course,' said Inspector Hummbugg, and the sigh he gave as he contemplated the crammed stocking at the foot of the marital bed floated like a gale down the telephone line.

But eventually Mrs Craggs showed his bulky form, and that of the pale young sergeant who came with him, into the hall where Mr Ebenezer in his tall chair, a bullet hole in his head, sat surrounded by the high-piled Christmas crackers beneath the sheet of paper bearing the words 'Old Scratch has got his own at last.'

It was this that seemed to puzzle Inspector Hummbugg most.

'Old Scratch?' he said. 'Now who on earth can Old Scratch be? Find out that, and, mark my words, sergeant, we'll have our murderer under our thumb.'

For a long moment he comtemplated that thumb, a formidable piece of pig-pink flesh.

'Scrooge, sir,' said the pale sergeant.

Inspector Hummbugg's little porcine eyes darted him a look of quick suspicion.

'It's Dickens, sir,' the sergeant said, with haste.

215

'His story, *A Christmas Carol.* Sir, it's about a man called Scrooge, and—'

'I'll thank you not to teach your grandfather to suck eggs, sergeant. I know who Scrooge is, if you please.'

'Yes, sir. But—' He was a courageous young man, this pallid sergeant. 'Sir, in that story by Charles – In it, sir, when the Spirit of Times Yet to Come is showing old Scrooge the future they hear a City merchant saying just those words, sir.'

'Just what words, sergeant? What are you blathering on about now?'

But that pale sergeant was a very courageous young man.

'Just "Old Scratch has got his own at last", sir. They're in the book, *A Christmas Carol.* Look, there's a copy in that bookcase over there. I'll show you.'

He advanced towards a tailor-made bookcase containing each and every one of the works of Charles Dickens, old Mr Ebenezer's favourite author, as he had been of his parents before him. Hence Mr Ebenezer's addiction to old Christmas and all its traditions, right down to steaming bowls of bishop.

'Stop,' said Mrs Craggs.

'Stop?'

'Don't you touch that book, sonny.'

Inspector Hummbugg bristled. He might treat his sergeant as if he were a schoolboy, but he did not at all care for anyone else doing so.

'I'll thank you,' he said to Mrs Craggs, 'not to come between me and a piece of vital evidence.'

'Vital it may be,' Mrs Craggs retorted. 'But it won't be 'alf so vital if the sergeant o' yours puts 'is fingerprints all over the ones what's probably there already. Can't you see that Christmas Carol book's the one that's sticking a bit out from the row? Like as not, the person what wrote that silly note on the chair went to that book to find the words for it. So you'd better get out your fingerprint set. If you remembered to bring it.'

'Sergeant,' said Inspector Hummbugg. 'Prints apparatus. In the car. Get it, lad. Get it.'

But just as the sergeant returned Mrs Craggs addressed Inspector Hummbugg once more.

'O' course,' she said, 'them fingerprints won't lead you to the one what done it, not necessarily. I mean, what about the clue o' the thousand crackers?'

'The thousand—'

Hummbugg, and his sergeant, turned to look at the great heap of crackers almost burying Mr Ebenezer's dead body.

'One thousand,' said the inspector. 'How do you know there's a thousand there?'

'I don't, though I dare say I'm not far out. But what I do know is that only yesterday afternoon one o' the seven folk old Ebenezer invited 'ere, an' threatened to cut out o' his will, said to 'im, "I 'ope I see you buried under your damn Christmas crackers".'

'Sergeant,' said Inspector Hummbugg. 'Notebook.'

Mrs Craggs waited till the sergeant's pencil was poised.

'Young woman by the name o' Yettercumb,' she said.

The sergeant coughed.

'Would you be so kind as to spell that?'

'For heaven's sake, man,' Hummbugg exploded. 'Didn't they even teach you spelling at school?'

'Yeh,' said Mrs Craggs. 'I'd better spell it. Funny old name.'

Letter by letter she spelt it out.

'That is funny all right,' the sergeant commented.

'I'll give you funny,' Hummbugg snapped. 'Just put down what you're told, and keep your mouth shut.'

'An' you know why it's funny, that name,' Mrs Craggs went on, just as if Hummbugg's huge pink bulk was not there at all.

'Will you kindly get on with it, woman,' Hummbugg boomed.

'I am. If you'd listen. That name, Yettercumb, remind you of anything sonny? You've read that old Christmas Carol story, didn't yer say? Just like I was brought up on it.'

Slowly light dawned on the sergeant's pale face.

'Yettercumb,' he said. 'Yet to come. The Spirit of Times Yet to Come.'

'You got it. That's why old Ebenezer 'ere even knew 'er, the silly young chit. Collected 'em up, 'e did. Names in that story. We ain't only got young Fifi Yettercumb. We got Mr Parst, what speculates in what they calls Stock Exchange futures whatever they may be, an' we got Mr Pressent, what's a theatrical angel, which I takes ter be a real-life devil. Times Past an' Times Present. An' more. We got Marylee Jacob, actress an' no better nor what she ought ter be.'

'Marylee Jacob?'

The sergeant's pallid face wore a frown. And then cleared.

'Jacob Marley,' he exclaimed. 'Old Scrooge's dead partner, Jacob Marley, just turned around.'

'All right then,' Mrs Craggs went on. ''Ow about Mrs Feswick, failed authoress so I 'eard 'er called?'

'Easy. Wife of Jolly old Mr Fezziwig, Scrooge's employer when he was an apprentice.'

'You're doing all right, son. So let me tell you

that old Mr Ebenezer acksherly 'appened to 'ave a nephew name o' Fred. Readymade, as you might say.'

'Yes, yes, Scrooge's nephew was called Fred. As least I think he was. Any others?'

'Just the one. Try the Hon. Robert Crayshett-Clark.'

The frown on the sergeant's face deepened and deepened.

Then with a snort that would have done credit to a prize porker Inspector Hummbugg broke in. 'Bob,' he said. 'Bob Cratchit. I remember seeing it all on the stage when I was a kid. Bob Cratchit, clerk. But where's his son, Tiny Tim, then? He was the one I really liked. "God bless us every one".'

Hastily he wiped away a pair of tears that had oozed one from each of his piggy little eyes.

'What about Tiny Tim?'

'You'll 'ave to make do with Tiny Tom, the valet,' Mrs Craggs replied. 'Only other living soul in the 'ouse last night when that snow was a-falling. He's a regular muttonhead, but that's the best we got.'

But a ferocious gleam had suddenly come into Inspector Hummbugg's little eyes.

'Sergeant,' he said, 'get that fellow in here. Always suspect the butler. First rule of investigation. And I reckon a valet's as good as a butler any day.'

'O' course,' Mrs Craggs told Mrs Milhorne, 'when that Hummbugg 'eard as 'ow Tiny Tom, God bless us every one, 'ad 'ad that annuity of 'is fer years already 'e put 'im out of account straightaway.'

'Yaiss,' said Mrs Milhorne. 'Yaiss, 'e – hhhe'd hhhave to, wouldn't 'e?'

'Not but what old Tom didn't do 'im a bit o' good.'

'I saw him though, I saw him,' Tiny Tom said as Inspector Hummbugg waved him exasperatedly away.

'Saw who, man? For heaven's sake, speak up if you've got anything to say.'

'Saw the one what done it, Inspector.'

'Saw him? Saw him? Then why the heck didn't you say so?'

'Couldn't, Inspector.'

'I'll give you couldn't. It's an offence, you know. Withholding evidence. Now, who did you see?'

'Santa Claus, Inspector.'

'Santa—'

But Mrs Craggs stepped in and deflected the mighty porcine wrath.

'I get it,' she said. 'It's this. The whole blooming lot of 'em came down 'ere with Santa outfits, saw 'em meself doing out the rooms. Wanting ter please the old devil, I suppose. An' what Tiny Tom 'ere's saying is the one what crep' down an' shot 'im wore that outfit to do it.'

'Then we'll have each manjack of them in and—'

'Oh, no, Inspector,' Mrs Craggs interrupted again. 'It ain't manjack. It's womanjack as well. Behind one o' them bit white beards it could 'ave been a woman just as well as a man. An' I tell you something else. They're all of a height. Each an' every one of 'em. Noticed it yesterday. So there'd be no telling one from another, dressed up like that.'

'Bother,' said Inspector Hummbugg.

But his pendulous pig-cheeks did not stay droopily despondent for long.

'Ha,' he exclaimed scarcely five minutes after the door had eventually closed behind Tiny Tom. 'Something was said about a threat. I haven't forgotten. Someone in this house threatened to bury the late Mr Ebenezer under one thousand of his Christmas crackers, and I want to know who.'

'Yettercumb,' Mrs Craggs answered. 'I was telling yer.'

'Sergeant. Why isn't Miss Yettercumb here? You're never going to solve cases, me lad, if you don't follow up a clue pretty sharpish. I'll tell you that for nothing.'

'No, sir. Yes, sir.'

And in no time at all little blonde Fifi Yettercumb

222

was confronting the inspector in Mr Ebenezer's next-door study. On the broad desk the ancient typewriter had been thrust aside in favour of a generous sample of the Christmas crackers together with the sheet of paper from the top of the chair. Once again the sergeant's pencil was poised.

Inspector Hummbugg pounced.

'So,' he said, glaring ferociously at the black leather-clad curvaceous little creature in front of him, 'You buried Mr Ebenezer's body under a pile of his Christmas crackers after all, did you? Afraid he'd cut you out of your hundred thousand pounds soon as Christmas was over, eh?'

'No, Inspector, no. No, I never.'

'No use denying it, my girl. Saying "No, I never" won't get you out of trouble. Not here, and not in court.'

'But it's the truth, most like.'

It was Mrs Craggs, stepping out from the dark shadows of the oak-panelled room where she had been careful to hide to get a ringside view.

'What do you mean it's the truth?' Inspector Hummbugg thundered.

'Look,' said Mrs Craggs. 'If you was going to murder a bloke what was going to cut you out of 'is will, would you go an' do to 'is corp just what everyone 'ad 'eard you threaten to do? I didn't think it was very likely all along, an' when I 'eard the young lady deny it I was sure.'

'But – But – But why were those crackers there if she didn't put them there as per her threat?'

'Simple,' said Mrs Craggs. 'It was because the real murderer wanted to put the blame on 'er. Make 'is or 'er share o' the dibbins all the bigger, wouldn't it, if this young lady was found guilty?'

'Yes,' Fifi Yettercumb put in with palpitating haste. 'It musta been one of the others, trying to put the blame on a girl. I mean, have you thought about that mysterious typewritten note there, Inspector? That's words out of that Christmas Carol thing, ain't it? And joo know somethink?'

Inspector Hummbugg blew down his nose till the crackers on the desk began to tumble to the ground below.

'I dare say I know more than you think, my girl,' he said.

'Well then, what joo know?'

For a moment, for a good many moments, Inspector Hummbugg did not speak. Then at last he looked at Fifi again.

'Suppose you tell me,' he said.

'Well, last night when we were all sitting round that Yule log thingy, and the nails in it going off every few seconds like ever so many pistol shots, old

Eb asked us if we'd all read that Christmas Carol book. And only one of us said right out they had. I mean, who could get through all that?'

'Right then,' said Hummbugg. 'Who was this person?'

'That Mrs Feswick,' Fifi replied promptly. 'Her and her sarky remarks.'

So it was just a few minutes later that Inspector Hummbugg had in front of him at the late Mr Ebenezer's desk Mrs Bonny Feswick, fiftyish, bouncy, tweeds-clad.

'Jolly good, Inspector,' she said. 'Thought you'd want to see me. Interviewing all round, what? Well, here I am. Always ready to do my duty. Spread a little happiness, don't you know.'

Hummbugg's huge pink face assumed an expression of immense cunning.

'Glad to hear that, madam,' he said. 'And I think you can indeed help us. We're interested in this note found on the chair above Mr Ebenezer's body.'

Mrs Feswick looked at the sheet.

'It's a quotation from *A Christmas Carol*,' she said, rather slowly. 'What someone says about Scrooge after he's dead. In the future, you know. Bit awful, what?'

'Mrs Feswick,' Hummbugg said with a sudden ferocious glace. 'What would you answer if I told

you that of all the people in this house you are the
only one to know that story through and through?'

'I – I—'

'And what would you say if I added that I
strongly suspect this note was typed on this very
machine in here?'

And Mrs Feswick gave a huge smile.

'I'd tell you to look at the note a little more
closely, Inspector,' she replied. 'I think you'll find
that it wasn't produced on a typewriter at all. I think
you'll find it was produced on a word-processor.'

At this the sergeant peered forward and examined the sheet that hitherto Inspector Hummbugg
had kept as his personal possession.

'Yes, sir,' he said. He was a very, very young sergeant. 'That's quite right, sir. You can easily tell that
sort of word-processor print. Dot matrix.'

'Dot – Dot – I'll dot you one in a moment,
my lad.'

But the inspector did turn to Mrs Feswick.

'Thank you, madam,' he said. 'That will be all.'

'Oh,' said Mrs Feswick. 'But aren't you going to
ask me if I know whether anybody in this house has
a word-processor?'

'I was about to put that question to you when you
elected to depart.'

'Well then, let me tell you in confidence,

Inspector, that Miss Marylee Jacob has a word-processor in her room, wrapped up in sheets of paper with snowmen on them. She intends to give it for Christmas to Bob Crayshett-Clark, the sweet boy. As if that would do any good . . .'

And out she flounced.

'I think,' said Hummbugg, 'it'd be no bad thing to have a word with Miss Jacob, Marylee.'

It was Mrs Craggs who was despatched to find this new witness, not to say suspect.

And once again Hummbugg, that man of cunning incarnate, adopted shock tactics.

'Tried out your nice little present for Mr Crayshett-Clark, did you?' he asked without preliminary.

But Marylee Jacob, brassy as a brass door knocker – and, thought the sergeant, who young as he was had a good vulgar streak hidden away inside him, with a pretty good pair of knockers on her, too – showed not the least sign of guilt or dismay at the shot-out question.

'Oh, no, Inspector,' she said. 'I mean, I wouldn't know how to work something like that. No, all I did was to creep into Bob's room late last night, all dressed up as Santa Claus if you can imagine, and leave my little present for him to find this morning. It did look as if the paper round it had been disturbed, though. Perhaps that was what made you think I'd tried it out.'

She gave the inspector a sweet, sweet smile. If hammered brass can smile sweetly.

'Nevertheless,' he said, ignoring the smile, 'a certain note found not a foot away from the corpse was written on a word-processor. You can tell by the print, you know. What we call dot mattress.'

'Matrix, sir,' said the sergeant, who despite his notions about knockers was a very innocent young sergeant.

'Well, Inspector,' Marylee answered. 'All I can suggest is that somebody very naughty tapped out that note on the word-processor before I gave it to sweety-pie Bob.'

'And why would they do that?'

'Oh, Inspector, haven't you worked that out yet? If whoever murdered that awful old man can pin it on someone else it means all the bigger share of what he's left, doesn't it?'

'I am quite capable of working out whatever I have to work out for myself, madam,' Hummbugg answered, giving no credit at all to Mrs Craggs who had pointed this out to him in the first place. 'But that leaves the question of who, in fact, did murder Mr Ebenezer.'

'And haven't you worked that out either,

Inspector? I mean, you've surely only got to find the weapon, and there'll be some nice, nice fingerprints on it for you. It'll be easy as falling off a Yule log, and I'm sure you can manage that.'

Exit Miss Marylee Jacob.

'Sergeant,' roared Hummbugg. 'Find the weapon.'

It took the sergeant, who despite his youth and innocence was a very active young man, just seven and a half minutes to find the gun that had put that bullet so neatly into Mr Ebenezer's forehead. It was down at the back of the tub in which stood Mr Ebenezer's enormous Christmas tree. Carefully taking it out, the sergeant blew powder on to it from his insufflator and revealed even to the naked eye splendidly clear fingerprints. Expertly he photographed them, and then, zooming off like a demented ice-skater, he secured in no time the prints of each of the seven suspects.

And it was clear beyond doubt that the ones on the gun belonged to none other than Mr Ebenezer's nephew Fred.

'I shall make the arrest at the very spot where the deed took place,' Inspector Hummbugg announced, leading the way, swaying and swinging, back into the holly decorated hall.

Nephew Fred was brought before him, sleepy-eyed and yawning.

'Don't know how it is,' he said easily, 'but I just dropped off. Always doing it, you know, having a bit of a zizz. And it's not as if I don't go off at night. I do. From ten o'clock on I'm out to the wide. Always have been. Dare say I always will be.'

Solemnly Inspector Hummbugg interrupted these self-revelations.

'Mr Frederick Ebenezer,' he began.

But before he could pronounce another word Mrs Craggs, who had been taking a good look at the gun with those clear, clear prints on it, called out.

''Ere, wait a sec.'

Deflated as if by a suddenly injected pin, Inspector Hummbugg wheeled round.

'What—'

'You 'ave another dekko at these 'ere finger marks,' Mrs Craggs said. 'I've taken 'old of enough brush 'andles in me time to know where your fingers come on 'em, and I tell yer this: nobody never 'eld this 'ere gun in a way they could of shot anybody with it, not never.'

Inspector Hummbugg peered. Nephew Fred peered. The pale sergeant peered.

It was this last who had the temerity to speak.

'She's quite right, sir, now you come to look.'

'Yes, yes,' said Nephew Fred. 'I promise you I never touched that gun. But I'll tell you what did happen to me. I was fast asleep last night, dreaming of something. Forget what. And then – this has hardly ever happened to me before – I woke up. I woke up and had the distinct impression somebody had been holding my hand.'

He gave a violent blush.

'Thought it might have been Bonny Feswick,' he said. 'Afraid she's rather keen on me. Or it might have been Marylee. Afraid she's a bit keen on me, too.'

'What you're telling me,' Inspector Hummbugg said, 'is that somebody came into your room last night while you were sound asleep and put your fingerprints on the weapon here.'

'Yes, yes, old boy, that is what I was telling you. Got it in one.'

He gave a tremendous yawn.

'Well,' he said, 'I suppose as those fingerprints have been sort of disposed of I may as well take the gun. Belongs to me now, you know. Uncle Ebenezer always said I'd get the house and everything in it. Only trouble was he was never too sure about leaving me enough actual cash to keep the old place going. Said I was too lazy. Can't think why.'

With another prodigious yawn he picked up the gun and wandered out.

'But then,' said Mrs Craggs, 'a funny thing 'appened.'

'No? What?' said Mrs Milhorne, eyes popping.

'Sleepy-clogs came back in again in just a brace o' shakes an' asked old Hummbugg did 'e know something about that gun.'

Inspector Hummbugg knew nothing about the gun. To judge from his massive silence.

So his sergeant evidently felt it up to him to save the honour of the country police.

'We know you were making off with the weapon in a somewhat suspicious manner, Mr Frederick Ebenezer,' he said, drawing himself up to his full formal height.

'Oh, no, old boy. It's just this. You see, there aren't any more bullets in it, and Uncle always kept it fully loaded. Happen to know that.'

'And so?' the redoubtable Hummbugg came trundling in.

'Well, and so, Inspector, find the bullets taken out of the gun, and I'd say you'd found your murderer.'

Fred yawned again.

'Sergeant, search the house.'

It took the sergeant, who in spite of his pallor, was a robustly active youth, only two and a half hours to search the house. But at last he came back to the study with in his hand five fat revolver bullets.

'Well,' Hummbugg grunted, 'where d' you find 'em? Took you long enough.'

'In the bedroom assigned to the Hon. Robert Crayshett-Clark,' the sergeant replied. 'Hidden.'

'Then why haven't you brought Bob Cratchit back down with you, lad? He'll have made his escape by now.'

'He's just outside, sir.'

'Then why isn't he standing here in front of me? Jump to it, lad, jump to it.'

The sergeant jumped. Bob Crayshett-Clark, man-about-town, debonair, not quite wearing an eyeglass, was standing in front of Inspector Hummbugg.

'God bless us every one,' Hummbugg said, sadly shaking his great pink head. 'I'm disappointed in you, Crayshett, father of a boy as good in every way as Tiny—'

'Father?' Bob Crayshett-Clark exclaimed. 'I assure you, Inspector, I have never even contemplated matrimony. Much less . . . Well, much less.'

'That is as may be, sir,' said Hummbugg, loudly blowing his snout to remove the two tears that had crept from his eyes at the thought, however mistaken, of Tiny Tim. 'But there's still the matter of certain bullets concealed in your room.'

Bob Crayshett-Clark flicked a minute scrap of lint from his beautifully tailored suit.

'Come, Inspector,' he said, 'I'm not such an idiot as to hide bullets from a gun I'd just shot someone with in my own room.'

'That's what I calls common sense,' Mrs Craggs put in from the shadows.

'Well, then—' Hummbugg began.

But the Hon. Bob at once answered the question the inspector would eventually have got round to asking.

'Last night,' he said, 'a person dressed as Santa Claus entered my room thinking I was asleep. I cannot name a name, but I feel it my duty to mention that that fellow Parst, hardly one's idea of a gentleman, had been going about all morning searching for his spectacles. Should you by chance have seen a pair at the scene of the crime, I think I can leave you to draw your own conclusions.'

He withdrew.

Mrs Craggs, still watching from the shadows, drew her conclusions. The pale sergeant drew his conclusions. They waited. At length Inspector Hummbugg arrived at his conclusions.

'Sergeant,' he said thoughtfully, 'have you observed anything in the hall in the nature of a pair of spectacles?'

'Yes, sir. I have just been looking. There's a pair

caught up in the Christmas tree. And, sir, I have asked Mr Parst to step in.'

Mr Parst, blinking so distractedly that his future as a speculator in futures seemed particularly in doubt, forestalled the question working its way up Inspector Hummbugg's capacious gullet.

'You're a policeman,' he said. 'Ought to be good at finding things. You noticed my glasses anywhere? Can't see a damn thing without them.'

'Yes, sir,' Hummbugg said portentously. 'A pair of spectacles has been found caught in the Christmas tree not five yards from the body of the late lamented Mr Ebenezer.'

'Ah, good. Well done. Credit to the force. Let me have them, will you?'

'It will be my duty,' Hummbugg pronounced, yet more portentously, 'to retain them as evidence in any criminal trial that may or may not take place.'

'Ah,' said Mr Parst, 'so you've got someone in your sights, eh? Good work. Spotted something clenched in the corpse's fist, I dare say. Fine piece of detection.'

Another question was perhaps moving slowly up Inspector Hummbugg's gullet. But before it had reached the air Mr Parst had gone.

The sergeant coughed. A pale cough, but enough to draw attention.

'Shall I take a close look at the corpse, sir?' he asked. 'At his fists, or something?'

'No, lad, you will not. If a close search is in order, it'd better be done by an expert.'

The three of them returned to Mr Ebenezer's body, still half-buried in bright Christmas crackers. Ponderously Inspector Hummbugg peered at both the fists, which were every bit as clenched as Mr Parst had indicated.

'Nothing,' he said at last. 'Trying his tricks, mark my words. Sergeant, have you ever seen a man arrested for murder? Well, if you haven't, you're just about to see that happening to a certain Mr Parst.'

'Only one moment,' said Mrs Craggs. 'If you'd spent as much o' your life a-looking fer little bits o' dirt as what I 'ave, you'd of seen what's just peeking out between them third an' fourth fingers there.'

Inspector Hummbugg returned to the corpse. His sergeant peered over his massive shoulder.

'Why, yes, sir,' he said. 'A tiny bit of green material. And, sir, when I was taking fingerprints I saw that Mr Pressent – he's the one who's a theatrical angel, sir, backs shows and that – though dressed in a green country suit, with green socks and even a green handkerchief in the pocket was wearing a pink bow-tie.'

'An' when 'e arrived 'ere,' added Mrs Craggs, ''e

was wearing a green 'un. You can draw a conclusion from that, if you like.'

'Sergeant,' said Inspector Hummbugg, 'didn't I tell you five minutes ago to bring Mr Pressent down here?'

'No, sir, you – Yes, sir. Yes, Inspector, you did.' The sergeant was learning, perhaps.

Soon Mr Pressent, green as the holly decorating the hall, was brought in.

'Charles Pressent,' Hummbugg began without preliminary, 'I am arresting—'

''Ere,' said Mrs Craggs, 'shouldn't you be asking 'im, afore you go saying who you was a-going to arrest, why 'e put all them crackers round the corpse?'

'And why,' said Hummbugg, before he had time to think, 'did you put all them – that is, all those crackers round the corpse?'

Green-clad Mr Pressent went green to the gills.

'Ask 'im if it weren't to make it look like Fifi Yettercumb done the murder,' said Mrs Craggs.

'Was it to make it looks as if Fifi Yett – Was it to create the appearance of Miss Yettercumb – er – doing the murder?'

Mr Pressent turned from green to blushful red.

'Look, Inspector,' he said, 'I happened to be coming down here last night to – to see if Ebenezer, whom we had left half-asleep in his chair, was all right, and—'

'Or p'raps,' said Mrs Craggs, 'you was creeping down dressed up as a Santa to see if it was a good time to put the poor old devil out of 'is Christmas misery.'

'Inspector, never mind why I was coming down. The fact of the matter is I found Ebenezer dead, and I thought that the police might, well, might suspect me myself.'

'Which,' said Mrs Craggs, 'seeing as 'ow it was probably your intention to murder the poor old feller anyhow was pretty much on the cards.'

'Be that as it may, Inspector. The thing is I – er – thought it better your attention should be directed elsewhere, and recalling that awful little Fifi's threat earlier in the evening I decided to put all Ebenezer's crackers where she had said she would like to see them. Why, it is quite probable she did in fact kill him.'

At which the door burst open and that awful little Fifi flung herself in.

'You rotten swine,' she said, 'what for joo pick on me? I may've thought old Eb was a bloody bore, yacking on about Christmas and that. But I wouldn't ever have murdered him, not however much I could do with a hundred thousand quid.'

'Well, I don't know what to say,' Inspector Hummbugg murmured.

'But I do,' said Mrs Craggs. 'I got this to say to you, Miss Fifi. If you think it's so bad o' Mr Pressent 'ere to try to plant the job on you, why did you go an' write that note on old Ebenezer's typewriter an' put it on the chair to make it look as if it was Mrs Feswick what done it?'

Now it was the turn of Fifi Yettercumb to look ashamed, though she hardly managed as deep a blush as Mr Pressent.

'Oh,' she said, 'might as well own up. What I did was look through and through that book till I found some good words, and then I picked them out on old Eb's typewriter. I thought that'd teach that snobby bitch to say I didn't even know how to read.'

'But, wait a moment,' the sergeant broke in, his pale face alight with intellectual triumph. 'That note wasn't typed. It was written on a word-processor. Dot matrix.'

'O' course it was,' Mrs Craggs said. 'An' who do you think by? That Mrs Feswick, o 'course.'

At once the door opened, and Bonny Feswick stood there. 'Well,' she said, 'when I came down to the hall here, dressed up as Santa Claus I don't mind admitting, and found someone had already done the deed and tried to make it look as if it was me, I wasn't going to take it lying down.'

'Do you mean to say, madam,' the young sergeant jumped in with youthful outrage, 'that you went up to Miss Marylee Jacob's room and used her word-processor?'

'Look,' Bonny Feswick replied cheerfully, 'I wasn't going to let her cut me out with that dishy young man if I could help it, was I?'

And then to the surprise of everyone – except perhaps Mrs Craggs – the door burst open again and Marylee Jacob came storming in.

'You bitch,' she said to Bonny Feswick. 'Why, if—' She got no further.

Mrs Craggs had a word to say.

'Just a minute. Suppose you tells us who it was what crep' into young Fred's room, knowing the way he slep' an' slep', an' put 'is fingers round the gun. After you 'ad come down 'ere, all in your Santas too I dare say, an' found old Ebenezer dead with a clue pointing to you?'

Marylee was made of too much brass ever to blush. But she did look a little put out.

'All right,' she said. 'But I didn't like the way Fred kept hinting I had a thing about him. As if I would. When he'd fall asleep before I'd even . . .'

'Sergeant,' said Inspector Hummbugg, going a

pinker shade of pink, 'suppose you go and fetch Mr Frederick. I dare say you'll find him dozing off somewhere. Ho, ho, ho.'

'In an armchair next-door, sir,' the sergeant said, half a minute later, leading in a yawning, stretching Fred.

And this time Hummbugg turned directly to Mrs Craggs.

'Well?'

'Now let's 'ave the truth,' Mrs Craggs said to Fred. 'When the inspector 'ere accused you o' the murder just now you thought you'd better be on the safe side an' make it look like someone else done it, didn't yer? So you went off an' put them bullets in Bob Crayshett-Clark's room. That gun was never as empty as what you made out, was it?'

'Got it in one,' Fred said, with a rueful shake of his head. 'Not very decent to try and pin it on old Bob. But I couldn't think of anything else.'

And the door burst open. Once again.

It was the Hon. Robert Crayshett-Clark.

'Well, damn it all,' he said, 'I do think you might have hit on somebody else. I mean, a fellow doesn't like to be accused of murder, even if he hasn't done it.'

'Then why,' said Mrs Craggs, stepping smartly forward, 'did you go an' pinch poor old Mr Parst's spectacles from 'is room an' leave them a-dangling on that there tree?'

'How do you know that?'

'Well, stands to reason Mr Parst couldn't never 'ave shot old Ebenezer, not without 'is glasses, 'im being blind as a bat when 'e ain't got 'em on. So someone must 'ave tried to plant the job on 'im. An' you was as likely as any, seeing there ain't 'ardly no one else left.'

The Hon. Bob looked round the room.

'There's Mr Pressent,' he said. 'He is, ha, ha, present.'

Now Inspector Hummbugg, almost all the suspects eliminated, moved into resolute action.

'So, Mr Pressent,' he said, 'suppose you account for the dead man having in his clenched fist a tiny piece of green material, which I happened have to observed. Taking into account you are no longer wearing your green bow-tie.'

Mr Pressent went pink as the tie beneath his chin.

But Mrs Craggs came at once to his rescue.

'That green tie, which I 'appened to point out to yer, Inspector, bein' clutched in the dead man's 'and, can't mean our friend 'ere murdered 'im. Old Ebenezer was shot, you know, 'e couldn't 'ardly 'ave wrenched off the tie o' the man what shot 'im, could 'e?'

'No,' said the young sergeant, careless at last of all promotion. 'Of course he couldn't have. So how did that tie get there?'

Mrs Craggs went over to the door and jerked it open. Mr Parst, speculator, was standing there, ear pressed to a panel attempting to see the future without having to speculate.

'Well?' said Mrs Craggs.

'Oh, well, dash it. Might as well admit it. When I found my specs had been taken from my bedside table I wondered if they'd been made away with for a purpose. So I came down here, and could just make out that poor old Ebenezer was dead. Not moving, you see. So I groped my way up to the first room I came to – I suppose it was Present's – grabbed an article of clothing and managed to stuff it into the body's fist. Did I get it all in?'

'You did, you swine,' remarked Mr Pressent.

And now from somewhere inside Inspector Hummbugg there came a curious, querulous rumbling.

'Well,' he said at last, 'if none of them murdered Mr Ebenezer, who for heaven's sake did?'

'Why,' said Mrs Craggs, 'simple enough. Tiny Tom's the one. 'Im an' 'is talk o' seeing a Santa creeping in. Nothing to 'ave stopped 'im being the killer 'imself. An' as to motive, provided for 'e may 'ave been but 'ow well was 'e provided for? Not with a hundred thousand quid. You can bet yer boots on that. So when 'e 'ears all this lot was getting that much each, what should 'e do but shoot the mean old Scrooge what gave 'im such a pittance.'

'And hhhad he done it, that Tom?' Mrs Milhorne asked, blinking.

'I told yer, didn't I?'

'Yaiss. Yaiss, but what I can't understand is I never saw nothing about hhhim in the paper. On trial and that.'

'Nah. Well, you wouldn't 'ave done, would yer? Not with old Hummbugg needing almost till New Year's Eve to catch on. Tiny Tom just 'opped on the nearest reindeer, I reckon, 'an skedaddled. 'Cos 'e ain't never been seen since.'

Death on the Air

On the 25th of December at 7:30 a.m. Mr. Septimus Tonks was found dead beside his wireless set.

It was Emily Parks, an under-housemaid, who discovered him. She butted open the door and entered, carrying mop, duster, and carpet-sweeper. At that precise moment she was greatly startled by a voice that spoke out of the darkness.

"Good morning, everybody," said the voice in superbly inflected syllables, "and a Merry Christmas!"

Emily yelped, but not loudly, as she immediately realised what had happened. Mr. Tonks had omitted to turn off his wireless before going to bed. She drew back the curtains, revealing a kind of pale murk which was a London Christmas dawn, switched on the light, and saw Septimus.

He was seated in front of the radio. It was a small but expensive set, specially built for him. Septimus sat in an armchair, his back to Emily, his body tilted towards the radio.

His hands, the fingers curiously bunched, were on the ledge of the cabinet under the tuning and volume knobs. His chest rested against the shelf below and his head leaned on the front panel.

He looked rather as though he was listening intently to the interior secrets of the wireless. His head was bent so that Emily could see his bald top with its trail of oiled hairs. He did not move.

"Beg pardon, sir," gasped Emily. She was again greatly startled. Mr. Tonks's enthusiasm for radio had never before induced him to tune in at seven-thirty in the morning.

"Special Christmas service," the cultured voice was saying. Mr. Tonks sat very still. Emily, in common with the other servants, was terrified of her master. She did not know whether to go or to stay. She gazed wildly at Septimus and realised that he wore a dinner-jacket. The room was now filled with the clamour of pealing bells.

Emily opened her mouth as wide as it would go and screamed and screamed and screamed . . .

Chase, the butler, was the first to arrive. He was a pale, flabby man but authoritative. He said: "What's the meaning of this outrage?" and then saw Septimus. He went to the armchair, bent down, and looked into his master's face.

He did not lose his head, but said in a loud voice: "My Gawd!" And then to Emily: "Shut your face." By this vulgarism he betrayed his agitation. He seized

Emily by the shoulders and thrust her towards the door, where they were met by Mr. Hislop, the secretary, in his dressing-gown. Mr. Hislop said: "Good heavens, Chase, what is the meaning—" and then his voice too was drowned in the clamour of bells and renewed screams.

Chase put his fat white hand over Emily's mouth.

"In the study if you please, sir. An accident. Go to your room, will you, and stop that noise or I'll give you something to make you." This to Emily, who bolted down the hall, where she was received by the rest of the staff who had congregated there.

Chase returned to the study with Mr. Hislop and locked the door. They both looked down at the body of Septimus Tonks. The secretary was the first to speak.

"But—but—he's dead," said little Mr. Hislop.

"I suppose there can't be any doubt," whispered Chase.

"Look at the face. Any doubt! My God!"

Mr. Hislop put out a delicate hand towards the bent head and then drew it back. Chase, less fastidious, touched one of the hard wrists, gripped, and then lifted it. The body at once tipped backwards as if it was made of wood. One of the hands knocked against the butler's face. He sprang back with an oath.

There lay Septimus, his knees and his hands
in the air, his terrible face turned up to the light.
Chase pointed to the right hand. Two fingers and
the thumb were slightly blackened.

Ding, dong, dang, ding.

"For God's sake stop those bells," cried Mr. Hislop. Chase turned off the wall switch. Into the sudden silence came the sound of the door-handle being
rattled and Guy Tonks's voice on the other side.

"Hislop! Mr. Hislop! Chase! What's the matter?"

"Just a moment, Mr. Guy." Chase looked at the
secretary. "You go, sir."

So it was left to Mr. Hislop to break the news to
the family. They listened to his stammering revela-
tion in stupefied silence. It was not until Guy, the
eldest of the three children, stood in the study that
any practical suggestion was made.

"What has killed him?" asked Guy.

"It's extraordinary," burbled Hislop. "Extraordinary. He looks as if he'd been—"

"Galvanised," said Guy.

"We ought to send for a doctor," suggested
Hislop timidly.

"Of course. Will you, Mr. Hislop? Dr. Meadows."

Hislop went to the telephone and Guy returned
to his family. Dr. Meadows lived on the other side of
the square and arrived in five minutes. He examined

the body without moving it. He questioned Chase and Hislop. Chase was very voluble about the burns on the hand. He uttered the word "electrocution" over and over again.

"I had a cousin, sir, that was struck by lightning. As soon as I saw the hand—"

"Yes, yes," said Dr. Meadows. "So you said. I can see the burns for myself."

"Electrocution," repeated Chase. "There'll have to be an inquest."

Dr. Meadows snapped at him, summoned Emily, and then saw the rest of the family—Guy, Arthur, Phillipa, and their mother. They were clustered round a cold grate in the drawing-room. Phillipa was on her knees, trying to light the fire.

"What was it?" asked Arthur as soon as the doctor came in.

"Looks like electric shock. Guy, I'll have a word with you if you please. Phillipa, look after your mother, there's a good child. Coffee with a dash of brandy. Where are those damn maids? Come on, Guy."

Alone with Guy, he said they'd have to send for the police.

"The police!" Guy's dark face turned very pale. "Why? What's it got to do with them?"

"Nothing, as like as not, but they'll have to be

notified. I can't give a certificate as things are. If it's electrocution, how did it happen?"

"But the police!" said Guy. "That's simply ghastly. Dr. Meadows, for God's sake couldn't you—?"

"No," said Dr. Meadows, "I couldn't. Sorry, Guy, but there it is."

"But can't we wait a moment? Look at him again. You haven't examined him properly."

"I don't want to move him, that's why. Pull yourself together, boy. Look here. I've got a pal in the CID—Alleyn. He's a gentleman and all that. He'll curse me like a fury, but he'll come if he's in London, and he'll make things easier for you. Go back to your mother. I'll ring Alleyn up."

That was how it came about that Chief Detective-Inspector Roderick Alleyn spent his Christmas Day in harness. As a matter of fact he was on duty, and as he pointed out to Dr. Meadows, would have had to turn out and visit his miserable Tonkses in any case. When he did arrive it was with his usual air of remote courtesy. He was accompanied by a tall, thick-set officer—Inspector Fox—and by the divisional police-surgeon. Dr. Meadows took them into the study. Alleyn, in his turn, looked at the horror that had been Septimus.

"Was he like this when he was found?"

"No. I understand he was leaning forward with

his hands on the ledge of the cabinet. He must have slumped forward and been propped up by the chair arms and the cabinet."

"Who moved him?"

"Chase, the butler. He said he only meant to raise the arm. *Rigor* is well established."

Alleyn put his hand behind the rigid neck and pushed. The body fell forward into its original position.

"There you are, Curtis," said Alleyn to the divisional surgeon. He turned to Fox. "Get the camera man, will you, Fox?"

The photographer took four shots and departed. Alleyn marked the position of the hands and feet with chalk, made a careful plan of the room and turned to the doctors.

"Is it electrocution, do you think?"

"Looks like it," said Curtis. "Have to be a PM, of course."

"Of course. Still, look at the hands. Burns. Thumb and two fingers bunched together and exactly the distance between the two knobs apart. He'd been tuning his hurdy-gurdy."

"By gum," said Inspector Fox, speaking for the first time.

"D'you mean he got a lethal shock from his radio?" asked Dr. Meadows.

"I don't know. I merely conclude he had his hands on the knobs when he died."

"It was still going when the housemaid found him. Chase turned it off and got no shock."

"Yours, partner," said Alleyn, turning to Fox. Fox stooped down to the wall switch.

"Careful," said Alleyn.

"I've got rubber soles," said Fox, and switched it on. The radio hummed, gathered volume, and found itself.

"No-o-el, No-o-el," it roared. Fox cut it off and pulled out the wall plug.

"I'd like to have a look inside this set," he said.

"So you shall, old boy, so you shall," rejoined Alleyn. "Before you begin, I think we'd better move the body. Will you see to that, Meadows? Fox, get Bailey, will you? He's out in the car."

Curtis, Hislop, and Meadows carried Septimus Tonks into a spare downstairs room. It was a difficult and horrible business with that contorted body. Dr. Meadows came back alone, mopping his brow, to find Detective-Sergeant Bailey, a fingerprint expert, at work on the wireless cabinet.

"What's all this?" asked Dr. Meadows. "Do you want to find out if he'd been fooling round with the innards?"

"He," said Alleyn, "or—somebody else."

"Umph!" Dr. Meadows looked at the Inspector. "You agree with me, it seems. Do you suspect—?"

"Suspect? I'm the least suspicious man alive. I'm merely being tidy. Well, Bailey?"

"I've got a good one off the chair arm. That'll be the deceased's, won't it, sir?"

"No doubt. We'll check up later. What about the wireless?"

Fox, wearing a glove, pulled off the knob of the volume control.

"Seems to be OK," said Bailey. "It's a sweet bit of work. Not too bad at all, sir." He turned his torch into the back of the radio, undid a couple of screws underneath the set, lifted out the works.

"What's the little hole for?" asked Alleyn.

"What's that, sir?" said Fox.

"There's a hole bored through the panel above the knob. About an eighth of an inch in diameter. The rim of the knob hides it. One might easily miss it. Move your torch, Bailey. Yes. There, do you see?"

Fox bent down and uttered a bass growl. A fine needle of light came through the front of the radio.

"That's peculiar, sir," said Bailey from the other side. "I don't get the idea at all."

Alleyn pulled out the tuning knob.

"There's another one there," he murmured.

"Yes. Nice clean little holes. Newly bored. Unusual, I take it?"

"Unusual's the word, sir," said Fox.

"Run away, Meadows," said Alleyn.

"Why the devil?" asked Dr. Meadows indignantly. "What are you driving at? Why shouldn't I be here?"

"You ought to be with the sorrowing relatives. Where's your corpseside manner?"

"I've settled them. What are you up to?"

"Who's being suspicious now?" asked Alleyn mildly. "You may stay for a moment. Tell me about the Tonkses. Who are they? What are they? What sort of a man was Septimus?"

"If you must know, he was a damned unpleasant sort of a man."

"Tell me about him."

Dr. Meadows sat down and lit a cigarette.

"He was a self-made bloke," he said, "as hard as nails and—well, coarse rather than vulgar."

"Like Dr. Johnson perhaps?"

"Not in the least. Don't interrupt. I've known him for twenty-five years. His wife was a neighbour of ours in Dorset. Isabel Foreston. I brought the children into this vale of tears and, by jove, in many ways it's been one for them. It's an extraordinary household. For the last ten years Isabel's condition has been the sort that sends these psycho-jokers dizzy with rapture. I'm only an out-of-date GP, and I'd just say she is in an advanced stage of hysterical neurosis. Frightened into fits of her husband."

"I can't understand these holes," grumbled Fox to Bailey.

"Go on, Meadows," said Alleyn.

"I tackled Sep about her eighteen months ago. Told him the trouble was in her mind. He eyed me with a sort of grin on his face and said: 'I'm surprised to learn that my wife has enough mentality to—' But look here, Alleyn, I can't talk about my patients like this. What the devil am I thinking about."

"You know perfectly well it'll go no further unless—"

"Unless what?"

"Unless it has to. Do go on."

But Dr. Meadows hurriedly withdrew behind his professional rectitude. All he would say was that Mr. Tonks had suffered from high blood pressure and a weak heart, that Guy was in his father's city office, that Arthur had wanted to study art and had been told to read for law, and that Phillipa wanted to go on to the stage and had been told to do nothing of the sort.

"Bullied his children," commented Alleyn.

"Find out for yourself. I'm off." Dr. Meadows got as far as the door and came back.

"Look here," he said, "I'll tell you one thing.

There was a row here last night. I'd asked Hislop, who's a sensible little beggar, to let me know if anything happened to upset Mrs. Sep. Upset her badly, you know. To be indiscreet again, I said he'd better let me know if Sep cut up rough, because Isabel and the young had had about as much of that as they could stand. He was drinking pretty heavily. Hislop rang me up at ten-twenty last night to say there'd been a hell of a row; Sep bullying Phips—Phillipa, you know; always call her Phips—in her room. He said Isabel—Mrs. Sep—had gone to bed. I'd had a big day and I didn't want to turn out. I told him to ring again in half an hour if things hadn't quieted down. I told him to keep out of Sep's way and stay in his own room, which is next to Phips's, and see if she was all right when Sep cleared out. Hislop was involved. I won't tell you how. The servants were all out. I said that if I didn't hear from him in half an hour I'd ring again and if there was no answer I'd know they were all in bed and quiet. I did ring, got no answer, and went to bed myself. That's all. I'm off. Curtis knows where to find me. You'll want me for the inquest, I suppose. Goodbye."

When he had gone Alleyn embarked on a systematic prowl round the room. Fox and Bailey were still deeply engrossed with the wireless.

"I don't see how the gentleman could have got

a bump-off from the instrument," grumbled Fox. "These control knobs are quite in order. Everything's as it should be. Look here, sir."

He turned on the wall switch and tuned in. There was a prolonged humming.

". . . concludes the programme of Christmas carols," said the radio.

"A very nice tone," said Fox approvingly.

"Here's something, sir," announced Bailey suddenly.

"Found the sawdust, have you?" said Alleyn.

"Got it in one," said the startled Bailey.

Alleyn peered into the instrument, using the torch. He scooped up two tiny traces of sawdust from under the holes.

"Vantage number one," said Alleyn. He bent down to the wall plug. "Hullo! A two-way adapter. Serves the radio and the radiator. Thought they were illegal. This is a rum business. Let's have another look at those knobs."

He had his look. They were the usual wireless fitments, Bakelite knobs fitting snugly to the steel shafts that projected from the front panel.

"As you say," he murmured, "quite in order. Wait a bit." He produced a pocket lens and squinted at one of the shafts. "Ye-es. Do they ever wrap blotting-paper round these objects, Fox?"

"Blotting-paper!" ejaculated Fox. "They do not."

Alleyn scraped at both the shafts with his pen-knife, holding an envelope underneath. He rose, groaning, and crossed to the desk. "A corner torn off the bottom bit of blotch," he said presently. "No prints on the wireless, I think you said, Bailey?"

"That's right," agreed Bailey morosely.

"There'll be none, or too many, on the blotter, but try, Bailey, try," said Alleyn. He wandered about the room, his eyes on the floor; got as far as the window and stopped.

"Fox!" he said. "A clue. A very palpable clue."

"What is it?" asked Fox.

"The odd wisp of blotting-paper, no less." Alleyn's gaze travelled up the side of the window curtain. "Can I believe my eyes?"

He got a chair, stood on the seat, and with his gloved hand pulled the buttons from the ends of the curtain-rod.

"Look at this." He turned to the radio, detached the control knobs, and laid them beside the ones he had removed from the curtain-rod.

Ten minutes later Inspector Fox knocked on the drawing-room door and was admitted by Guy Tonks. Phillipa had got the fire going and the family was gathered round it. They looked as though they had not moved or spoken to one another for a long time.

It was Phillipa who spoke first to Fox. "Do you want one of us?"

"If you please, miss," said Fox. "Inspector Alleyn would like to see Mr. Guy Tonks for a moment, if convenient."

"I'll come," said Guy, and led the way to the study. At the door he paused. "Is he—my father—still—?"

"No, no, sir," said Fox comfortably. "It's all ship-shape in there again."

With a lift of his chin Guy opened the door and went in, followed by Fox. Alleyn was alone, seated at the desk. He rose to his feet.

"You want to speak to me?" asked Guy.

"Yes, if I may. This has all been a great shock to you, of course. Won't you sit down?"

Guy sat in the chair farthest away from the radio.

"What killed my father? Was it a stroke?"

"The doctors are not quite certain. There will have to be a post-mortem."

"Good God! And an inquest?"

"I'm afraid so."

"Horrible!" said Guy violently. "What do you think was the matter? Why the devil do these quacks have to be so mysterious? What killed him?"

"They think an electric shock."

"How did it happen?"

"We don't know. It looks as if he got it from the wireless."

"Surely that's impossible. I thought they were fool-proof."

"I believe they are, if left to themselves."

For a second undoubtedly Guy was startled. Then a look of relief came into his eyes. He seemed to relax all over.

"Of course," he said, "he was always monkeying about with it. What had he done?"

"Nothing."

"But you said—if it killed him he must have done something to it."

"If anyone interfered with the set it was put right afterwards."

Guy's lips parted but he did not speak. He had gone very white.

"So you see," said Alleyn, "your father could not have done anything."

"Then it was not the radio that killed him."

"That we hope will be determined by the post-mortem."

"I don't know anything about wireless," said Guy suddenly. "I don't understand. This doesn't seem to make sense. Nobody ever touched the thing except my father. He was most particular about it. Nobody went near the wireless."

"I see. He was an enthusiast?"

"Yes, it was his only enthusiasm except—except his business."

"One of my men is a bit of an expert," Alleyn said. "He says this is a remarkably good set. You are not an expert, you say. Is there anyone in the house who is?"

"My young brother was interested at one time. He's given it up. My father wouldn't allow another radio in the house."

"Perhaps he may be able to suggest something."

"But if the thing's all right now—"

"We've got to explore every possibility."

"You speak as if—as—if—"

"I speak as I am bound to speak before there has been an inquest," said Alleyn. "Had anyone a grudge against your father, Mr. Tonks?"

Up went Guy's chin again. He looked Alleyn squarely in the eyes.

"Almost everyone who knew him," said Guy.

"Is that an exaggeration?"

"No. You think he was murdered, don't you?"

Alleyn suddenly pointed to the desk beside him.

"Have you ever seen those before?" he asked abruptly. Guy stared at two black knobs that lay side by side on an ashtray.

"Those?" he said. "No. What are they?"

"I believe they are the agents of your father's death."

The study door opened and Arthur Tonks came in.

"Guy," he said, "what's happening? We can't stay cooped up together all day. I can't stand it. For God's sake what happened to him?"

"They think those things killed him," said Guy.

"Those?" For a split second Arthur's glance slewed to the curtain-rods. Then, with a characteristic flicker of his eyelids, he looked away again.

"What do you mean?" he asked Alleyn.

"Will you try one of those knobs on the shaft of the volume control?"

"But," said Arthur, "they're metal."

"It's disconnected," said Alleyn.

Arthur picked one of the knobs from the tray, turned to the radio, and fitted the knob over one of the exposed shafts.

"It's too loose," he said quickly, "it would fall off."

"Not if it was packed—with blotting-paper, for instance."

"Where did you find these things?" demanded Arthur.

"I think you recognised them, didn't you? I saw you glance at the curtain-rod."

"Of course I recognised them. I did a portrait of Phillipa against those curtains when—he—was away last year. I've painted the damn things."

"Look here," interrupted Guy, "exactly what are you driving at, Mr. Alleyn? If you mean to suggest that my brother—"

"I!" cried Arthur. "What's it got to do with me? Why should you suppose—"

"I found traces of blotting-paper on the shafts and inside the metal knobs," said Alleyn. "It suggested a substitution of the metal knobs for the Bakelite ones. It is remarkable, don't you think, that they should so closely resemble one another? If you examine them, of course, you find they are not identical. Still, the difference is scarcely perceptible."

Arthur did not answer this. He was still looking at the wireless.

"I've always wanted to have a look at this set," he said surprisingly.

"You are free to do so now," said Alleyn politely. "We have finished with it for the time being."

"Look here," said Arthur suddenly, "suppose metal knobs were substituted for Bakelite ones, it couldn't kill him. He wouldn't get a shock at all. Both the controls are grounded."

"Have you noticed those very small holes drilled

through the panel?" asked Alleyn. "Should they be there, do you think?"

Arthur peered at the little steel shafts. "By God, he's right, Guy," he said. "That's how it was done."

"Inspector Fox," said Alleyn, "tells me those holes could be used for conducting wires and that a lead could be taken from the—the transformer, is it?—to one of the knobs."

"And the other connected to earth," said Fox. "It's a job for an expert. He could get three hundred volts or so that way."

"That's not good enough," said Arthur quickly; "there wouldn't be enough current to do any damage—only a few hundredths of an amp."

"I'm not an expert," said Alleyn, "but I'm sure you're right. Why were the holes drilled then? Do you imagine someone wanted to play a practical joke on your father?"

"A practical joke? On *him*?" Arthur gave an unpleasant screech of laughter. "Do you hear that, Guy?"

"Shut up," said Guy. "After all, he is dead."

"It seems almost too good to be true, doesn't it?"

"Don't be a bloody fool, Arthur. Pull yourself together. Can't you see what this means? They think he's been murdered."

"Murdered! They're wrong. None of us had the

nerve for that, Mr. Inspector. Look at me. My hands are so shaky they told me I'd never be able to paint. That dates from when I was a kid and he shut me up in the cellars for a night. Look at me. Look at Guy. He's not so vulnerable, but he caved in like the rest of us. We were conditioned to surrender. Do you know—"

"Wait a moment," said Alleyn quietly. "Your brother is quite right, you know. You'd better think before you speak. This may be a case of homicide."

"Thank you, sir," said Guy quickly. "That's extraordinarily decent of you. Arthur's a bit above himself. It's a shock."

"The relief, you mean," said Arthur. "Don't be such an ass. I didn't kill him and they'll find it out soon enough. Nobody killed him. There must be some explanation."

"I suggest that you listen to me," said Alleyn. "I'm going to put several questions to both of you. You need not answer them, but it will be more sensible to do so. I understand no one but your father touched this radio. Did any of you ever come into this room while it was in use?"

"Not unless he wanted to vary the programme with a little bullying," said Arthur.

Alleyn turned to Guy, who was glaring at his brother.

"I want to know exactly what happened in this house last night. As far as the doctors can tell us, your father died not less than three and not more than eight hours before he was found. We must try to fix the time as accurately as possible."

"I saw him at about a quarter to nine," began Guy slowly. "I was going out to a supper-party at the Savoy and had come downstairs. He was crossing the hall from the drawing-room to his room."

"Did you see him after a quarter to nine, Mr. Arthur?"

"No. I heard him, though. He was working in here with Hislop. Hislop had asked to go away for Christmas. Quite enough. My father discovered some urgent correspondence. Really, Guy, you know, he was pathological. I'm sure Dr. Meadows thinks so."

"When did you hear him?" asked Alleyn.

"Some time after Guy had gone. I was working on a drawing in my room upstairs. It's above his. I heard him bawling at little Hislop. It must have been before ten o'clock, because I went out to a studio party at ten. I heard him bawling as I crossed the hall."

"And when," said Alleyn, "did you both return?"

"I came home at about twenty past twelve," said Guy immediately. "I can fix the time because we had gone on to Chez Carlo, and they had a midnight stunt there. We left immediately afterwards. I came home in a taxi. The radio was on full blast."

"You heard no voices?"

"None. Just the wireless."

"And you, Mr. Arthur?"

"Lord knows when I got in. After one. The house was in darkness. Not a sound."

"You had your own key?"

"Yes," said Guy. "Each of us has one. They're always left on a hook in the lobby. When I came in I noticed Arthur's was gone."

"What about the others? How did you know it was his?"

"Mother hasn't got one and Phips lost hers weeks ago. Anyway, I knew they were staying in and that it must be Arthur who was out."

"Thank you," said Arthur ironically.

"You didn't look in the study when you came in?" Alleyn asked him.

"Good Lord, no," said Arthur as if the suggestion was fantastic. "I say," he said suddenly, "I suppose he was sitting here—dead. That's a queer thought." He laughed nervously. "Just sitting here, behind the door in the dark."

"How do you know it was in the dark?"

"What d'you mean? Of course it was. There was no light under the door."

267

"I see. Now do you two mind joining your mother again? Perhaps your sister will be kind enough to come in here for a moment. Fox, ask her, will you?"

Fox returned to the drawing-room with Guy and Arthur and remained there, blandly unconscious of any embarrassment his presence might cause the Tonkses. Bailey was already there, ostensibly examining the electric points.

Phillipa went to the study at once. Her first remark was characteristic. "Can I be of any help?" asked Phillipa.

"It's extremely nice of you to put it like that," said Alleyn. "I don't want to worry you for long. I'm sure this discovery has been a shock to you."

"Probably," said Phillipa. Alleyn glanced quickly at her. "I mean," she explained, "that I suppose I must be shocked but I can't feel anything much. I just want to get it all over as soon as possible. And then think. Please tell me what has happened."

Alleyn told her they believed her father had been electrocuted and that the circumstances were unusual and puzzling. He said nothing to suggest that the police suspected murder.

"I don't think I'll be much help," said Phillipa, "but go ahead."

"I want to try to discover who was the last person to see your father or speak to him."

"I should think very likely I was," said Phillipa composedly. "I had a row with him before I went to bed."

"What about?"

"I don't see that it matters."

Alleyn considered this. When he spoke again it was with deliberation.

"Look here," he said, "I think there is very little doubt that your father was killed by an electric shock from his wireless set. As far as I know the circumstances are unique. Radios are normally incapable of giving a lethal shock to anyone. We have examined the cabinet and are inclined to think that its internal arrangements were disturbed last night. Very radically disturbed. Your father may have experimented with it. If anything happened to interrupt or upset him, it is possible that in the excitement of the moment he made some dangerous readjustment."

"You don't believe that, do you?" asked Phillipa calmly.

"Since you ask me," said Alleyn, "no."

"I see," said Phillipa; "you think he was murdered, but you're not sure." She had gone very white, but she spoke crisply. "Naturally you want to find out about my row."

"About everything that happened last evening," amended Alleyn.

"What happened was this," said Phillipa; "I came into the hall some time after ten. I'd heard Arthur go out and had looked at the clock at five past. I ran into my father's secretary, Richard Hislop. He turned aside, but not before I saw . . . not quickly enough. I blurted out: 'You're crying.' We looked at each other. I asked him why he stood it. None of the other secretaries could. He said he had to. He's a widower with two children. There have been doctor's bills and things. I needn't tell you about his . . . about his damnable servitude to my father nor about the refinements of cruelty he'd had to put up with. I think my father was mad, really mad, I mean. Richard gabbled it all out to me higgledy-piggledy in a sort of horrified whisper. He's been here two years, but I'd never realised until that moment that we . . . that . . ." A faint flush came into her cheeks. "He's such a funny little man. Not at all the sort I've always thought . . . not good-looking or exciting or anything."

She stopped, looking bewildered.

"Yes?" said Alleyn.

"Well, you see—I suddenly realised I was in love with him. He realised it too. He said: 'Of course, it's quite hopeless, you know. Us, I mean. Laughable, almost.' Then I put my arms round his neck and kissed him. It was very odd, but it seemed quite natural. The point is my father came out of his room into the hall and saw us."

"That was bad luck," said Alleyn.

"Yes, it was. My father really seemed delighted. He almost licked his lips. Richard's efficiency had irritated my father for a long time. It was difficult to find excuses for being beastly to him. Now, of course . . . He ordered Richard to the study and me to my room. He followed me upstairs. Richard tried to come too, but I asked him not to. My father . . . I needn't tell you what he said. He put the worst possible construction on what he'd seen. He was absolutely foul, screaming at me like a madman. He was insane. Perhaps it was dt's. He drank terribly, you know. I dare say it's silly of me to tell you all this."

"No," said Alleyn.

"I can't feel anything at all. Not even relief. The boys are frankly relieved. I can't feel afraid either." She stared meditatively at Alleyn. "Innocent people needn't feel afraid, need they?"

"It's an axiom of police investigation," said Alleyn and wondered if indeed she was innocent.

"It just *can't* be murder," said Phillipa. "We were all too much afraid to kill him. I believe he'd win even if you murdered him. He'd hit back somehow." She put her hands to her eyes. "I'm all muddled."

"I think you are more upset than you realise. I'll

be as quick as I can. Your father made this scene in your room. You say he screamed. Did anyone hear him?"

"Yes. Mummy did. She came in."

"What happened?"

"I said: 'Go away, darling, it's all right.' I didn't want her to be involved. He nearly killed her with the things he did. Sometimes he'd . . . we never knew what happened between them. It was all secret, like a door shutting quietly as you walk along a passage."

"Did she go away?"

"Not at once. He told her he'd found out that Richard and I were lovers. He said . . . it doesn't matter. I don't want to tell you. She was terrified. He was stabbing at her in some way I couldn't under-stand. Then, quite suddenly, he told her to go to her own room. She went at once and he followed her. He locked me in. That's the last I saw of him, but I heard him go downstairs later."

"Were you locked in all night?"

"No. Richard Hislop's room is next to mine. He came up and spoke through the wall to me. He wanted to unlock the door, but I said better not in case—he—came back. Then, much later, Guy came home. As he passed my door I tapped on it. The key was in the lock and he turned it."

"Did you tell him what had happened?"

"Just that there'd been a row. He only stayed a moment."

"Can you hear the radio from your room?"

She seemed surprised.

"The wireless? Why, yes. Faintly."

"Did you hear it after your father returned to the study?"

"I don't remember."

"Think. While you lay awake all that long time until your brother came home?"

"I'll try. When he came out and found Richard and me, it was not going. They had been working, you see. No, I can't remember hearing it at all unless—wait a moment. Yes. After he had gone back to the study from mother's room I remember there was a loud crash of static. Very loud. Then I think it was quiet for some time. I fancy I heard it again later. Oh, I've remembered something else. After the static my bedside radiator went out. I suppose there was something wrong with the electric supply. That would account for both, wouldn't it? The heater went on again about ten minutes later."

"And did the radio begin again then, do you think?"

"I don't know. I'm very vague about that. It started again sometime before I went to sleep."

273

"Thank you very much indeed. I won't bother you any longer now."

"All right," said Phillipa calmly, and went away.

Alleyn sent for Chase and questioned him about the rest of the staff and about the discovery of the body. Emily was summoned and dealt with. When she departed, awestruck but complacent, Alleyn turned to the butler.

"Chase," he said, "had your master any peculiar habits?"

"Yes, sir."

"In regard to the wireless?"

"I beg pardon, sir. I thought you meant generally speaking."

"Well, then, generally speaking."

"If I may say so, sir, he was a mass of them."

"How long have you been with him?"

"Two months, sir, and due to leave at the end of this week."

"Oh. Why are you leaving?"

Chase produced the classic remark of his kind.

"There are some things," he said, "that flesh and blood will not stand, sir. One of them's being spoke to like Mr. Tonks spoke to his staff."

"Ah. His peculiar habits, in fact?"

"It's my opinion, sir, he was mad. Stark, staring."

"With regard to the radio. Did he tinker with it?"

"I can't say I've ever noticed, sir. I believe he knew quite a lot about wireless."

"When he tuned the thing, had he any particular method? Any characteristic attitude or gesture?"

"I don't think so, sir. I never noticed, and yet I've often come into the room when he was at it. I can seem to see him now, sir."

"Yes, yes," said Alleyn swiftly. "That's what we want. A clear mental picture. How was it now? Like this?"

In a moment he was across the room and seated in Septimus's chair. He swung round to the cabinet and raised his right hand to the tuning control.

"Like this?"

"No, sir," said Chase promptly, "that's not him at all. Both hands it should be."

"Ah." Up went Alleyn's left hand to the volume control. "More like this?"

"Yes, sir," said Chase slowly. "But there's something else and I can't recollect what it was. Something he was always doing. It's in the back of my head. You know, sir. Just on the edge of my memory, as you might say."

"I know."

"It's a kind—something—to do with irritation," said Chase slowly.

"Irritation? His?"

"No. It's no good, sir. I can't get it."

"Perhaps later. Now look here, Chase, what happened to all of you last night? All the servants, I mean."

"We were all out, sir. It being Christmas Eve. The mistress sent for me yesterday morning. She said we could take the evening off as soon as I had taken in Mr. Tonks's grog-tray at nine o'clock. So we went," ended Chase simply.

"When?"

"The rest of the staff got away about nine. I left at ten past, sir, and returned about eleven-twenty. The others were back then, and all in bed. I went straight to bed myself, sir."

"You came in by a back door, I suppose?"

"Yes, sir. We've been talking it over. None of us noticed anything unusual."

"Can you hear the wireless in your part of the house?"

"No, sir."

"Well," said Alleyn, looking up from his notes, "that'll do, thank you."

Before Chase reached the door Fox came in.

"Beg pardon, sir," said Fox, "I just want to take a look at the *Radio Times* on the desk."

He bent over the paper, wetted a gigantic thumb, and turned a page.

"That's it, sir," shouted Chase suddenly. "That's what I tried to think of. That's what he was always doing."

"But what?"

"Licking his fingers, sir. It was a habit," said Chase. "That's what he always did when he sat down to the radio. I heard Mr. Hislop tell the doctor it nearly drove him demented, the way the master couldn't touch a thing without first licking his fingers."

"Quite so," said Alleyn. "In about ten minutes, ask Mr. Hislop if he will be good enough to come in for a moment. That will be all, thank you, Chase."

"Well, sir," remarked Fox when Chase had gone, "if that's the case and what I think's right, it'd certainly make matters worse."

"Good heavens, Fox, what an elaborate remark. What does it mean?"

"If metal knobs were substituted for Bakelite ones and fine wires brought through those holes to make contact, then he'd get a bigger bump if he tuned in with *damp* fingers."

"Yes. And he always used both hands. Fox!"

"Sir."

"Approach the Tonkses again. You haven't left them alone, of course?"

"Bailey's in there making out he's interested in

the light switches. He's found the main switchboard under the stairs. There's signs of a blown fuse having been fixed recently. In a cupboard underneath there are odd lengths of flex and so on. Same brand as this on the wireless and the heater."

"Ah, yes. Could the cord from the adapter to the radiator be brought into play?"

"By gum," said Fox, "you're right! That's how it was done, Chief. The heavier flex was cut away from the radiator and shoved through. There was a fire, so he wouldn't want the radiator and wouldn't notice."

"It might have been done that way, certainly, but there's little to prove it. Return to the bereaved Tonkses, my Fox, and ask prettily if any of them remember Septimus's peculiarities when tuning his wireless."

Fox met little Mr. Hislop at the door and left him alone with Alleyn. Phillipa had been right, reflected the Inspector, when she said Richard Hislop was not a noticeable man. He was nondescript. Grey eyes, drab hair; rather pale, rather short, rather insignificant; and yet last night there had flashed up between those two the realisation of love. Romantic but rum, thought Alleyn.

"Do sit down," he said. "I want you, if you will, to tell me what happened between you and Mr. Tonks last evening."

"What happened?"

"Yes. You all dined at eight, I understand. Then you and Mr. Tonks came in here?"

"Yes."

"What did you do?"

"He dictated several letters."

"Anything unusual take place?"

"Oh, no."

"Why did you quarrel?"

"Quarrel!" The quiet voice jumped a tone. "We did not quarrel, Mr. Alleyn."

"Perhaps that was the wrong word. What upset you?"

"Phillipa has told you?"

"Yes. She was wise to do so. What was the matter, Mr. Hislop?"

"Apart from the . . . what she told you . . . Mr. Tonks was a difficult man to please. I often irritated him. I did so last night."

"In what way?"

"In almost every way. He shouted at me. I was startled and nervous, clumsy with papers, and making mistakes. I wasn't well. I blundered and then . . . I . . . I broke down. I have always irritated him. My very mannerisms—"

"Had he no irritating mannerisms, himself?"

"He! My God!"

279

"What were they?"

"I can't think of anything in particular. It doesn't matter, does it?"

"Anything to do with the wireless, for instance?"

There was a short silence.

"No," said Hislop.

"Was the radio on in here last night, after dinner?"

"For a little while. Not after—after the incident in the hall. At least, I don't think so. I don't remember."

"What did you do after Miss Phillipa and her father had gone upstairs?"

"I followed and listened outside the door for a moment." He had gone very white and had backed away from the desk.

"And then?"

"I heard someone coming. I remembered Dr. Meadows had told me to ring him up if there was one of the scenes. I returned here and rang him up. He told me to go to my room and listen. If things got any worse I was to telephone again. Otherwise I was to stay in my room. It is next to hers."

"And you did this?" He nodded. "Could you hear what Mr. Tonks said to her?"

"A—a good deal of it."

"What did you hear?"

"He insulted her. Mrs. Tonks was there. I was just thinking of ringing Dr. Meadows up again when she and Mr. Tonks came out and went along the passage. I stayed in my room."

"You did not try to speak to Miss Phillipa?"

"We spoke through the wall. She asked me not to ring Dr. Meadows, but to stay in my room. In a little while, perhaps it was as much as twenty minutes—I really don't know—I heard him come back and go downstairs. I again spoke to Phillipa. She implored me not to do anything and said that she herself would speak to Dr. Meadows in the morning. So I waited a little longer and then went to bed."

"And to sleep?"

"My God, no!"

"Did you hear the wireless again?"

"Yes. At least I heard static."

"Are you an expert on wireless?"

"No. I know the ordinary things. Nothing much."

"How did you come to take this job, Mr. Hislop?"

"I answered an advertisement."

"You are sure you don't remember any particular mannerism of Mr. Tonks's in connection with the radio?"

"No."

"And you can tell me no more about your interview in the study that led to the scene in the hall?"

"No."

"Will you please ask Mrs. Tonks if she will be kind enough to speak to me for a moment?"

"Certainly," said Hislop, and went away.

Septimus's wife came in looking like death. Alleyn got her to sit down and asked her about her movements on the preceding evening. She said she was feeling unwell and dined in her room. She went to bed immediately afterwards. She heard Septimus yelling at Phillipa and went to Phillipa's room. Septimus accused Mr. Hislop and her daughter of "terrible things." She got as far as this and then broke down quietly. Alleyn was very gentle with her. After a little while he learned that Septimus had gone to her room with her and had continued to speak of "terrible things."

"What sort of things?" asked Alleyn.

"He was not responsible," said Isabel. "He did not know what he was saying. I think he had been drinking."

She thought he had remained with her for perhaps a quarter of an hour. Possibly longer. He left her abruptly and she heard him go along the passage, past Phillipa's door, and presumably downstairs. She had stayed awake for a long time. The wireless could not be heard from her room. Alleyn showed her the curtain knobs, but she seemed quite unable to take in their significance. He let her go, summoned Fox, and went over the whole case.

"What's your idea on the show?" he asked when he had finished.

"Well, sir," said Fox, in his stolid way, "on the face of it the young gentlemen have got alibis. We'll have to check them up, of course, and I don't see we can go much further until we have done so."

"For the moment," said Alleyn, "let us suppose Masters Guy and Arthur to be safely established behind cast-iron alibis. What then?"

"Then we've got the young lady, the old lady, the secretary, and the servants."

"Let us parade them. But first let us go over the wireless game. You'll have to watch me here. I gather that the only way in which the radio could be fixed to give Mr. Tonks his quietus is like this: Control knobs removed. Holes bored in front panel with fine drill. Metal knobs substituted and packed with blotting-paper to insulate them from metal shafts and make them stay put. Heavier flex from adapter to radiator cut and the ends of the wires pushed through the drilled holes to make contact with the new knobs. Thus we have a positive and negative pole. Mr. Tonks bridges the gap, gets a mighty wallop as the current passes through him to the earth. The switchboard fuse is blown almost immediately. All this is rigged by murderer while Sep was upstairs bullying wife and daughter. Sep revisited study some time after ten-twenty. Whole thing was made ready between ten, when Arthur went out, and the time Sep returned—say, about ten-forty-five. The murderer reappeared, connected radiator with flex, removed wires, changed back knobs, and left the thing tuned in. Now I take it that the burst of static described by Phillipa and Hislop would be caused by the short-circuit that killed our Septimus?"

"That's right. It also affected all the heaters in the house. *Vide* Miss Tonks's radiator."

"Yes. He put all that right again. It would be a simple enough matter for anyone who knew how. He'd just have to fix the fuse on the main switchboard. How long do you say it would take to—what's the horrible word?—to recondition the whole show?"

"M'm," said Fox deeply. "At a guess, sir, fifteen minutes. He'd have to be nippy."

"Yes," agreed Alleyn. "He or she."

"I don't see a female making a success of it," grunted Fox. "Look here, Chief, you know what I'm thinking. Why did Mr. Hislop lie about deceased's habit of licking his thumbs? You say Hislop told you he remembered nothing and Chase says he overheard him saying the trick nearly drove him dippy."

"Exactly," said Alleyn. He was silent for so long that Fox felt moved to utter a discreet cough.

"Eh?" said Alleyn. "Yes, Fox, yes. It'll have to be done." He consulted the telephone directory and dialled a number.

"May I speak to Dr. Meadows? Oh, it's you, is it? Do you remember Mr. Hislop telling you that Septimus Tonks's trick of wetting his fingers nearly drove Hislop demented. Are you there? You don't? Sure? All right. All right. Hislop rang up at ten-twenty, you said? And you telephoned him? At eleven. Sure of the times? I see. I'd be glad if you'd come round. Can you? Well, do if you can."

He hung up the receiver.

"Get Chase again, will you, Fox?"

Chase, recalled, was most insistent that Mr. Hislop had spoken about it to Dr. Meadows.

"It was when Mr. Hislop had flu, sir. I went up with the doctor. Mr. Hislop had a high temperature and was talking very excited. He kept on and on, saying the master had guessed his ways had driven him crazy and that the master kept on purposely to aggravate. He said if it went on much longer he'd . . . he didn't know what he was talking about, sir, really."

"What did he say he'd do?"

"Well, sir, he said he'd—he'd do something desperate to the master. But it was only his rambling, sir. I daresay he wouldn't remember anything about it."

"No," said Alleyn, "I daresay he wouldn't." When Chase had gone he said to Fox: "Go and find out about those boys and their alibis. See if they can put you on to a quick means of checking up. Get Master Guy to corroborate Miss Phillipa's statement that she was locked in her room."

Fox had been gone for some time and Alleyn was still busy with his notes when the study door burst open and in came Dr. Meadows.

"Look here, my giddy sleuth-hound," he shouted, "what's all this about Hislop? Who says he disliked Sep's abominable habits?"

"Chase does. And don't bawl at me like that. I'm worried."

"So am I, blast you. What are you driving at? You can't imagine that . . . that poor little broken-down hack is capable of electrocuting anybody, let alone Sep?"

"I have no imagination," said Alleyn wearily.

"I wish to God I hadn't called you in. If the wireless killed Sep, it was because he'd monkeyed with it."

"And put it right after it had killed him?"

Dr. Meadows stared at Alleyn in silence.

"Now," said Alleyn, "you've got to give me a

straight answer, Meadows. Did Hislop, while he was semi-delirious, say that this habit of Tonks's made him feel like murdering him?"

"I'd forgotten Chase was there," said Dr. Meadows.

"Yes, you'd forgotten that."

"But even if he did talk wildly, Alleyn, what of it? Damn it, you can't arrest a man on the strength of a remark made in delirium."

"I don't propose to do so. Another motive has come to light."

"You mean—Phips—last night?"

"Did he tell you about that?"

"She whispered something to me this morning. I'm very fond of Phips. My God, are you sure of your grounds?"

"Yes," said Alleyn. "I'm sorry. I think you'd better go, Meadows."

"Are you going to arrest him?"

"I have to do my job."

There was a long silence.

"Yes," said Dr. Meadows at last. "You have to do your job. Goodbye, Alleyn."

Fox returned to say that Guy and Arthur had never left their parties. He had got hold of two of their friends. Guy and Mrs. Tonks confirmed the story of the locked door.

"It's a process of elimination," said Fox. "It must be the secretary. He fixed the radio while deceased was upstairs. He must have dodged back to whisper through the door to Miss Tonks. I suppose he waited somewhere down here until he heard deceased blow himself to blazes and then put everything straight again, leaving the radio turned on."

Alleyn was silent.

"What do we do now, sir?" asked Fox.

"I want to see the hook inside the front door where they hang their keys."

Fox, looking dazed, followed his superior to the little entrance hall.

"Yes, there they are," said Alleyn. He pointed to a hook with two latch-keys hanging from it. "You could scarcely miss them. Come on, Fox."

Back in the study they found Hislop with Bailey in attendance.

Hislop looked from one Yard man to another.

"I want to know if it's murder."

"We think so," said Alleyn.

"I want you to realise that Phillipa—Miss Tonks—was locked in her room all last night."

"Until her brother came home and unlocked the door," said Alleyn.

"That was too late. He was dead by then."

"How do you know when he died?"

"It must have been when there was that crash of static."

"Mr. Hislop," said Alleyn, "why would you not tell me how much that trick of licking his fingers exasperated you?"

"But—how do you know? I never told anyone."

"You told Dr. Meadows when you were ill."

"I don't remember." He stopped short. His lips trembled. Then, suddenly he began to speak.

"Very well. It's true. For two years he's tortured me. You see, he knew something about me. Two years ago when my wife was dying, I took money from the cash-box in that desk. I paid it back and thought he hadn't noticed. He knew all the time. From then on he had me where he wanted me. He used to sit there like a spider. I'd hand him a paper. He'd wet his thumbs with a clicking noise and a sort of complacent grimace. Click, click. Then he'd thumb the papers. He knew it drove me crazy. He'd look at me and then . . . click, click. And then he'd say something about the cash. He'd never quite accused me, just hinted. And I was impotent. You think I'm insane. I'm not. I could have murdered him. Often and often I've thought how I'd do it. Now you think I've done it. I haven't. There's the joke of it. I hadn't the pluck. And last night when Phillipa showed me she cared, it was like Heaven—unbelievable. For the first time since I've been here I *didn't* feel like killing him. And last night someone else *did*!"

He stood there trembling and vehement. Fox and Bailey, who had watched him with bewildered concern, turned to Alleyn. He was about to speak when Chase came in. "A note for you, sir," he said to Alleyn. "It came by hand."

Alleyn opened it and glanced at the first few words. He looked up.

"You may go, Mr. Hislop. Now I've got what I expected—what I fished for."

When Hislop had gone they read the letter.

Dear Alleyn,

Don't arrest Hislop. I did it. Let him go at once if you've arrested him and don't tell Phips you ever suspected him. I was in love with Isabel before she met Sep. I've tried to get her to divorce him, but she wouldn't because of the kids. Damned nonsense, but there's no time to discuss it now. I've got to be quick. He suspected us. He reduced her to a nervous wreck. I was afraid she'd go under altogether. I thought it all out. Some weeks ago I took Phips's key from the hook inside the front door. I had the tools and the flex and wire all ready. I knew where the main switchboard was

and the cupboard. I meant to wait until they all
went away at the New Year, but last night when
Hislop rang me I made up my mind at once. He
said the boys and servants were out and Phips
locked in her room. I told him to stay in his room
and to ring me up in half an hour if things hadn't
quieted down. He didn't ring up. I did. No answer,
so I knew Sep wasn't in his study.

I came round, let myself in, and listened. All
quiet upstairs but the lamp still on in the study,
so I knew he would come down again. He'd said
he wanted to get the midnight broadcast from
somewhere.

I locked myself in and got to work. When Sep
was away last year, Arthur did one of his modern
monstrosities of painting in the study. He talked
about the knobs making good pattern. I noticed
then that they were very like the ones on the radio
and later on I tried one and saw that it would fit
if I packed it up a bit. Well, I did the job just as
you worked it out, and it only took twelve minutes.
Then I went into the drawing-room and waited.

He came down from Isabel's room and
evidently went straight to the radio. I hadn't
thought it would make such a row, and half
expected someone would come down. No one came.
I went back, switched off the wireless, mended

the fuse in the main switchboard, using my torch.
Then I put everything right in the study.

There was no particular hurry. No one would
come in while he was there and I got the radio
going as soon as possible to suggest he was at it.
I knew I'd be called in when they found him. My
idea was to tell them he had died of a stroke. I'd
been warning Isabel it might happen at any time.
As soon as I saw the burned hand I knew that
cat wouldn't jump. I'd have tried to get away
with it if Chase hadn't gone round bleating about
electrocution and burned fingers. Hislop saw the
hand. I daren't do anything but report the case
to the police, but I thought you'd never twig the
knobs. One up to you.

I might have bluffed through if you hadn't
suspected Hislop. Can't let you hang the blighter.
I'm enclosing a note to Isabel, who won't forgive
me, and an official one for you to use. You'll find
me in my bedroom upstairs. I'm using cyanide.
It's quick.

I'm sorry, Alleyn. I think you knew, didn't
you? I've bungled the whole game, but if you will
be a supersleuth . . . Goodbye.

Henry Meadows

Stuffing

There are several people concerned in this story whom it is impossible within a limited space to describe. If you are on friendly terms with the great men of Scotland Yard you may inspect the photographs and fingerprints of two—Harry the Valet and Joe the Runner.

Lord Carfane's picture you can see at intervals in the best of the illustrated weeklies. He was once plain Ferdie Gooberry, before he became a contractor and supplied the army with odds and ends and himself with a fortune and a barony.

In no newspaper, illustrated or otherwise, do the names of John and Angela Willett appear. Their marriage at a small registrar's office had excited no public comment, although he was a BA of Cambridge and she was the grand-niece of Peter Elmer, the shipping magnate, who had acknowledged his relationship by dictating to her a very polite letter wishing her every happiness.

They lived in one furnished room in Pimlico, this good-looking couple, and they had the use of the kitchen. He was confident that he would one day be a great engineer. She also believed in miracles.

Three days before Christmas they sat down calmly to consider the problem of the great annual festival and how it might best be spent. Jack Willett scratched his cheek and did a lightning calculation.

"Really, we ought not to spend an unnecessary penny," he said dolefully. "We may be a week in Montreal before I start work, and we shall need a little money for the voyage."

They were leaving on Boxing Day for Canada; their berths had been taken. In Montreal a job was awaiting Jack in the office of an old college friend: and although twenty-five dollars' per did not exactly represent luxury, it was a start.

Angela looked at him thoughtfully.

"I am quite sure Uncle Peter is going to do something awfully nice for us," she said stoutly.

Jack's hollow laugh was not encouraging.

There was a tap at the door, and the unpleasant but smiling face of Joe the Runner appeared. He occupied an attic bedroom, and was a source of worry to his landlady. Once he had been in the newspaper business, running evening editions, and the name stuck to him. He had long ceased to be associated with the Press, save as a subject for its crime reporters, but this the Willetts did not know.

"Just thought I'd pop in and see you before I went, miss," he said. "I'm going off into the country to do a bit of work for a gentleman. About that dollar, miss, that you lent me last week."

Angela looked uncomfortable.

"Oh, please don't mention it," she said hastily.

"I haven't forgotten it," said Joe, nodding solemnly. "The minute I come back, I'll bring it to you." And with a large and sinister grin he vanished.

"I lent him the money because he couldn't pay his rent," said Angela penitently, but her husband waved her extravagance away.

"Let's talk about Christmas dinner. What about sausages . . . !"

"If Uncle Peter—" she began.

"Let's talk about sausages," said Jack gently.

Foodstuffs were also the topic of conversation between Lord Carfane and Prince Riminoff as they sat at lunch at the Ritz-Carlton. Lord Carfane emphasized his remarks with a very long cigar.

"I always keep up the old English custom of distributing food to the poor," he said. "Every family on my estate on Christmas Eve has a turkey from my farm. All my workers," he corrected himself carefully, "except old Timmins. Old Timmins has been very rude to me, and I have had to sack him. All the tenants assemble in the great hall . . . But you'll see that for yourself, Prince."

Prince Riminoff nodded gravely and tugged at his short beard. That beard had taken Harry the Valet five months to grow, and it was so creditable a production that he had passed Chief Inspector Mailing in the vestibule of the Ritz-Carlton and had not been recognized.

Very skilfully he switched the conversation into more profitable channels.

"I do hope, my dear Lord Carfane, that you have not betrayed my identity to your guests?"

Ferdie smiled.

"I am not quite a fool," he said, and meant it.

"A great deal of the jewellery that I am disposing of, and of which you have seen specimens, is not mine. I think I have made that clear. I am acting for several of my unfortunate compatriots, and frankly it would be embarrassing for me if it leaked out that I was the vendor."

Ferdie nodded. He suspected that a great deal of the property which he was to acquire had been secured by underhand means. He more than suspected that, for all his princely origin, his companion was not too honest.

"That is why I have asked that the money you pay should be in American currency. By the way, have you made that provision?" Lord Carfane nodded. "And, of course, I shall not ask you to pay a single dollar until you are satisfied that the property is worth what I ask. It is in fact worth three times as much."

Lord Carfane was nothing if not frank.

"Now, I'm going to tell you, my dear chap," he said, "there will only be one person at Carfane Hall who will know anything whatever about this little transaction of ours. He's an expert jeweller. He is an authority, and he will examine every piece and price it before I part with a single bob!"

His Highness heartily, but gravely, approved of this act of precaution.

Lord Carfane had met his companion a few weeks before in a highly respectable night club, the introduction having been effected through the medium of a very beautiful lady who had accidentally spilt a glass of champagne over his lordship's dress trousers. She was so lovely a personage that Lord Carfane did no more than smile graciously, and a few minutes later was introduced to her sedate and imposing presence.

Harry the Valet invariably secured his introductions by this method. Usually he worked with Molly

Kien, and paid her a hundred pounds for every introduction.

He spoke no more of jewels smuggled from Russia and offered at ridiculous prices, but talked sorrowfully of the misfortunes of his country; spoke easily of his estates in the Crimea and his mines in the Urals, now, alas! in Bolshevik hands. Lord Carfane was immensely entertained.

On the following evening, Harry drove down in Lord Carfane's limousine to Berkshire, and was introduced to the glories of Carfane Hall; to the great banqueting chamber with its high-raftered roof; to the white-tiled larder where petrified turkeys hung in rows, each grisly corpse decorated with a gay rosette . . .

"My tenants come in on Christmas Eve," explained Lord Carfane, "and my butler presents each one with a turkey and a small bag of groceries—"

"An old feudal custom?" suggested the Prince gravely.

Lord Carfane agreed with equal gravity.

The Prince had brought with him a large, heavily locked and strapped handbag, which had been deposited in the safe, which was the most conspicuous feature of Ferdie's library. The expert jeweller was arriving on the morrow, and his lordship looked forward, with a sense of pleasurable anticipation, to a day which would yield him 400 per cent profit on a considerable outlay.

"Yes," said Ferdie at dinner that night, "I prefer a combination safe. One can lose keys, but not if they're here"—he tapped his narrow forehead and smiled.

Harry the Valet agreed. One of his greatest charms was his complete agreement with anything anybody said or did or thought.

Whilst he dwelt in luxury in the halls of the great, his unhappy confederate had a more painful task. Joe the Runner had collected from a garage a small, light trolley. It was not beautiful to look upon, but it was fast, and under its covered tilt, beneath sacks and amidst baskets, a man making a swift getaway might lie concealed and be carried to London without exciting attention.

Joe made a leisurely way into Berkshire and came to the rendezvous at the precise minute he had been ordered. It was a narrow lane at the termination of a footpath leading across the Carfane estate to the house. It was a cold, blue-fingered, red-nosed job, and for three hours he sat and shivered. And then, coming across the field in the blue dusk, he saw an old man staggering, carrying a rush basket in one hand and an indescribable something in the other.

He was evidently in a hurry, this ancient. From time to time he looked back over his shoulder as though he expected pursuit. Breathlessly, he mounted the stile and fell over rather than surmounted it.

Stumbling to his feet, he saw Joe sitting at the wheel of the van, and gaped at him toothlessly, his eyes wide with horror. Joe the Runner recognized the signs.

"What have you been doin'?" he demanded sternly.

For a few minutes the breathless old man could not speak; blinked fearfully at his interrogator; and then:

"He's fired me," he croaked. "Wouldn't give me no turkey or nothin, so I went up to the 'All and pinched one."

"Oh!" said Joe judiciously.

It was not an unpleasant sensation, sitting in judgement on a fellow creature.

"There was such a bother and a fuss and shouting going on . . . what with the safe bein' found broke open, and that foreign man being caught, that nobody seed me," whimpered the elderly Mr Timmins.

"Eh?" said Joe. "What's that—safe broken open?"

The old man nodded.

"I heered 'em when I was hiding in the pantry.

300

His lordship found that the safe had been opened an' money took. He sent for the constable, and they've got the prince locked up in a room, with the undergardener and the butler on guard outside the door—"

He looked down at the frozen turkey in his red, numbed hand; and his lips twitched pathetically.

"His lordship promised me a turkey and his lordship said I shouldn't have—"

Joe Runner was a quick thinker. "Jump up in the truck," he commanded roughly. "Where do you live?"

"About three miles from here," began Mr Timmins.

Joe leaned over, and pulled him up, parcel, bag and turkey.

"Get through into the back, and keep quiet."

He leapt down, cranked up the engine with some difficulty, and sent the little trolley lumbering on to the main road. When he passed three officers in a police car speeding towards Carfane Hall his heart was in his mouth, but he was not challenged. Presently, at the urgent desire of the old man, he stopped at the end of a row of cottages.

"Gawd bless you, mister!" whimpered Mr Timmins. "I'll never do a thing like this again—"

"Hi!" said Joe sternly. "What do I get out of this?"

And then, as the recollection of a debt came to him:

"Leave the turkey—and hop!"

Mr Timmins hopped.

It was nine o'clock on Christmas morning, and Angela Willett had just finished her packing.

Outside the skies were dark and cheerless, snow and rain were falling together, so that this tiny furnished room had almost a palatial atmosphere in comparison with the drear world outside.

"I suppose it's too early to cook the sausages—by the way, our train leaves at ten tonight, so we needn't invent ways of spending the evening—come in."

It was Joe the Runner, rather wet but smiling. He carried under his arm something wrapped in an old newspaper.

"Excuse me, miss," he said, as he removed the covering, "but a gent I met in the street asked me to give you this."

"A turkey!" gasped Angela. "How wonderful . . . who was it?"

"I don't know, miss—an old gentleman," said Joe vaguely. "He said 'Be sure an' give it to the young lady herself—wishin' her a happy Christmas'."

They gazed on the carcase in awe and ecstasy.

As the front door slammed, announcing Joe's hasty departure:

"An old gentleman," said Angela slowly. "Uncle Peter!"

"Uncle grandmother!" smiled John. "I believe he stole it!"

"How uncharitable you are!" she reproached him. "It's the sort of thing Uncle Peter would do. He always had that Haroun al Raschid complex—I wrote and told him we were leaving for Canada tonight. I'm sure it was he."

Half-convinced, John Willett prodded at the bird. It seemed a little tough.

"Anyway, it's turkey," he said, "And, darling, I adore turkey stuffed with chestnuts. I wonder if there are any shops open—"

There was a large cavity at one end of the bird, and as he lifted the turkey up by the neck, the better to examine it, something dropped to the table with a flop. It was a tight roll of paper. He shook the bird again and a second fell from its unoffending body.

"Good God!" gasped John.

With trembling hands he cut the string that bound the roll—

"It's money!" she whispered.

John nodded.

"Hundred dollar bills . . . five hundred of them at least!" he said hollowly.

Their eyes met.

"Uncle Peter!" she breathed. "The darling!"

Mr Peter Elmer, the eminent shipowner, received the following day a telegram which was entirely meaningless:

Thank you a thousand times for your thought and generosity. You have given us a wonderful start and we shall be worthy of your splendid kindness.

It was signed "Angela". Mr Peter Elmer scratched his head.

And at that moment Inspector Mailing was interrogating Harry the Valet in the little police station at Carfane.

"Now come across, Harry," he said kindly. "We know you got the money out of the safe. Where did you plant it? You couldn't have taken it far, because the butler saw you leaving the room. Just tell us where the money is, and I'll make it all right for you when you come up in front of the old man."

"I don't know what you're talking about," said Harry the Valet, game to the last.